Tom Winter has always made his living from words, first as an editor and writer in magazine publishing, and then as an advertising copywriter and speech writer. His debut novel, *Lost & Found,* was published in five languages. He lives in Berlin, with a potted plant and a variety of noisy neighbours.

Also by Tom Winter

Lost & Found

ARMS WIDE OPEN

Tom Winter

corsair

Constable & Robinson Ltd.
55–56 Russell Square
London WC1B 4HP
www.constablerobinson.com

First published in the UK by Corsair,
an imprint of Constable & Robinson Ltd., 2014

Copyright © Tom Winter, 2014

The right of Tom Winter to be identified as the author of this
work has been asserted by him in accordance with the
Copyright, Designs and Patents Act 1988

All rights reserved. This book is sold subject to the condition
that it shall not, by way of trade or otherwise, be lent, resold,
hired out or otherwise circulated in any form of binding or cover
other than that in which it is published and without a similar condition
including this condition being imposed on the subsequent purchaser.

This is a work of fiction. Names, characters,
places and incidents are either the product of the author's imagination
or are used fictitiously, and any resemblance to actual persons,
living or dead, or to actual events or locales is entirely coincidental.

A copy of the British Library Cataloguing in
Publication Data is available from the British Library

ISBN: 978-1-4721-0168-6 (paperback)
ISBN: 978-1-4721-1096-1 (ebook)

Printed and bound in the UK

1 3 5 7 9 10 8 6 4 2

For Stefano and Iside
My kind of crazy

GLASGOW LIFE GLASGOW LIBRARIES	
C005245499	
Bertrams	12/03/2015
F/WIN	£7.99
PW	GEN

1

Meredith

It's a Thursday afternoon and Meredith is staring at a pot of yogurt. It's been in the fridge for almost a year, left there by her husband on the same day he left her too. It sits unopened and untouched. Preserved like evidence from a crime scene. Covered with the invisible fingerprints of a man she still loves.

Of course, her two children have complained about it over the months. It's been easy to dismiss Jemima's disgust for the simple reason that she's a teenager; everything horrifies her. The time will doubtless come when even *having* a refrigerator will affront one of her new-found sensibilities: a fleeting sympathy for Chinese factory workers, perhaps, or a dislike of capitalist societies and their self-indulgent white goods.

Luke's critique was more surprising, all the more so coming from an eleven-year-old boy who rarely expresses an opinion about anything. Unlike his sister, he didn't think it 'gross', 'perverse' or 'proof of a monumental midlife crisis'. He just thought it 'unhealthy'. And in that simple diagnosis, Meredith momentarily felt naked and transparent, unsure whether he was talking about the yogurt or her.

Yet here it is, all this time later, still sitting in the refrigerator.

And Meredith still finds herself staring at it on a regular basis, not even sure any more what it represents, but certain that whatever is happening to its contents is a fitting parallel of her own life: a slow liquefaction, the irreversible death of something good. And it's all happening beneath a pristine exterior. A bacterial Armageddon perfectly contained by a cheerful plastic pot and a shiny foil lid.

Jemima

Jemima gets home from school to find her mother like this, staring into the refrigerator, so absorbed she doesn't even notice she's being watched.

Saying nothing, Jemima quietly retreats to her bedroom, thinking of her father as she climbs the stairs two at a time. It would be wrong to say he left a year ago; in many ways, he left them a long time before that, was possibly never even with them in the first place. An astronomy professor, he'd made no secret of the fact that outer space was more appealing than family dramas; that the complexities of planetary physics made more sense to him than the thoughts and actions of his own children.

In the long months since he had left them to move in with another woman, Jemima's found other ways to fill his place. It was just a joke at first: using a picture she'd copied from a website; pretending to be Lucy, a twenty-something blonde girl with the kind of smile that means many things to many people. But Lucy was an instant hit on dating sites, and overnight Jemima went from being a girl ignored by her father to a woman surrounded by men, all of whom have been happy to lend a hearing ear and a shoulder to cry on. Yes, it's true they do it in the expectation that Lucy will one day be on all fours paying it back with interest, but hope springs eternal, and for every man who tires of the chase, a new one starts to woo her.

In the privacy of her bedroom, Jemima turns on her computer, checks her mail. There's a message from one of her newest admirers urging her to meet for a drink as soon as possible. She knows her reply so well, she types it almost without thinking: 'I would love to meet, but I've been hurt in a previous relationship and I'd prefer to take things slow.'

It's a useful line, but it's hard to keep using it month after month as confidences are shared and intimate subjects broached. Only last week, after nearly six months of correspondence, she'd told one of her most loyal suitors that she still couldn't meet because she'd just got back from India with a bad case of chlamydia. And though she later insisted she'd meant cholera, the damage had been done. Such are the perils of pretending to be old before one's years.

Jack
Jack's not just having a difficult year, he's having a *Hindenburg* moment: in recent months, he's learnt the hard way that life is made of a highly flammable material. After seeing his career crash and burn, he's watched the flames spread to every other part of his carefully orchestrated life, melting it into something so distorted it almost takes a forensic skill to see the link between past and present.

He ponders this as he peers at himself in the bathroom

mirror, unshaven and bleary-eyed, barely out of bed in the middle of the afternoon.

Until twenty minutes ago he'd at least still had a girlfriend, but she's just ended the relationship with a cocktail of terminal contempt: a generous fistful of expletives shaken over ice and served straight up. And as the door slammed behind her, Jack's only thought was that he couldn't even remember her name.

His arrival at the office goes unnoticed. It's commonly accepted that he's on some kind of extended leave, prone to drifting in and out purely because he's one of the agency's founding partners and can do whatever he likes.

The newer recruits assume this is the leisured life of a successful man. Only his contemporaries know better. In their mouths, words like 'taking a break' are mere euphemisms for having lost his edge, the man who once blew creative ideas like an oil rig now finding the well has run dry.

Jack is busy with a game of Angry Birds when Harry, his business partner, pops his head through the open doorway. 'Right, Jack? I didn't expect to see you back so soon.'

Jack knows this is Harry-speak for 'Please leave before you do something terrible.' In the final months before he had agreed to take a break, Jack had resorted to ever more desperate measures to get the ideas flowing, a sort of creative fracking in which he drank larger and larger amounts of alcohol in the hope of triggering a response. The ideas didn't come, but the embarrassments quickly began to pile up, so that for a while his presence in the office was as welcome as airborne tuberculosis.

'How was St Lucia?' says Harry, his body language – leaning awkwardly through the doorway, half in, half out – suggesting that this is purely a brief catch-up before Jack goes away and does something. Anywhere but here.

'Hot,' replies Jack, struggling to think of something more profound to say about a holiday he hadn't enjoyed. 'Good cocktails.' He notices Harry's expression. 'Not that I had many.'

'Look, the guys are getting ready for a big pitch next week. They're not going to have much time for socializing.'

'Sure, I just wanted, you know, to be back here for a while.' Silence. 'It's been a rough day.'

'Tell you what, you should go away again.' The atmosphere stiffens. 'I'm not saying that being here is a bad idea . . .' And now he flounders because they both know that bad ideas have become Jack's hallmark in recent months. 'What I mean,' he adds, trying a little too hard to sound chummy and reassuring, 'is you'll be back on the job soon enough. And then there'll be no time, so *carpe diem*! Go skiing or something. Sail around Tahiti.'

Jack stares at him, sober enough to realize that this is his cue to leave for another month, two, maybe even more. 'Yeah,' he replies. 'Perhaps you're right.' And even though there's nowhere he wants to go, nowhere really left to go, he forces a smile. 'I'll send you a postcard.'

Luke

It's not just a cigarette butt, it's a story, Luke is certain of that. He crouches on the ground beside the phone booth and peers closer. It wasn't merely stubbed out, it was *mashed* into the concrete with a force that seems almost vengeful.

5

Luke wonders if the person had been talking on the phone to someone who made them angry. Or perhaps they just felt guilty about smoking: one last puff and then they wanted to destroy the evidence. As he carefully lifts the shreds of paper, he sees smudges of lipstick – and what lipstick! The kind of colour that makes him think of fairground rides and party balloons.

He puts it in a Ziploc bag for safe keeping, knows before he even looks up that he has an audience yet again: the same old woman who often stands in her living-room window and watches as he inspects the ground around the phone booth. Occasionally even stands there with the same blank gaze as some of the other kids from school punch him or throw his bag over the nearest wall.

He and the old lady make eye contact for a few seconds but, as ever, Luke can't decide if she's interested in his presence or worried by it.

Not for the first time he considers waving hello, but then he wonders if she might mistake it for some other kind of hand gesture. And, yes, he could just smile, but with the distance between them it would have to be such a theatrical, over-the-top smile, he'd probably end up appearing even more threatening. So instead he walks away, pondering now what *she* knows about the mystery cigarette smoker.

Luke's biggest discovery of the day comes a couple of streets from home. Parked beneath a tree, a car like Uncle Jack's. On closer inspection, it not only *is* Uncle Jack's car, but Uncle Jack is sitting in it, staring at the empty street.

Luke stands beside the passenger door, observes him for a moment, but it's clear Jack's mind is far away. Finally, he knocks on the window.

'Shit!' yells Jack, so obviously startled that Luke decides he and his uncle may be kindred spirits after all.

Moments later, Jack is opening the passenger door and Luke is scrambling in.

'I think,' says Luke, 'you're not supposed to use language like that in front of me.'

'Nonsense. There are many situations in which a good swear word is the only appropriate response.'

Luke locks the door behind himself, as much for Jack's benefit as his own. 'We don't live on this street.'

'Yes, thank you, Luke. I am actually on the way to your house.' Perhaps aware that even a child can see that the car is stationary, he adds, 'I'm just ... just getting in the right frame of mind.'

They sit in silence for a few moments. Two men in a place of refuge.

Jack grimaces at the street, at its neatly trimmed hedges and shiny Volvos. 'One day, you'll realize how much you hate this place. And from that moment on, your life will never be the same.'

Unsure what to make of this advice, Luke concentrates instead on the way Jack says it: how his voice drifts off into a sad silence, so that Luke can't decide whether Jack is trying to tell him that one day he'll find something or lose it for ever.

2

Meredith is nowhere to be seen when Jack and Luke get home, but evidence of her recent presence is all over the kitchen: a large basket of laundry, so fresh it scents the air; an aborted attempt at housework, the steam iron unplugged but still warm to the touch.

Jack goes to the window, already knows she'll be out in the concrete expanse of her back garden, tending one of the small troughs that pass for flowerbeds in her world.

When Meredith and her husband had first moved in, they had optimistically called the garden 'entertaining space' but, being realistic, it's more like a miniature execution yard: the perfect place to bring people together, then gun them down. And yet there's Meredith, working with such reverence, it's as though she alone can see what's really there: not a sad concrete trench but, rather, a magic garden, an invisible kingdom.

Jack calls to her: 'You have a guest for dinner.'

'Hello, stranger! What a lovely surprise.' She clambers upright and wraps him in a big hug. 'I'm making fish pie tonight, but it's such a breeze I thought I'd do a little gardening first.' They stand in silence for a few seconds, looking at a flowerbed that contains little more than cold, dark mud and a few dead plants. 'It's winter, of course, so there's not much to see right now. But there's still work to do.'

She brushes a strand of hair from her face and unknowingly smears mud across her brow. Before Jack can say anything, Meredith's elderly neighbour, Edna, steps from her house. She steadies herself against the doorframe and starts to mumble at the sky.

'Bloody hell, she's still alive,' says Jack.

'She's a sweet old thing, really.'

'You know, I might go and see if she needs anything.' Meredith stares at him, clearly too shocked for words. 'I was thinking on the way down here I should start doing some charity work. To show people my good side and … and, you know, reach out to sad, tragic people.' He glances at the old woman again. 'There's no time like the present, surely.'

Unfortunately for Jack, Edna wants only to talk about the Second World War – which she's convinced continues to rage on all around them.

'It's more of those flying bombs,' she says. They watch as a British Airways jet passes overhead on its way to Heathrow. 'It's when the engines stop you have to worry.'

'I think we're all agreed on that one,' replies Jack.

Edna's dog joins them, an ageing mutt with milky white cataracts and creeping patches of mange.

'Your dog looks quite poorly,' says Jack.

'Reggie? He's going to die.'

'Is that what the vet said?'

9

'What do I need a vet for? One look and you can tell he's not long for this world.'

She mutters her disgust at Jack's obvious stupidity and gazes skyward again, scanning the clouds for more signs of doom.

The only note of sympathy is from Reggie. He cocks his head to the sound of Jack's voice, peering up in his general direction. Jack gives him an encouraging smile, aware that a blind dog won't get much from the gesture, but it seems the right thing to do.

They stand like that for a few moments, Edna gazing at the heavens while her dog tries to make sense of the world with his few remaining faculties.

'So, is there anything I can do for you?' says Jack, growing impatient now.

Edna gasps as a Qantas A380 comes into view. 'Dear God, is there no end to Hitler's madness?'

Before he's even aware of what he's saying, Jack can hear himself shouting at Edna, in the same voice that an over-worked teacher might use in a school for the deaf, 'Why don't you join us for dinner tonight?'

Jack would be the first to admit that his understanding of women is limited. Through years of practice he's become attuned to their pleasure, in all its forms, but beyond that they're emotionally kaleidoscopic and confusing.

This is certainly the case as he watches Meredith prepare dinner. Until a short while ago, she'd appeared genuinely pleased to see him: now her every move is redolent of a sigh.

The last time she was like this was during a much earlier visit when he had drunkenly broken one of her favourite vases. Yes, she'd said she forgave him but, much like the vase itself, their relationship gained an air of restoration: the faint whiff of glue and a patchwork of telltale cracks.

'What if she'd agreed to come?' says Meredith. 'I can't imagine what you were thinking.'

'After a reaction like that, I would have gone back and told her we'd changed our minds.'

'Jack!'

'She probably doesn't even remember I asked.'

'Is this how you plan to be with all your charity work? Taking disabled children to the park, perhaps, then leaving them there because you've changed your mind?'

'Why does everyone talk to me like I'm some kind of monster?' He raises his voice to make sure she can't respond. 'Ask yourself, would a monster invite an old lady to dinner?'

'I think that depends on the monster's motives.'

'It's about giving and receiving, isn't it? There's more joy in giving.'

'So the invitation was actually for your benefit?'

'No,' he says, in a voice that means yes. 'Perhaps I just need to feel some joy right now. Perhaps I've come to you, my only family, because I'm in the grip of a joy recession. Is that okay?'

Meredith appears to consider the words, softens a little. 'To be honest, I'm surprised you even have time for us.'

'I've taken a few months off work.'

'Well, how generous of you to be here when you could be sitting on a beach in the Caribbean.'

'I got back last week.' He sees the indignation in her face, quickly speaks again. 'Look, is this about the vase?'

'Jack, what are you talking about? That was years ago.'

'But you haven't forgiven me, have you?'

'Of course I have.'

'Melly ...'

'It was Victorian! It had survived two wars, not to mention a couple of children, which, if you were a family man, you'd know is a good deal more remarkable. And then you come along. A hundred and thirty years of perfection destroyed by my drunken, middle-aged brother.'

Jack looks hurt. 'I'm not middle-aged.'

'You're forty-three. How long do you really expect to live?' An uneasy silence descends on the room. 'Anyway, you should look on the bright side. You're my twin brother and yet somehow you manage to look five years younger than me.'

Jack's tempted to say, 'It's closer to ten years,' but this doesn't seem the right moment. Instead, he watches as she fills a baking tray with layer upon layer of fish fingers and grated cheese, eventually covering the whole thing with mashed potato. 'When you said we were having fish pie, that wasn't quite what I had in mind.'

Meredith appears to take this as a compliment. 'I know, it's so simple, isn't it?' She looks at the tray with genuine pleasure. 'It really takes no time at all.'

'If you like, I can do the cooking tomorrow.'

'You didn't say anything about staying.'

'Is it not all right?'

'No, it's fine. It's perfect, in fact. The kids are going away with their father on Saturday.' She doesn't seem to notice the look of alarm on his face. 'I'll be grateful for the company.' She starts to attack the washing-up with the efficiency of a machine. 'And I'm visiting Mummy tomorrow. She'd love to see you.'

'She'd probably love to remember who we are, too, but that's not going to happen, is it?'

'Jack, she's dying.'

'Only in the sense we're all dying.' He bites a fingernail, a childhood habit he's returned to in recent months. 'It's a slow-motion loss of life called ageing.'

'Please, you know it's more than that. Even though she can't talk, I'd like to think she's still in there somewhere. That she's aware of us. That she remembers.'

Jack looks at her and, for the first time today, feels only pity: for this grown woman who still wants to believe in their mother's goodness; an eternal child who can be knocked down again and again and yet still go back in the hope of a hug.

'Melly,' he says, 'if I was her, I think I'd rather forget.'

Five years earlier, 2007

There's a grotesque sense of carnival about it, barging into this place of silence with two young children in the throes of a tantrum, not to mention a husband who keeps saying how much he hates coming here. Meredith feels the entire nursing-home irradiated by his displeasure: only just arrived and already eager to leave.

'I just don't understand why we're here,' he says, this man who seemingly knows everything, who understands what holds the very universe together, but who doesn't grasp the connection between Meredith and her mother.

'She still understands sometimes,' is Meredith's only reply.

They thread their way across the lounge, each of its orthopedic chairs containing the remnants of a life, and join her mother by the sash windows on the far side of the room.

She's mumbling something about carrots as Meredith stoops to kiss her, the children and their father standing at a safe distance, horrified spectators to the carnage of old age.

'Happy birthday, Mummy.'

Still the mumbling continues, like a machine that no longer does what it's intended to do but at least the parts still move. And as Meredith listens to the nonsensical monologue, the faint echoes and stray radio waves of a mind now gone, it seems appropriate that fewer and fewer people want to come here because, in truth, there's less and less of her mother to visit.

'Is that Grandpa?' says Luke, pointing to one of the other residents, an aged man whose gaze remains fixed on the sky.

'No, darling,' replies Meredith, already feeling the sadness of the words that follow. 'Grandpa died a long time ago.' The words come wrapped in a pain that she still can't comprehend: a man she never met; a limb she never had but still misses.

Wanting to distract herself, she glances at the potted plants on one of the side tables. 'They're looking a little forlorn, aren't they? I'd have brought a few with me, if I'd thought of it.'

'For Christ's sake,' says her husband, Alastair. 'Is it not enough to bring a spouse, two children and a cake? Would you have us buy them some new furniture too?'

'It's just I like plants, you know that.'

'I certainly do,' he replies, the statement carried on an audible sigh, his disapproval so obvious, she doesn't even need to check that he's rolling his eyes.

The children begin to look happy only when the birthday cake is lifted from its box, the sight of smooth fondant icing managing to illuminate their young faces. Even Meredith smiles at it: an edible work of art.

'Dear God, how much did you spend on that?' says Alastair, no trace of awe in his voice.

'It's a special occasion.' She avoids looking at him as she says it; isn't even sure if she means it or simply wishes it were true. Had her mother been a different sort of person, a moment like this could at least have been a celebration of a life well lived. Instead they're here for – what? It's supposed to be love, but that can't be true because it's not love she's feeling right now.

She hands plates of cake to the children, carries another to her mother. 'Here you are, Mummy …' She scoops up a forkful, watches as her mother begins to chew, no recognition in her face that this is an expensive cake rather than, say, a jalapeño chilli or a bar of soap. 'I'm sorry Jack isn't here. He's very busy with work at the moment. But I'm sure he's thinking of you.'

Her mother fixes her with pale blue eyes, a fleeting moment of lucidity. 'Jack …' she says, the word clumsy and tumbling. 'Always such a disappointment.'

Buried secrets

3

It's been less than six months since Luke started senior school and it's gone as well as anyone expected: akin to watching Bambi trying to cross a busy motorway. After several near-misses, he's now escorted to school each morning by Jemima, the idea being that her teenage hormones are more than a match for his bullies.

This morning she takes pleasure in hurrying him through his breakfast, enjoys seeing the sheer terror in his face when she threatens to leave without him. He's still eating a slice of toast when she herds him from the house, driving him out to the street, like an animal that needs a firm hand.

Less than five minutes later, it's the car exhaust she hears first: a deep, throaty growl. Moments later, Jack pulls up alongside them in his Maserati, crawling along the kerb in a way that would doubtless seem predatory to uninformed observers. He winds down the passenger window, shouts to them, 'Let me drive you to school.'

'No, thanks,' she replies.

'Jem, this is a sports car. You're a teenager. What have I missed?'

'Aren't you a little old to be driving a car like that?'

Jack appears so stunned by the comment, he momentarily falls behind. Jemima keeps up her pace, goading Luke onwards.

With another throaty growl, Jack pulls back alongside. 'Look, I don't just want to give you a ride. I also want to talk.'

'About what?'

'I want you to take the day off. Both of you. We'll go and do something.'

'Okay,' says Luke.

Jemima punches his arm, turns to Jack again. 'You mean, take the day off *school*?'

'Don't children do that kind of thing any more?'

'Only the ones who want to spend their lives stacking shelves.'

'It's the last day before half-term. I hardly think it's going to make the difference between a stellar career and a lifetime of failure.'

'Did you skip school when you were young?'

'Sure, sometimes.'

'Well, there you go. Look at you now.'

'I'm driving a Maserati!'

'With no job to go to. And a bad case of bed head.' She watches him check his reflection in the mirror. 'This is what it's like to be jobless, isn't it? You drink too much, sleep late.'

'Piss off. I'm not jobless.' He scrambles for his wallet. 'There's twenty quid for each of you if we can just spend the day together. I'll even write a note for your teachers.'

It occurs to Jemima that she should really feel sorry for him, this man who's so desperate for company he's prostituting himself to two minors, but she also smells weakness and it seems wrong – in a fundamental, Darwinian sense – not to take advantage of that.

'Fifty,' she says.

'Bloody hell!'

'What's an extra thirty to you? You've probably spent more than that on petrol in the last five minutes.'

'Fine, you know what? I'll give both of you a hundred quid to spend the day with me.'

Jemima stares at him, dumbstruck.

'I'll take that as a yes,' he says, pushing open the passenger door. 'All I ask is we never tell your mum ...'

4

As usual, Meredith finds her mother sitting near the window, her body a tad slumped, her eyes fixed on some indeterminate point near the skirting board. Seen in proximity to the tall sash windows like this, she appears more like a miniature person, a faulty toy.

'It's a little chilly out there today,' says Meredith, giving her a kiss. 'But it's not raining, so we can't grumble, can we?'

She sits down with a cup of tea, beaming at her mother as though they're about to have a wonderful conversation; to watch them from a distance, one could almost imagine the old woman is merely playing a game, entertaining her daughter with a very convincing impression of catatonia.

Meredith passes on the children's greetings, sharing them as if they're heartfelt messages of love rather than mere inferences. She considers mentioning Jack too, but decides against it.

'The children are going away with their father tomorrow. Off to France for a week, the lucky devils. Though it's funny, Luke's excited only at the prospect of getting a beret. When you think of all that wonderful food and wine, France seems rather wasted on children, don't you think?' For a moment she's relieved her mother can't talk back: can't remind her of all the places she once dreamt of visiting, places she will never see now.

Unsure what to say next, Meredith eats a chocolate biscuit, one of the few perks of this place. 'The car is still making that funny noise whenever I change gear ...' She has a sip of tea, can feel herself succumbing to the contagious silence, every breath taking the infection deeper.

'I must say, it's strange to think of the children going off without me. I try to remind myself they'll be on holiday, that it's a happy occasion, but I've never been without them before ...' The words stick in her throat, and suddenly even the prospect of another chocolate biscuit offers no consolation. 'I know what you'd say. That I've let a good man slip away. To be honest, it's not at all how I'd imagined things turning out, and with Luke still so young ...'

She looks to her mother for comfort, but there's only the slight rise and fall of her chest to suggest she's even alive. And that's when Meredith's deepest fear comes rushing at her: that one day she, too, may be like this, unable even to recognize her own children.

Overwhelmed now, she closes her eyes, flailing for reassurance, anything, that her life is not falling apart: that her husband *will* come back to her, even if he doesn't know it yet; that her mother can sense her presence, maybe even hear her words, and that she's grateful for it.

Marigolds. Those are the first things Meredith sees emerging from the darkness. It's just a few at first, their petals catching the sunlight as they lap against the shores of her sorrows. But then more and more: a spring tide of marigolds filling every inch of the room around her, rising up and engulfing her. Her mind becomes still as she remembers how good it feels to push her fingers into the damp soil of the garden, tending living things in the certainty that she'll reap what she sows; a rhythm and cycle that can be relied on and trusted when so much in life cannot.

Eyes still shut to the world, she sits now with the hint of a smile, each passing moment making the world seem a little less forbidding.

Meanwhile

The petting zoo was Jack's idea, and he was enthusiastic about it until they got inside. At that moment, faced with a few pens of sad-looking goats and rabbits on a cold winter's day, he started making references to it being 'a tragic idea'. And for some reason, the word 'idea' seemed to make him unhappier, so that for a while Luke and Jemima simply followed him around out of pity.

Finally, Jack speaks: 'I find your silence very disturbing.'

'We're too busy having a good time,' replies Jemima.

'Christ, now I really do feel bad. A teenager trying to protect my feelings. You *are* allowed to be honest.'

Jemima twitches like a predator downwind from prey. 'You mean, we can tell the truth and you'll still give us the money?' Jack nods, but still Jemima looks wary. 'And you won't, I don't know, slash your wrists or something?'

'You have my word.'

'Fine. This place sucks.'

'Sorry, I thought kids liked this stuff.'

'I'm fifteen.'

'But you can still stroke the animals. Experience some unconditional love ...' He wanders towards a pen of sheep. They glance at him with ovine contempt and continue munching hay.

While Jack tries to call one over, Luke moves to his side. 'Are you okay?'

'I'm fine,' replies Jack, unaware that it isn't a question but, rather, the observation of an eleven-year-old boy that he's definitely not okay.

'Look,' says Jemima, 'you've bribed two children into spending the day with you, just so we can come to— God, I don't even know what this place is. Brain Damage Central. These are not the actions of a happy man. Besides which, you're old and basically unemployed—'

'Okay, okay, thank you. That's as much honesty as I'd like just for now.'

Perhaps out of pity, one of the sheep wanders across to him. It stands there, woolly and stoic, while Jack rubs it behind the ears. 'There,' he says, 'that's better, isn't it?' the words coming so softly, it's hard to tell if he's saying them to the sheep or himself. He continues the massage, the animal now lifting its head, its eyes half closed in some private reverie. Jack glances at Luke, his rhythm unbroken. 'In New Zealand, this would be considered foreplay.' Before Luke can ask about this intriguing new word, Jack has turned to the sheep again, appears distracted. 'If you must know, things haven't been going too well recently. Not just with work. With everything.'

'Does that mean,' says Jemima, 'you've been dumped by another girlfriend?'

'You know what? I think I preferred the silent Jem, the one who felt sorry for me.'

'You'll have a whole week of silence while we're away.'

'That's not exactly what I want either. Are you looking forward to it?'

'Not really,' she replies.

'It's a chance to spend some time with your dad.'

'You make it sound like he's fun to be with.'

'He's alive. I would have liked to spend some time with my dad.'

Evidently bored by the prospect of his sentimentality, Jemima takes out her phone, begins scrolling through messages.

'I visited his grave with Mummy last month,' says Luke. 'We took him some flowers. She looked very sad.' He moves closer to Jack. 'Was he a nice man?'

'I hope so, but I don't really know. He died before I was born.'

Jemima says, without looking up: 'I wish ours would die.'

'You don't mean that,' snaps Jack, the tone sharp and reproachful. 'Even if you think you do, you don't.'

'There's no need to get angry about it. He's *my* dad.'

'And you're *my* niece. I'm allowed to get angry when you say bloody stupid things.'

From behind them, a man's voice: 'You'll find a picture's a lovely way to remember the day.' They all turn to see a rotund, balding man in his fifties carrying a tray of disposable cameras. He steps closer, tries again. 'How about a picture to capture the happy moment?'

Jack glares at him. 'Does it look like we're having a happy moment?'

'Still a memory, isn't it?' He stands there, obviously planning to stay put until they buy something, anything.

'Look,' says Jack, taking out his wallet, 'if I buy one, will you piss off?'

'I'll go one better than that. I'll give you three for the price of two.' Perhaps aware that his luck can take him no further, he hurriedly tears a camera from its plastic wrapper. 'I'll even take your first picture for you.' Gripping the plasticky little thing in fat fingers, he gestures for them to huddle together. 'Perfect,' he says. 'This'll be a lovely souvenir.' Three people looking angry, confused, bored. And behind them all, a sheep in the throes of rejection. 'Everyone say, "Cheese"!'

That afternoon

It's an impromptu visit: an antidote to the nursing-home. Meredith stands beside her father's grave and marvels at the way in which the silence of this place is so full of life – birdsong and the rattle of wind in the bare trees – whereas life in the nursing-home is full only of silence.

'It's rather lovely here, isn't it?' says Meredith, unconcerned that she's talking to a headstone. 'I suppose some people wouldn't approve of saying that about a graveyard, but it's true.'

She looks at the bunches of fresh flowers laid on nearby graves, incongruous bursts of colour in this place of granite and marble.

'I saw Mummy this morning. She's doing well. Under the circumstances, I mean. I'm sure she'd send her greetings if she could.' She hesitates over the statement, not at all sure if it's true; still not sure, in fact, even after all these years, how her mother really felt about this man. She can be certain only of her own feelings for him: a man who would surely have loved her from the day she was born, and who would be so proud of the woman she's become.

'To be honest,' she says, 'it's been a bit of a challenging morning, but I'm feeling much better now. I really do think Alastair will come back to us soon. And that's not just wishful thinking, it's logic. He needs to sow some wild oats. It's what he should have done years ago. Before he met me, I mean. But he's spent his whole life with his head stuck in books, that's the trouble. He's . . .'

She notices a woman on the far side of the graveyard, her hair a shock of red, her clothes redolent of beach parties in Goa. The woman wanders from headstone to headstone, occasionally stopping to read an epitaph.

Meredith tries to focus on her father, but a monologue like this feels wrong in the presence of the living.

'So I'm sure Alastair will be back soon enough ...' Again, she glances at the woman and her ignition-flash of red hair. 'Frankly, I think a week with the kids will be sufficient to scare off that girl he's been seeing. Holidaying with children is not for the faint of heart.'

The woman wanders closer, is obviously engrossed in the graves, but her proximity alone is enough to spoil the moment for Meredith.

'You know what? I should probably be going ...' She looks at her watch apologetically, as though even the dead participate in the slow dance of English etiquette. 'I'm sorry I couldn't stay longer.' She takes a step back, stops. 'How about I bring you some nice potted plants next time?' She smiles at the thought. 'I might not do a very good job of it, but I suppose I could even grow them myself. Marigolds, perhaps.' And now her heart beats faster: at all the things she could conjure from tiny seeds; at what she could achieve with a little faith and some patience. 'I might even buy some seeds on the way home.'

Twenty minutes later

By the time Jack announces they're visiting a graveyard, nothing about the day would surprise Jemima. She'd imagined they'd hit rock bottom at the petting zoo, the family day-trip equivalent of sleeping in a shop doorway and eating out of bins. But after that they'd drifted on to an equally dismal lunch, during which Jack criticized everyone's food with the eye of a keen chef. And then he'd insisted on visiting a super-market because he couldn't bear the thought of Meredith 'trying to cook dinner again'.

'I'll say this,' says Jemima, as they slowly pull through the gates of the cemetery. 'You have a weird idea of a fun day out.'

'We don't have to stay long,' replies Jack.

'What do I care? You're paying for my time.'

'It's just I haven't been here in ages. It'd be nice to see the old man again.'

'If you want, I can take a picture of Grandpa for you,' says

Luke, one of the disposable cameras in hand. 'You can frame it and have it at home.'

'Thanks for the offer, Luke, but people tend not to put pictures of graves on the wall.'

The car advances at a sedate pace through the sea of the dead. In the distance, an open expanse of lawn awaits the mortal remains of people who possibly don't even know they'll be gone soon.

Jemima tries not to look, focuses instead on the leather of the car's dashboard. 'I know he's your father and everything . . .'

'And your grandfather,' adds Jack.

'Yes, but it's not like you ever knew him. It's not like you can visit his grave and remember all the good times you had together.'

'I don't come often.'

'Mum does.'

Jack takes his time to respond so that for a while the only sound is the purr of the engine. 'Just because we never met him, he's still our father. Sometimes it's nice to come here and just imagine how different things might have been.'

There's a moment of reverent silence as they pull to a stop, and then Luke speaks: 'Who's that at Grandpa's grave?'

Jemima cranes her neck, can see only a head of bright red hair bobbing about among the headstones.

'That's not his grave,' says Jack.

'It is,' replies Luke. 'And she's doing something to it.'

For a man who thinks Luke's wrong, Jack gets out of the

car surprisingly fast. Jemima and Luke follow, tearing after him as he zigzags through the headstones.

'Can I help you?' he shouts, as it becomes obvious that Luke was right: that this mystery woman *is* crouching at his father's grave, and *is* doing something to it.

The woman stands up, a piece of tracing paper and a crayon in hand. 'I'm just taking a rubbing. For my records.'

Jack looks confused. 'Did you know Mr Cooper?'

'Not personally, no. I'm working on my doctoral thesis and …' She evidently decides this is not the time or place. 'Can I ask what your link is to him?'

'He was my father.'

'I – I wasn't aware he had any family,' replies the woman, the words coming out in much the way a psychiatrist might try to talk a patient off a high ledge.

'Yes, my sister and I. He died before we were born.'

'So you're also Mr Cooper?'

'Well, no, we use our mother's surname.'

'But his name is on your birth certificate?'

Jack begins to sound irritable. 'No, they still hadn't married when he died. Can you tell me where this is going?'

'I'm sorry, I meant no offence. It's just … How should I say this? Mr Cooper here … he was black.'

Ten years earlier, 2002

Strip lights. Meredith's certain that's what she'll remember from these weeks, these months. Over-lit waiting rooms crowded with people expecting bad news. The endless corridors. The smell of disinfectant.

In some ways it's a blessing her mother's forgetfulness becomes worse by the week. After enduring an hour or two of doctors and tests, all the while complaining bitterly, she goes home and doesn't remember a thing.

Meredith wouldn't admit it to anyone – can barely admit it to herself – but there are times when she likes her mother more this way: a woman whose complaints are momentary and fleeting. It's as though nature is correcting some error in her; that it has determined her tyres were over-inflated, for instance, and in letting a little air out has made her a softer, more yielding person. Given enough time, it seems feasible that she could yet become the parent Meredith needs. Has always needed.

With all of this waiting in crowded hospital corridors, Meredith's thoughts often drift to her father, a man conjured from fantasy rather than fact. If he was here, she imagines they would pass the time fetching one another cups of milky tea, the stewed and bitter taste sweetened with lots of sugar and a warm smile; a simple touch that says, 'It's okay, we have each other.'

When Meredith tells people she has a twin brother, they always seem to assume that life has given her a mind-reading *doppelgänger* to atone for everything else it has not. Then they meet Jack and she can see in their faces the same question she often asks herself: how could the two of them have spent nine months together in their mother's womb yet be so different? This man who looks nothing like her, who thinks differently about all things. Two eggs, two sperm, two moments in time, and the rest seemingly counts for nothing: the months of hearing one another's heartbeats, of feeling one another kick.

As ever, he's made his apologies for not being here, but in the same tone that Meredith uses when excusing herself from an event she doesn't want to attend. He's busy, it's true, but even if he wasn't, he wouldn't be here, they both know that.

A nurse's voice rouses her, the words spoken softly, apologetically. 'Mrs Thomson, the doctor is ready for you now.'

This is when she wishes there was a hand to reach for. The warm, firm grip of someone older and wiser. Sitting here, she feels its absence: a father-shaped hole in the room.

'The dementia is early-onset,' the doctor explains. 'It's a rare form that tends to progress far quicker than normal dementia.'

'Will it kill her?'

'It's not the dementia that kills a patient. It's the loss of everything else – the mobility and the other bodily functions – all of which naturally has an impact on the immune system …' The words flow in a patient monotone, as though a diet of constant sickness and misery has made him impervious to the tragedy he's describing. '… and I need you to understand that, unlike normal dementia, early-onset is a genetic condition. Which means it can be hereditary.'

The room suddenly seems quieter.

'You're saying I may get it too?'

'I'm saying you may have the gene. Is dementia very common in your mother's family? In your grandparents, your aunts, your uncles?'

'I don't know,' she replies, aware only of a rising sense of panic. 'My mother preferred not to keep in touch with them.'

'Well, I'd certainly recommend that you and …' he glances at his notes '… your brother have a test to find out if you're carrying the gene. It's a very simple procedure.'

'And my children?' The words come too fast, too loud, this small, windowless room feeling more and more like a cabin in a stricken ship. Out of sight, water is surely rushing through the corridors, blocking all escape routes as the entire vessel begins to sink beneath the waves.

And yet still the doctor sits there, his hands neatly folded over files that foretell the destruction of everything Meredith holds dear.

'I see no reason to test your children at such an early age. Even early-onset dementia is very unusual before one's forties.'

'I'm already thirty-three.'

'Which is why a test would help put your mind at rest.'

'Unless I have the gene.'

34

The doctor hesitates, a hint of pity in his eyes. 'In which case it will give you valuable time for contingency planning.'

The car drives itself, that's how it feels. Meredith simply sits behind the wheel, going through the motions while the world slides past.

She glances at little Luke in the rear-view mirror, the back of his baby seat appearing to arc out from his body like angel's wings. He gurgles and coos at her, clearly overjoyed to have been rescued from the babysitter, the two of them out on another adventure together.

'I can't tell your father. At least, not until I've told Uncle Jack.' Luke looks confused, not at the words – he's still so young, words are mere music – but rather at her tone: as though he's being reproached for something. 'No, no, darling, everything's fine. It's just . . . Mummy's had some bad news. Something she ought to tell Daddy. Something she *will* tell Daddy. Just ... just not yet.'

Now that the words are out, she knows they're a lie. She'll tell him if he asks, but that's the thing about Alastair: he never will. She glances at Luke again, already feeling guilty that she's made him party to her deceit. 'Don't worry, darling, Daddy loves us very much. He really, really does.'

Yet still Luke stares at her with the same confusion, seemingly aware of nothing but her own doubt.

Fears and distractions

5

Meredith hadn't planned to buy quite so many seeds, quite so many pots, but now that she's in the back garden, with her purchases strewn all around her, she's certain that everything is as it should be; that there's nothing more important for her to be doing than this.

Her hands dirty with cold, damp soil, she wonders if this is the key to not forgetting: the creation of something that she will see, smell and touch for years to come; a tangible connection to the past. Perhaps if her mother could smell her youth or feel the joy of happier days between her fingers, a lifetime of memories would come flooding back, and with it an awareness of the here and now.

She notices Jack is there only when he opens the back door, his face several shades paler than usual.

'Melly, we need to talk.'

'I didn't hear you get back,' she says, downing her pots and following him indoors.

'We only arrived a few minutes ago.'

'We?'

'I, er, picked the kids up from school.'

'Well, they must love you.' She notices the bags of shopping on the kitchen table. 'What's all this for?'

'Melly, ignore that. We need to talk about Dad's grave.'

'What about it? I was there—'

'It's not his.'

Little pots of mud can't help her now, Meredith knows that much. No amount of marigolds can remedy the sensation that the ground beneath her feet has disappeared and now she's in free-fall.

Even as Jack recounted the events of the afternoon, she wanted to point out that the woman could be wrong. After all, if one should be wary of strangers, how much more so of a stranger with bright red hair?

But then the dénouement. 'She's doing some kind of doctoral thesis on slavery and ... I don't know, I lost track.'

'Slavery?'

He nods. 'George Cooper was a descendant of black slaves. A *black* descendant ...'

'Then where's our father? And why would Mummy lie to us all these years?'

'Come on, Melly, it's in character when you think about it. It's always been pretty obvious our mother saw the family tree as something to be pruned rather than nurtured.'

'But if George Cooper isn't our father, then the only person who knows the truth—'

'Is our mother.'

Meredith steadies herself against the kitchen sink. 'In which case we'll never know.'

'Harry, my partner at the agency, he used a private investigator for his divorce last year. I'm going to get the guy's details, put him onto it.'

He reaches into one of the shopping bags and takes out a can of dog food.

'What are you doing?' says Meredith.

'What I always do when I'm stressed.' He pulls open the tin and empties it onto a plate. 'I'm going to find comfort in feeding some decent food to a fellow living thing.'

Still dazed, Meredith follows Jack out to the back garden and across to Edna's house. When they reach her back door, he doesn't even bother knocking, just gently turns the knob.

'Jack, I don't think we should be breaking into an old woman's home.'

'We're feeding her dog.' The door swings open. 'Anyway, look, no breaking involved.'

They advance into the gloom, the whole house in such blackout conditions it feels like the small hours of the morning. It's immediately apparent that it's not just Edna who's stuck in the 1940s. The place is a veritable time capsule, an insight on what it meant to have no taste seventy years ago.

'Hello?' calls Jack, nearing the hallway now.

The only sound is the loud ticking of a grandfather clock at the foot of the stairs.

'God, that smell,' he whispers.

'I certainly think there's a damp problem in here.'

'Yes, but is it the house, the dog or Edna?'

Up ahead, an open doorway, a dull glow.

Meredith steels herself, tries to banish the thought that, today of all days, they're about to find Edna dead, or may actually find her alive but scare her to death.

Moving slowly, they peer into the living room. Edna sits fast asleep in a threadbare chair, the only light coming from a small table lamp. Reggie sprawls at her feet, his blind eyes wide open; his head slumped on the floor in a way that doesn't suggest slumber so much as hopelessness.

'Reggie,' says Jack, in a conspicuous whisper.

The grandfather clock begins to chime the half-hour: a sound so deep and rich, Meredith can picture Edna waking up at any second, not to mention the panicked screaming that will surely follow.

'Reggie,' says Jack, again.

Reggie's left ear pricks up.

'Yes, come on …'

He lifts his head, sniffs the air, Edna still fast asleep beside him.

'Come on, Reggie, this way …'

While Reggie rises on weary legs, Jack and Meredith retrace their steps to the kitchen.

By the time Reggie enters the room, the plate of food is on the floor, Jack standing over it with such pride anyone would think he'd cooked it himself.

Reggie hovers over the plate for several seconds, breathing in its meaty vapours. And then the eating starts, small mouthfuls at first, his tastebuds clearly unaccustomed to food like this. It quickly escalates to frantic gulps, a hungry animal in sensory overload. Even long after the food has gone, he continues licking the plate so thoroughly it's easy to believe he'll take the pattern off too.

'That was a very nice thing to do,' says Meredith.

'Well, after a day like this …' He sighs. 'It'll be a trip to the vet next.'

'Anyone would think he's our dog.'

'Perhaps he should be.' Reggie turns to him, his eyes no less expressive for being blind. 'Would you like that?'

As he gives Reggie an affectionate rub, it becomes apparent that the dog is starved of much more than food. He responds to Jack's touch by nuzzling into him, his crusty skin crackling against the fabric of Jack's jeans.

'I think he might have some greyhound in him,' says Meredith.

'I think he's got some of everything. Even a bit of water buffalo wouldn't surprise me.' He keeps stroking, seems to need it as much as Reggie. 'I promise you, Melly, we're going to find the truth about Dad. Christ knows how, but whether he's dead or alive, we're going to find him.'

6

Tonight, more than ever, Jemima needs the distraction of Lucy and her harem. Even without the trip to France tomorrow, which now looms over her like a death sentence, it's troubling to think that a long-dead relative may actually be alive, as though he's merely been mislaid for the last forty years. She isn't sure what this says about her family – or her grandfather, for that matter – but she's certain it's not good.

She escapes into her world of online suitors, gently encouraging some, dashing the hopes of others. The only downside is that the more she does it, the more the men seem like playthings, rather than real human beings.

Case in point, her newest supplicant, Brian. He's just sent her a very unflattering picture along with an impassioned message about being a widower and wanting to move on with his life. It seems vaguely sleazy that a man in his sixties wants to move on with *her*, but at least the age difference feels empowering.

Dear Brian, despite my youth and obvious beauty, I'm an old-fashioned kind of girl. Before I can agree to correspond with you, I need to know that you're serious in your intentions.

She leans back in her seat, picks the first thought that comes to mind.

I need you to send me a picture of yourself in your underwear, posing on all fours and growling for the camera like an unhappy pussycat. Please don't ask why this is important to me.

She adds a couple of kisses, hits the send button and starts clicking through her other messages, most of which are from men she's beginning to dislike: their bleating insistence that they're falling in love, all this blah, blah, blah about wanting to settle down and raise a family. She might have fallen for it last year, but she can see now that her father probably once said the exact same things.

Just as she's about to log off, a message comes in from someone new. She clicks on the picture first, in no mood to read more empty promises of affection and loyalty.

The photo was taken somewhere windswept and barren. In the centre of the frame, an athletic man smiles for the camera, a mischievous look in his eyes. Jemima leans forward and pores over the details, his broad shoulders and air of robust good health. He appears much younger than most of the men who write to her, could even be the same age as Lucy.

When she finally reads his message, she's all the more intrigued by its brevity:

I'm Tim and I'm definitely the man for you. But I think you already know that.

45

On the other side of the landing, also hidden behind a closed bedroom door, Luke, too, is sorting through secrets. He hadn't planned to take his bird to France, but it seems the right thing to do. He certainly doesn't want his mother finding it while he's gone.

It was intended to be a work of art, a *statement*, just like the dead shark and the dead cow he saw on television: lifeless animals staring out from big glass cases of bleach. Or, at least, he'd assumed it was bleach.

When he'd found a dead sparrow on the roadside last week, it was with total confidence that he brought it home and granted it immortality in an old jar full of Domestos. As it gazed out at him, preserved for all eternity, he dreamt of collecting many more specimens in the months to come; preserving them all for ever and ever right here in his bedroom.

In retrospect, bleach may not have been the right choice. Over the last week, the animal has begun to dissolve, gathering in a pink sludge at the bottom of the jar. Even by Luke's standards, it's a horrifying spectacle, yet the more he looks at it, the more certain he is that it still says something important about life. If not the bird's, then his.

Late that night
Despite the chill air, Meredith and Jack sit on the back doorstep, sharing a bottle of wine while Reggie lies at their feet.

Meredith drinks more quickly than usual, every thought seeming to lead to bigger, more daunting thoughts. 'I just can't stop wondering whether he's alive. Whether he even knows about us.'

'That's the thing, isn't it? If Mother lied to us, she might have lied to him too.'

'Think of it. All these years and maybe he never knew ...'

'And why did she choose that grave?'

'Maybe they were lovers ...'

'It's hard to imagine her being anyone's lover.'

They sit in silence now, both staring at the darkness of the garden. Finally, Jack speaks again: 'You really need to pull up all this bloody concrete.'

'Alastair likes it.'

'Alastair's gone.'

'Not for ever. He'll come back soon, I'm sure.' Jack lets the comment pass. 'Anyway,' she adds, shivering with the cold, 'it's a good space for—'

'Entertaining. I know. But how much entertaining have you actually done out here?'

'Well, there's the weather, isn't there? And Alastair doesn't really like to have people over.'

'Then get rid of it, for Christ's sake. Use your garden as a garden.'

'I've always fancied a French parterre garden.'

'The only French thing about that idea is the tragedy of it. You may as well just cut to the chase and install a guillotine.'

Meredith ignores him, takes another generous sip of wine, the edges of reality beginning to soften and blur. 'I'm dreading the kids going away tomorrow. I'm glad you'll be here.'

'Actually, I was thinking I may go back into town for a few days.' He avoids looking at her as he speaks. 'I want to talk to the investigator.'

'We do have a phone.'

'There's some other stuff I should get sorted too. You know how it is.'

'You don't want to be alone with me, do you?'

'Melly—'

'It's true. You want the entertainment of family life, but not the intimacy.'

'Thank you, Dr Freud.'

'And as for you cooking dinner this evening, that was just a very Jack way of saying I'm a crap cook, wasn't it?'

'Well, it's obvious your passions lie elsewhere.'

'Yes, and my biggest passion is my family.' Yet another mouthful of wine. 'This hasn't been a great year for family togetherness.'

'Things don't always work out the way we want, do they? That's just a fact of life.'

The mood begins to sour. 'You know, I sometimes marvel at your ability to be so detached. Like nothing matters except you.'

'Why do people seem to think I don't care about anyone but myself?'

'Because either you do a very good impression of it or it's true. You really don't.'

'I'm not Harry Potter, Mel. I don't have a wand to make the world a better place. Do you not think I would if I could?'

'I don't know. Not for Mummy, perhaps.'

'What – just because I see no point in sitting around a mausoleum of a nursing-home—'

'It's not that bad.'

'Yes, it is. It's like some avant-garde chapel of rest where they put the dead in armchairs rather than coffins.'

'Jack, it could be us one day. Doesn't that scare you?'

'Have you still not had the test?' Meredith looks away. 'Maybe you don't even have the gene.'

'True, but what if I do? I sometimes think uncertainty is the closest thing I have to hope.'

'Melly, you have kids. You *need* to know.'

'I would ask if you've had the test, but there's really no point. Everything always works out for you, doesn't it?' She becomes more animated, oblivious to Jack's offence. 'Could you not at least look your age? Is that too much to ask, that my perfect twin brother gets a few more wrinkles and starts to sag in all the wrong places?'

'Melly, I appreciate you're having a difficult day, a difficult year, but there's no need to be like this.'

'Like what?' she replies, a slight slur in her words now. 'I'm just being honest. That I sometimes feel like a very second fiddle to your continual ability to – to walk on water.' She finishes her wine. 'And, of course, it had to be *you* who found out about our father. The man who only bothers to come down here once in a blue moon and, bang, everything just falls at your feet.'

Jack puts the wine bottle out of her reach. 'I think you've had enough.'

'I've lost interest, thank you.' She stands up, a little unsteady.

'You know, Jack, it's odd to me. You're the man who has everything, and yet here you are, in this place you say you hate so much. It makes me wonder what you really want from us.'

'Trust me, Melly, you have nothing I want.'

'Even if that's true,' she says, heading indoors, 'I suspect we have something you need.'

7

The moment of the kids' departure has all the stoic Britishness of a wartime flick: as Meredith gives each of the children a hug and tells them to be good, the look in her eyes suggests that, in the days to come, the family home is likely to be reduced to rubble, doubtless while she's still in it.

It's the way she insists on hugging Alastair that's most telling: wrapping him in an embrace that's a little too long, a little too tight. Clenched like this, her face almost buried in his neck, she takes a deep breath. 'You always smell so nice,' she says. 'I love that aftershave.'

Finally, Alastair disentangles himself, takes a step back. 'Well, we'd better get going.' He shoos the kids towards the car, each of them trailing oversized bags full of things they probably don't need.

Meredith calls after them, 'I look forward to seeing all of you back here soon.'

Moments later, doors are being slammed and they're pulling away. And still Meredith stands in the doorway, waving goodbye until the car is out of sight.

When she eventually closes the front door, the emptiness of

the house feels suffocating, as though the kids have somehow taken all the oxygen with them too.

'I'll get going in the next few minutes,' says Jack.

'Look, I'm sorry about last night, I—'

'Forget it.'

'But I feel like I'm driving you away.'

'No, I should really spend some time back in town.' An awkward moment of silence. 'Will you be all right?' he says, aware that the answer is no.

Despite the panic in her eyes, the look of a woman dissolving in her own pain, she manages a cheery smile. 'Don't worry about me, I'll be fine.'

Fifteen years earlier, 1997

'How can you not want to know what sex it is?'

Meredith's mother makes it sound like a failing, akin to not being able to tie shoelaces or read.

'We want it to be a surprise.'

'Childbirth is no time for surprises. For all you know, it will come out with three legs. Then you'll be sorry for wanting a surprise.'

When Meredith had first revealed she was pregnant, her mother had been decidedly indifferent, almost as if she didn't think Meredith was up to the task of parenthood. But as the months have passed, and the bump has grown, she seems to have warmed to the idea of a grandchild. She's been especially helpful in recent weeks, attending to Meredith's needs in much the way that Meredith normally attends to hers. And yet still Meredith can't shake the feeling that her mother has ulterior motives: that she's staking her claim, not just as a family member but as part-owner.

'It's not twins,' her mother says, a critical eye on Meredith's bump. 'When I was carrying you and Jack, I thought the ground would buckle beneath me, you were such a heavy load. People call it the miracle of life, but you two nearly killed me.' She lights a cigarette, takes a long drag. 'Have you chosen names?'

'Luke if it's a boy. Jemima if it's a girl.'

She watches her mother through the haze of cigarette smoke, can see she dislikes both options.

'I hope for your sake it's a boy. Just not one that turns out like your brother.'

'What are you talking about? Jack's lovely.'

'Well, I never get to see him, I really wouldn't know.'

'How's Alastair dealing with the pregnancy?' says her mother, the cigarette break having morphed into an early lunch.

'Fine.' Meredith struggles to think what else she can say about her husband, a man prone to metronomic routine. The whole world could come to an end and he would still get up at the same time in the morning, dress in the same corduroy jacket and go off to work with some ham sandwiches and a banana. 'It's not him carrying the baby, is it?'

Her mother frowns. 'Is that some kind of feminist thing? This disinterest in your husband's happiness?'

'No, I just mean he's fine. He's always fine.'

'You even manage to make that sound like a bad thing.' She becomes more strident, as though Alastair is her child and Meredith is merely the daughter-in-law; an interloper who's not yet learnt the family's ways. 'You *need* a man who's solid and dependable.'

'Alastair is certainly solid. Sometimes I think he's frozen solid.'

'And that's a good thing.' She finishes making cheese

sandwiches, each of them just a slab of Cheddar between two barely buttered pieces of bread; the latest in a lifetime of meals that are as dry and joyless as the woman herself. 'You should consider yourself lucky to have him. Raising a family with a good man, that was never an option for me.'

Meredith accepts her lunch, begins to peck at it, hopeful that this small act of gratitude might encourage her mother to talk more about the past. 'Do you think you would have had more children if Dad hadn't died?'

'"Dad",' she says, an unmistakable snarl in her voice. 'You make it sound like you knew him.'

So Meredith concentrates on the sandwich instead, washing down every mouthful with a sip of water. Despite her uneasiness, the silence seems to have a restorative effect on her mother.

'I don't know if I would have had more children,' she says. 'It's cause and effect, isn't it? Given what most men want, I suppose it was quite likely.'

It's not exactly the fond remembrance that Meredith has in mind, but it's something. From this speck of gold dust, she chooses to believe that her father was a hot-blooded male. Everything that Alastair is not.

Her mother glances at her while she eats, the hint of a frown on her face. 'Next time you see fit to criticize your husband, I suggest you take a look in the mirror. Unless that baby is some kind of immaculate conception, he's obviously not as cold as you say.'

The truth bubbles up

8

It's the first time Meredith has been without the children – the first time she's ever been alone in this house – and it feels as though gravity itself has failed. Her entire life is beginning to float away from her, everything she wants to hold onto now moving out of reach.

It's only for one week, she keeps saying to herself, repeating it like a mantra over and over, desperate to invest the words with mystical power.

She ends up at the nursing-home for her own sake rather than her mother's. To fill the hours. To hide her loneliness in a cloak of filial duty.

At first they sit in silence, Meredith wishing she was like some of the psychics she's seen on TV dramas, able to divine the truth of her mother's history with a mere touch. It's such a compelling thought, so seductive in its simplicity, she pulls her chair closer and reaches for her mother's hand. As she takes it in her own, she braces herself for what may come, a thunderbolt of clarity, so that for a split-second Meredith will find herself standing face to face with the man she's dreamt of and grieved over for almost forty years.

But here she is, holding her mother's hand, and all she feels is the frailty of old age: a loose assembly of skin and bone.

Self-conscious now, she lets go, pretends she was merely saying hello.

'I saw Alastair today.' She surreptitiously pushes her chair back a little. 'He was looking well. I wish he could have come in for a cup of tea or something, but there was the other woman … Charlotte …' The name comes out like a cough, something bronchial and contagious. 'Not that there's any need to think of her, of course. I mean, she's really just a symptom of all the other stresses we'd accumulated in our lives. The way we never seemed to talk about any of our problems.'

She thinks back to the day he left, to the veritable spring-head of angry words that came rushing at her, a resentment that must have been percolating through the rock of their marriage for years.

'We were never very good at discussing difficulties … Or maybe it's just me. Maybe it's my problem.' She shifts in her seat, reluctant to say what she's thinking, but desperate to confess it to someone. 'You know, I worry I didn't say enough that day. Maybe it wouldn't have changed anything, but surely it's better to say too much than too little. After it blew up, all I did was watch him go, my husband of twenty years. I just stood there, too stunned to say anything at all …'

A nurse silently approaches, her footfall as gentle as her manner. 'You're looking like you could do with some help.'

Meredith, who naturally assumes she's talking to her, is unsure whether this is perceptive or plain insulting. But then

60

the nurse starts rearranging her mother's cushions, and all the while continuing in the same calm, kindly tone: 'We want to look our best for our visitor, don't we? A beautiful young lady like you.'

Meredith watches her work, listens to her voice of endless patience. This woman who knows better than most that this is the end of the line, a place of slow goodbyes, yet still has the energy and goodwill to make the moment feel hopeful.

'I won't be long,' she says to Meredith. 'Why don't you make yourself another cup of tea while I finish up?'

Out in the pantry, Meredith tries to busy herself with teabags and hot water, suddenly wishing she lived in some ancient Chinese dynasty, so she could spin the simple act of making a cup of tea into a long and time-consuming ritual. She doesn't notice the nurse standing behind her now, watching her hands fuss over teaspoons and sugar cubes, desperate for something to keep them busy.

'Old age is a bugger, isn't it?'

Startled, Meredith turns to face her. 'Excuse me?'

'Watching people you love fade away. It's a terrible thing. But you do a wonderful job of it. And there aren't many who come as often as you.'

'Thank you,' she replies, her only thought that she can't remember how many spoons of sugar she's already put in her tea.

They stare at one another for a moment.

'Well, I should get back to the grindstone,' says the nurse, backing away.

'How much longer do you think my mother will live?'

The nurse stops, gives her an encouraging smile. 'She's getting very frail, but I'll say this: she's a tough one. She's made of stern stuff.'

'Yes,' replies Meredith, the words tinged with sadness. 'Yes, she is.'

9

It had become obvious within minutes of leaving home that Jemima's father and Charlotte have a challenging relationship. First she criticized him for driving too fast, then for driving too slowly, and then came the announcement that just *being* in the car was making her feel ill, as though even the bends in the road were his fault. By the time they reached the coast, the Channel Tunnel seemed more like the gates to Hell, a dark, bottomless hole from which they would never return.

True, they now find themselves amid rolling Norman countryside, but in the kind of tense silence that only an unhappy family can achieve, pressing on with the trip despite every indication that it's doomed.

It doesn't take Charlotte long to decide that feeling nauseous on the road in England is infinitely preferable to feeling nauseous on the wrong side of the road in France.

'But it's the right side of the road *here*,' says Alastair, in the same tone of strained patience he uses when having to explain anything – from how to tie a knot, to the quantum mechanics of dark matter.

It's not a major problem while they're on the motorway – Charlotte keeps asking if there are airbags on her side of the car, but in general she remains pretty calm. It's when they progress to country roads that the real problem starts. At first she merely whimpers that it's disorienting to be sitting on the wrong side of the car: that she finds it disturbing to see oncoming vehicles hurtle towards her. Before long, however, she's worked herself into tearful hysteria, screaming that the approach of every car feels like a near-death experience.

By sunset Jemima's father gives up trying to reach the cottage, instead decides that they should spend their first night in a hotel, 'any damned hotel, as long as it means I can get out of this bloody car'.

This low requirement is evident in his choice: a place of hard mattresses and stained carpets, with a smell in the bathroom suggestive of bad plumbing and death.

It seems par for the course that Jemima's expected to share her room with Luke; might even have to share it with complete strangers by the time the night is through, stepping over squatters and drug addicts whenever she needs to use the toilet.

'There are two pairs of greasy handprints here,' says Luke, staring at his headboard. 'Why would people hold on to the headboard like that? And why were their hands greasy?'

'It's France, dumbo.'

'Do you think I can buy my berry near here?'

'One, it's a *beret*. And, two, I don't care.' She turns on her computer, gives thanks that a place like this has WiFi. 'If you make any more noise, you'll die in this room. Is that clear?'

After the rigours of the day, Lucy isn't just a diversion, she's a lifeline. And yet there's something about her picture that

64

Jemima finds offensive tonight. She's just too *innocent*, as though her only understanding of disappointment is when her favourite kind of cupcake is out of stock.

Jemima sets about rewriting Lucy's profile: 'I was raised by a string of foster parents,' she types, 'many of whom touched me in inappropriate ways.'

From the room next door, she hears her father and Charlotte raising their voices at one another, their words muffled and distorted by the carpeted walls.

As the voices grow louder, Jemima types faster: 'I have eleven different parents – fourteen if you include the heroin addicts and the rapists, but I don't keep in touch with those.'

From next door, the loud thud of a slamming door.

'It sometimes seems like everything is wrong,' she writes, no longer sure of the line between fact and fiction, between her own life and Lucy's. 'All I want is someone who can make me feel safe and loved.'

As soon as she's posted the new profile, she takes another look at Tim's picture, tries to imagine him being right here, right now, holding her in those strong arms, how nothing would seem daunting with him by her side. It's such a calming thought that she hammers out a message to him too, typing words she never thought she'd say:

I need to tell you something. The picture on my profile is fake. Here's my real picture. And I'm still a teenager. Is that a problem for you?

10

When Harry grasps that it's Jack on the phone, he replies in a loud voice, as though his words need the extra volume to reach Jack on the far side of the world.

But then Jack explains that he's in London. That he has, in fact, just got home from Surrey. And he's calling to invite Harry to dinner.

'You what?' says Harry, sounding more and more confused.

'Dinner. At my place.'

'Just the two of us?'

'For Christ's sake, it's dinner, not sodomy.'

'Jack, it's Saturday. I do have a life. My night was booked up weeks ago.'

'It's just I want to discuss something,' says Jack. 'In private, I mean. Just you and me.'

The silence that follows is ripe with anticipation. The last time Jack asked to talk privately like this, just the two of them at his place, it was ten years ago and he somehow convinced Harry they should set up their own agency. It was a mad, reckless, terrifying decision that saw them work longer hours than either of them had ever thought possible, but then, through some mystical combination of hard work, coke-fuelled arrogance and sheer dumb luck, the agency started winning big clients, big money. And the more successful they became, the more they found themselves in demand.

'So it's important, then?' says Harry.

'Yes, mate. It's important.'

'Fine,' he replies, clearly trying to hide his excitement. 'I'll come for a few pre-dinner cocktails.'

It's obvious when Harry arrives that he's expecting many things, but not to find Jack listening to Cliff Richard.

'I didn't know you were into … this kind of music,' he says, barely out of his coat and already looking worried.

'I'm not. Not really, anyway. I'll make us a drink.' He wanders towards the kitchen just as Cliff starts crooning about taking a summer holiday.

'For Christ's sake,' says Harry, following close behind, 'this is the musical equivalent of electro-shock therapy.'

'My father looked like Cliff Richard. Have I ever mentioned that?'

'He could *be* your father and it still wouldn't be a good excuse to listen to this.'

'I never met him.'

'Who? Cliff Richard?'

'No, my dad.' Jack starts to mix their drinks with all the reverence of a priest performing last rites. 'My mother never really spoke about him, but I remember she said a couple of times that he looked like Cliff Richard …' He glances at Harry, suddenly aware that the absence of a sarcastic retort is a bad sign. 'Do you think the music is too much?'

'No, no, it's fine,' replies Harry, evidently worried that some saccharine song may be all that stands between Jack and a full mental breakdown. 'Your dad died when you were young, right?'

'Before my sister and I were born. Or so our mother said.' He hands Harry a martini. 'But I've just found out she lied. About his grave, at least.'

'Jesus ...'

'That's why I asked you over. I want the name of that investigator you used last year.'

Harry chokes mid-sip. 'Is that all?' He sees the look on Jack's face. 'Not that this isn't important, of course, but you could have just emailed me or something.'

'This is my life we're talking about. It's existential stuff.'

'Yeah, course ...' He appears to listen to Cliff for a few moments, as if trying to divine something from the lyrics. 'I never knew it was so important to you. Your dad's absence, I mean.'

'Sure. I've always wondered what it's like to have a dad. My whole life.'

Harry swallows a hefty slug of his martini. 'You know what I think? That investigator is the wrong guy.'

'He worked out okay for you.'

'But that was an easy job. Any muppet could have followed Laura around. She was practically shagging in the park ...' Not consciously aware that this is still a painful memory, he drains his glass. 'I've heard about this other guy. He's like ex-Mossad or something.'

'For Christ's sake, I just want to find an old man, not assassinate someone.'

'And when you find the truth? Are you sure you're ready for it?'

'I don't know,' replies Jack, choosing not to look at Harry as he says it. 'All I know is I have to find out.'

Meanwhile, in Surrey

They're good listeners, those little pots of mud. And Meredith consoles herself that the monologue is good for *them* too; that the tiny seeds need her gentle, encouraging voice at this moment more than ever as, deep down, out of sight, they burst into life.

In truth, she'd started talking to the pot of yogurt first – standing at the open door of the refrigerator, gazing past rows of eggs and a bunch of wilting parsley – recalling how she'd first bought Alastair's aftershave as a birthday gift, back in the early days of their marriage, long before the children came along. How she'd struggled for weeks over what to buy him, not the man who had everything but the man who appeared to need so little.

It was only when the fridge alarm started bleating that Meredith closed the door and moved on to her pots of freshly planted seeds.

'Alastair's always been so disapproving of frippery that I was worried he'd hate the gift,' she tells them. 'And it's true, he did look a bit nonplussed when he finally opened it. So I told him the scent was "very distinguished, very virile".'

She smiles at the memory. How from that day forward he had sprayed it on each morning before going to work. How the smell of it lingering around the house became a reminder of their new life together, a comforting thought on all the long days she'd spent alone at home, trying to be the kind of wife he wanted.

In the silence that follows, she stares at the pots of mud and wonders if the story might have done the seeds more harm than good: if they feel anything like her, they probably just want to curl up and cry now.

'I might pop out for a while,' she says, the words instantly swallowed by the emptiness of the house. 'There's probably something I need from the shops …'

The only reason Meredith's come to the department store is to smell Alastair's aftershave again, but now that she's here she's so certain that it's a regressive, hopelessly neurotic thing to do that she spends the first hour looking at everything else instead: a process of elimination that inevitably ends at her brightly lit target, the air thick with the scent of myriad fragrances.

At first she just sprays Alastair's aftershave on a paper strip, sniffs it as though smelling it for the first time. There's a certain pleasure in this coy ritual, much like being on a first date – an exchange of mere flirtations rather than an immediate progression to full intercourse.

She takes another sniff, can picture the scene: a charming French café, sunlight coming through the trees; the two of them sitting at separate tables; strangers who've just made eye contact for the first time.

She's so swept up in the fantasy, she only notices the sales woman once she's standing right beside her, the white lab coat suggestive of a psychiatric facility.

'Do you need help?'

Unsure whether the woman wants to sell her perfume or medicate her, Meredith just stares, the aftershave enveloping them both in a cloud of amber top notes.

The woman inches closer. 'Is it for your husband? Or your father, maybe?'

'Yes, that's right,' replies Meredith, already reaching for her purse, wanting only to get away from this place of bright lights and personal questions. 'I'll take the smallest bottle.'

'So is that *two* bottles you want? One for your husband and one for your father?'

In the background, Meredith can hear a song playing for the third time since she got here: a fitting statement of her day, her life.

'My father's dead,' she says, the words coming out louder than she'd anticipated. 'Though he may not be, we're not sure any more. And my husband's just taken my children to France. With his new girlfriend. So I'll just take the one bottle, thank you.'

She's practically running by the time she nears the doors, overwhelmed by the thought that she wouldn't be here right now if her marriage had worked out differently; if she was a better, more lovable person.

As she pushes into the cold night air, the feeling of failure is visceral. It's a Saturday evening and she's become a mere spectator of the world around her: everyone seemingly going somewhere with someone, the night ahead sparkling with the promise of candlelit dinners, and beyond that a lazy Sunday full of snuggling and companionship.

Under the circumstances she does the only thing she can do: she stops off on her way home and buys several tins of dog food. And later that evening, when she's certain that Edna has once again fallen asleep, she goes back and feeds Reggie, spending much longer this time on the inevitable nuzzling that follows, wanting to bottle it, in fact, and take it away with her, the sensation of being loved and needed by another living thing.

When she finally returns to the silence of her home, she avoids saying anything to her plants; is certain that every word would have come laced with such sorrow, the plants would have been dead by morning. Instead, she retreats to her bedroom, taking the aftershave from its box and spritzing her sheets and pillow cases, trying to remember the pleasure of all those years when this smell represented the man she loved.

11

It's a new beginning. That's what Luke's father says the next morning as they prepare to leave the hotel. It's the first day of their holiday.

'I thought yesterday was the first day?' says Luke, confused by the way his father is saying everything in a bright, cheery manner at odds with his usual personality.

His father ignores him. 'Charlotte's decided she'd rather sit in the back for the ride to the cottage so, Jemima, you'll be sitting up front with me.'

He clears his throat, glares at Charlotte as though she's just missed her cue.

'Oh, sorry!' she says, turning to Luke with all the sincerity of a ham actor. 'That means you and I can get to know each other better. I can't wait.'

In Charlotte's defence, things go well at first. Luke can tell she's scared of being on the road again, but whenever she notices him looking at her, she tries to laugh it off, as if the journey is actually a fairground ride and being petrified is part of the fun.

It's when he opens his bag to look for some sweets that the day starts to unravel.

Charlotte notices the top of the bird jar. 'What's that?' she says.

'It's not important,' he replies, hurriedly shutting the bag.

'But it looked interesting.'

'You wouldn't like it.'

'You don't know that. I like all sorts of things.'

'But it's not really for show, it's … I couldn't put it in my suitcase because it's fragile.'

'Well, now you *have* to show me. I'm fascinated.'

'What's going on back there?' says Alastair.

'Luke is about to show me something very special.'

'Then go on, Luke. Reveal all.'

Certain that this is a bad idea, Luke nevertheless opens his bag again, holds the jar up for Charlotte.

The good news is that she no longer looks scared by the other cars on the road. Unfortunately, when she realizes what it is, she starts to scream.

It's such a blood-curdling scream that Luke's father turns in his seat, the car drifting into the path of oncoming traffic.

'Look out,' yells Jemima.

As the other cars begin to blare their horns, Alastair swerves back into the right-hand lane. He moves so sharply that the jar slips from Luke's hands, its lid coming loose as it falls to the floor beside Charlotte.

It's hard to say which is worse: the smell of bleach, the smell of the long-dead bird or the escalation of Charlotte's shrieking. It doesn't help that she's wearing Capri pants, the bleach and pink sludge splashing across her bare ankles.

By now, the car could drive off a cliff and she wouldn't notice.

'It's burning!' she screams. 'It's burning my skin!'

The next few minutes are a roadside blur, the car abandoned at an odd angle while Alastair rinses off Charlotte's feet with bottle after bottle of Evian. The passing cars honk noisily, everyone bemoaning these crazy English tourists who think they can park wherever they want.

Saving Charlotte's ankles was relatively easy compared to the task of extracting bird sludge from the back of the car. Charlotte sits at a distance, crying, and Jemima is even further away, her headphones on, her mind clearly elsewhere. Only Alastair and Luke stay with the vehicle, the air thick with the smell of ammonia and decay.

'What in Christ's name were you thinking?' says Alastair, trying to scoop up … something. 'Why would you bring this on holiday?'

'It's art. It's a reminder that life can be cruel sometimes, that when we're in the wrong place, we begin to disappear.'

'Luke, what utter nonsense are you talking? I don't—'

'What I mean is, it was an experiment,' says Luke, choosing to lie now. 'It was a *science* experiment.' Luke knows this is the magic word. He's pretty sure he could have brought anti-matter with him, could have accidentally wiped out all of Western Europe, and his father would still find it excusable in the name of science.

'Well, this isn't a laboratory,' he says, his tone already softening. 'This is supposed to be a holiday.'

'I just didn't want Mum finding it while I was gone.'

'I suspect she would have handled it better than Charlotte.'

They both glance in her direction again. Her face wet with tears, she's started shouting at the passing motorists and their incessant horns. 'Fuck off, all of you! *Je t'emmerde! Ta mère la pute!'*

'What is she saying?' says Luke.

His father seems reluctant to explain. 'It's nothing. She's fine.'

The rest of the journey is made in silence, all the windows down. Charlotte leans from the car in a doglike pose, but with no lolling tongue or wagging tail to suggest it's an enjoyable experience.

The cottage turns out to be a bucolic idyll – a half-timbered warren of beamed ceilings, soft beds and views of cows grazing in the meadows. But the atmosphere is so tense by now that everyone retreats to their room, no one wanting to speak.

Only Jemima breaks the silence, staring at her phone as though something's broken. 'I thought you said there was WiFi here?'

'I said no such thing,' replies her father. 'One of the specific selling points of this place is that there's not.'

'Not even a mobile signal?'

'We're on holiday, Jemima. You'll soon understand what a special and wonderful thing it is to be completely out of reach.'

12

Meredith wakes up that morning fully clothed on her bed, the scent of aftershave – much like the man it was supposed to represent – already fading.

She tries watching television to pass some time, but it seems to only heighten her sense of isolation, her connection to the world reduced to something two-dimensional and scripted. And books, which in other times have brought so much pleasure, offer surprisingly little solace today – though it doesn't help that every book seems to come with its own set of memories: family holidays on the beach, or leisurely afternoons on the sofa while Alastair worked beside her.

There's some satisfaction in watering the seeds, though she still doesn't feel emotionally equipped to coo over them in the manner they deserve.

Her aimless perambulation around the house ends at the kitchen sink, Meredith staring out at the back garden. In any other season she would already be out there getting mud under her nails, but even she has to admit there's only a certain amount that can be done to a few small flowerbeds in late winter.

*

Under the circumstances, it wasn't a difficult decision for Meredith to visit the garden centre, drawn there like a Catholic to the grotto of Lourdes.

She starts in the glass-roofed nursery, its aisles crowded with plants reaching out in all directions. The air is thick with the scent of damp earth, and even the sky looks different seen like this: framed as though it's a hundred works of art, each grey square subtly different from the one before.

Standing there, she decides she'd happily trade her entire home for a massive glasshouse. She and the children would live in tents beneath banana trees and pick fresh guavas for breakfast. They would be a suburban Swiss Family Robinson, the heavy, humid air swaddling them all like a warm hug.

Feeling more alive with every step, she moves deeper into the store, into aisles of garden tools, a hundred varieties dangling before her in virginal purity, all begging to be taken away and sullied. She lingers over the massive garden hoses and their sophisticated winding mechanisms, certain that her life would be richer if she owned one, not because she needs five hundred feet of kink-free hose, but because every time she looked at it she would remember that even the most unwieldy things in life can be reeled in and returned to a state of order.

She takes the longest time over the garden sheds – finds herself wondering if her father has one. The father she's never met. The father who may or may not still be alive.

As she enters one of the larger sheds, she tries to imagine that it's his, that the window doesn't look out at a sales assistant picking his nose but, rather, at a sea of sweet peas and forget-me-nots. If she'd known him in childhood, the smell of this shed, its heady scent of wood and creosote, would take her back to those times, to a gentle soul tinkering in here all day, but always happy to be distracted by mischievous young daughters and their fond kisses.

Reggie is waiting for her when she gets home, sitting outside her back door as though Edna is merely a part-time act of charity.

'Would you like to help me sort out my new plants?' she says, aware that he's a dog but so eager for conversation it's as much as she can do not to ask him about his homework and whether he's tidied his room yet.

He enters the kitchen, the floor covered with eight trays of plants: tiny things, barely more than zygotic shoots, each in a peaty little pot.

Even in the absence of sight, Reggie goes straight to them, the aromas of damp earth and chlorophyll bringing to life a world he cannot see.

'They were very cheap,' she says, as if Reggie is quietly judging her, though she decides not to explain how she ended up with so many – the way she had felt when she'd bought the first two, taking them out to the car with such a spring in her step, it had seemed wrong to drive away without buying more: so she had gone back and bought another three. By the time she had started arranging them in the boot, it had seemed more logical to buy enough to fill the entire space. 'They would have slid around otherwise,' she says, distracted now by the thought of how many other plants she could have got if she'd gone with a flat-bed truck, or an eighteen-wheel juggernaut.

Reggie licks her hand, rousing her from the daydream.

'Yes, I know,' she says, trying to find a patch of mange-free skin she can rub. 'We're going to make it look lovely in here, aren't we?' And although this suddenly strikes her as a cruel thing to say to a blind animal, he nevertheless rubs up against her, wagging his tail so happily that his whole body appears to be on the move.

13

Sunday morning in London, and although most of the city is still in bed with a hangover, Harry's private investigator agrees to meet Jack straight away.

Jack's always assumed that the guy must be fairly impressive if Harry chose him to spy on his wife. This is the same Harry, after all, who drives an Aston Martin. The same Harry whose coke dealer lives in Mayfair.

It comes as a surprise, then, to find the investigator has the look of a man who finds everyday life a frightening experience. Jack watches as he turns paler the more he learns about the case.

'Ah, well,' he says, fidgeting in his seat, 'that already sounds very complicated. If you can't even give me a name to go on, it's not like I can just look him up on Facebook, is it?'

'I'd imagined your techniques were rather more sophisticated than that.'

He looks offended. 'Of course they are. I have *many* different ways of hunting people down. It's just some are more effective than others.' He begins to scribble something in a notepad, though it looks more like an excuse to avoid eye contact.

'Have you ever handled a case like this?' says Jack.

'I've done it all, Mr Harris. You name it, I've done it. And it can be dangerous work, I'm telling you. I've even had my tyres slashed. A brand-new Fiat Panda, only a few hundred miles on the clock.' He looks sad for moment, as though his life hasn't been the same since.

Jack breaks the silence. 'So when do you think you might be able to tell me something?'

'How long is a piece of string? From what you've told me, this is going to be a highly complex mission. And, for all we know, it may even be risky.'

'This is an old man we're talking about.'

'Have you never seen *The Godfather*?'

'He's my dad.'

'You've just told me you don't even know his name. If you don't know something as fundamental as that, how can you be sure he's not involved in organized crime? That he's not got links to the Russian Mafia?' He clearly takes Jack's disbelief as a sign of contrition. 'This is the world I move in, Mr Harris. But you have my word, I'll give it my very best shot.'

It's afternoon by the time Jack returns to his empty, quiet apartment. After the rough and tumble of family life with Meredith and the kids, it doesn't just feel silent, it feels barren – a blank canvas still awaiting the imprint of real life.

He finds that Meredith has left several messages while he was out. Even though he doesn't want to hear from her right now, he still smiles at the sheer Meredith-ness of it: that she would choose to call his home rather than risk actually reaching him by calling his mobile; that her simple message of apology ran out of time not just once, but twice.

He listens to her voice echo through the apartment as he wanders around trying to figure out how he can make the place more homely.

'I feel so bad about what I said to you because it's just not true. Not about you not being successful, of course, because you are, but about finding it wrong, which it isn't and I don't. I need you to know I'm so proud of you for everything you've accomplished. You're like the North Star to my long, dark night.' She pauses. 'Actually, I'm not really sure what I mean by that, but it sounds nice, don't you think?' There's another pause, as though she's forgotten she's speaking to an answer machine and now expects a reply. 'Oh, where was I? Yes, of course … What I mean is, I'm calling to apologize, but only for sounding bitter, which I'm—'

The machine cuts her dead. Plays the next call.

'That's a very short amount of time for a message. It makes me think either I'm the only person who uses this machine, in which case it's been specifically engineered to frustrate me, or everyone else you know is just very succinct. Which I suppose they are, working in advertising. For all I know, you talk to each other in catchy slogans and jingles. No wonder you find the rest of us mundane. I suppose life down here must seem very boring by comparison.' She stops speaking again, perhaps realizing that she, too, now finds her life depressing. 'But that's why I love you, Jack. Because you've got on with your life and achieved things. God, more things than I would ever have thought possible. And what have I done? Other than having two wonderful children, of course, but I hardly think I can take credit for the miracle of life. It's not like I invented it. So, all I really did was screw up my marriage, probably by being the same sort of ninny I was with you the other day. I mean, who wants to spend their life with—'

Jack is standing by his bookshelves when the machine starts to play her third and final message. These are expensive, architectural shelves, and right now they have all the personality of a test tube; home to pristine books he's almost never touched. He thinks of Meredith's shelves and laughs to himself: the postcards and photos that jostle for attention alongside well-thumbed books, everything appearing to have been through some kind of war, and yet survived because it's loved.

'This machine really is out to get me, isn't it? Not that I'm being paranoid. In fact, that's why I'm calling. To say I'm not mad or paranoid or crazy. Not all the time, anyway. I'm just so, so proud of you. And I love you very much. Which is my whole point, really. That whatever the future holds, you and me and the children, we're family. And when I think of that, I think I'm the luckiest person alive.'

To her credit, she simply hangs up – perhaps understands that any attempt to say 'goodbye' or 'see you soon' would end up spilling across countless more messages.

Jack is standing in the window by the time silence returns to his orderly, sterile existence. Outside, London is awash with rain, the streets so grey and sodden it seems possible they will never dry out. This city has been home for more than twenty years, but as he stands there, it feels like someone else's history, not his own.

Before he's even aware of what he's doing, he's pulling on his jacket and picking up his car keys. There's only one place he should be right now. Only one thing he needs to say.

Less than an hour later
It's already getting dark when Meredith's front-door bell rings, the heavy rain adding to the sense that something terrible has happened.

Reggie escorts her to the door, his mangy frame and unseeing eyes unlikely to scare anyone, but he's a comforting presence nevertheless.

When she opens the door and sees Jack, she's so surprised that she momentarily forgets to invite him in. They just stare at one another as the rain soaks through his clothes, a sleek ensemble doubtless chosen for its form rather than its function.

He smiles at her, the same innocent smile she remembers from when they were kids; back when they were an army of two pitched against impossible odds. 'Hello, Melly.'

'Gosh, I didn't … Come in, come in. You'll catch your death of cold.' She hurries him inside, closes the door behind him with a reassuring clunk.

Dripping, he turns to her. 'We need to talk.'

'If this is about what I said …'

'Melly, I listened to all, I don't know, twenty-five minutes of your messages. Don't worry, the other day is history.'

'It's just I was so wrong to say what I did.'

'But you were right. You do have something I need.'

'And the way I said it. So jealous and … and *bitter.*'

'Look, it's okay.'

'Which I'm not, by the way. Bitter, I mean. I'm actually very proud of everything you've done.'

'Melly . . .'

'Very, very proud.'

'Melly, when I had the test—'

'But I need to make that clear. It's important to me.'

Jack raises his voice, talks over her: 'Melly, when I had the test ... it came back positive.'

Twenty years earlier, 1992

The trouble with having a twin is that Meredith is constantly reminded of her shortcomings. If Jack was a few years older than her, it would be easy to see his success as an attribute of age; she might even take some comfort in it, as though it were an indication that she, too, was destined for greatness. But Jack is not older. In fact, she was the first to come screaming from their mother's womb, something she used to tell him constantly when they were kids, back when being 'older' meant she had the biological, nay God-given, authority to boss him around.

And now here they are, twenty-three years old, and life is proving itself to be a much more sophisticated equation than she'd imagined. Jack has a job with a big advertising agency in London, a junior position with long hours and unremarkable pay, but he's responded to his new environment with all the ease of a fish in water. On the rare occasions she gets to see him, it strikes her that he hasn't found a job so much as a new life; that he's swimming away from her, slipping out of reach.

And what is Meredith's life by contrast? Her memories of university already have a distant, hazy quality. The only sense of continuity from those days is the precarious state of her finances, and the general dereliction of a flat she shares with two other people not far from where she grew up. Even that seems indicative of the fundamental difference between her and Jack: while he forges a path in the heart of London, her bold new life is still out in the commuter belt, a suburban purgatory.

Of course, that isn't what she tells people at the parties she attends: rooms full of similarly disenfranchised young people, everyone trying to smooth over their disappointments with an endless flow of cheap wine.

If she's had a bad day or a bit too much to drink, she might admit that she originally wanted to work in publishing. That she hadn't anticipated the gladiatorial nature of the process: that trying to get a foot in the door of one of London's top publishers is a blood sport, a fight to the death with frenzied hordes of the brightest and the best.

This makes it even harder, of course, to make it sound like she's happy with the job she's got, working in admin for a plastics manufacturer. 'I'm very lucky,' is her usual line, always delivered with a broad smile that she hopes will feel genuine one day. 'The office is right here in town, and it's a small company. Very friendly.'

Set against the backdrop of her working life – the chipped mugs, the worn carpet tiles, the dog-eared Pirelli calendar down in the loading bay – meeting Alastair is an epochal moment. A serious-minded man, six years older than her and redolent of an exotic, far-off land. A man whose life in academia is like some intellectual feedback loop, his intelligence growing ever-louder and more insistent.

'Is it love?' asks Jack, meeting her for the first time in months, the two of them sitting on a bench in Hyde Park.

'Yes. Yes, it is.' And now that she hears herself say it, she feels even more hopeful that it's true.

'Good. You deserve to be loved. Lord knows you've had to wait long enough for it.'

'And you?' she says, a leisurely Sunday unfolding all around them in picnics and fumbling games of frisbee. 'Are you dating?'

'I've been on a few,' he replies, with a smile.

'That's great.'

'All with different women, of course.' He evidently sees her disappointment. 'Marriage isn't high on my agenda right now.'

'I suppose not. How's the job?'

'Good. Great, actually. If the hours don't kill me, I think I might really achieve something.'

'Nice people?'

A nod, more evasive. 'Most of them are very bright, very sharp. There's one guy who started at the same time as me, Harry. He's a good mate.' He watches a lithe young woman in Lycra shorts stride past, her deep, purposeful breaths better suited to an antenatal class than a walk in the park. 'What does Mother have to say about your new man?'

'I haven't told her yet.'

He laughs. 'Don't admit you told me first. She won't forgive you for that one.'

'She's still too busy resenting me for moving out.' She

smiles at this small victory, but instantly regrets the honesty. 'Though she's much more relaxed, these days. I think maybe she was just menopausal before.'

'She can't have been menopausal for the last twenty years.'

'Then depressed, maybe. I can think of so many times in the past when she seemed so hopeless. I mean literally hopeless.'

'Melly, maybe she's just not a very nice person.' He doesn't wait for a reply. 'Anyway, she's sure to be happy about your new man. I suspect she'll be much happier with him than me.'

Hopes and dreams

14

It seems perfectly natural to Jemima that she should take her laptop everywhere she goes. It is, after all, just a bunch of wires in a plastic case. *Benign*, as her father might say. *Inanimate*. And yet, in the context of taking her laptop to a cheese farm, for instance, or on a tour of a cider brewery, he seems to find its very presence a portent of evil.

'I thought they might have WiFi here,' she explains, as once again he sighs at the very sight of it.

'And what in the life of a fifteen-year-old girl could be so important that it can't wait for a few days?'

Jemima ignores him, assumes it's a rhetorical question, but then he speaks again. 'Well?'

'You wouldn't understand.'

'Of course I wouldn't! After all, I only have two PhDs. What possible chance do I have of understanding the logic of a teenager?'

For a second, she wants to tell him exactly what she's thinking: that she's hoping to hear from a man who will do the job that he can't – love her and make her happy for ever and ever. Instead, she turns on Charlotte. 'You look awful today. I'm surprised you could even leave the house looking like that.'

Charlotte reacts much like a slug sprinkled with salt. While she visibly shrinks, Alastair appears to grow larger, his whole body inflating with anger. 'Apologize to Charlotte. This instant.'

'Why? I'm only telling the truth. You should be encouraging honesty, not attacking me for it.' She turns to Charlotte. 'You surely know how bad you look.'

Charlotte puts on a pair of large sunglasses. They go some way to covering her pallid skin, but do nothing for her lank hair. 'I'm not feeling well.'

'See?' says Jemima to her father. 'I was right.'

'Apologize, or I'm confiscating your computer and your telephone until we get back to England.'

'You can't do that.'

'I paid for them. I can do what I like.'

'But I've – I've got my exchange partner arriving from America in a couple of weeks—'

'Yet another luxury paid for by me.'

'What if she needs to email me about something urgent?'

'As inconceivable as it may sound, I'm sure she'll cope without your reply for just a few days.'

In the tense silence that follows, Luke speaks: 'What's foreplay?'

'Not now, Luke.'

'Your father really wouldn't know,' hisses Charlotte.

Alastair continues to stare down Jemima. 'So, young lady, we're all waiting for your apology.'

She glances at Charlotte, aware that this is a crucial moment in their relationship. 'Maybe you're right ...' she says.

For a fleeting moment, Charlotte seems to rally with the anticipation of her first victory. There's some satisfaction, then, in seeing her face as Jemima hands over her laptop and phone. 'But just for the record,' she says, 'I consider this a declaration of war.'

15

Jack wakes that morning with his hair sticking up in so many directions he has the appearance of a Renaissance Christ, a crown of thorns upon his head. Beside him, Reggie sleeps sprawled on his back, his four legs reaching skyward.

While Reggie sighs and slobbers through dreamtime, Jack does a mental run-through of his evening with Meredith. Until last night, he'd dreaded admitting the truth to anyone: not simply that he has the gene, but that at the age of forty-three he's already symptomatic. And yet lying here this morning, there's a sense of relief that someone else finally knows about his fleeting moments of confusion, knows that he's teetering on the edge of something dark and deep, simply waiting for gravity to do the rest.

Taking care not to wake Reggie, Jack tiptoes out to the landing and listens as Meredith moves about downstairs. Finally, a moment of silence. 'Melly?' he says, his voice low and gentle.

She hurries into view, appears concerned, as though Jack's circumspection is a possible symptom of dementia. 'Are you okay?'

'I'm fine. I just don't want to wake Reggie.'

'And too lazy to come downstairs?'

'Yes, that too.' He glances back at his bedroom. No sign of movement. 'I was thinking, how about we make a trip to the vet this morning?'

Even though it seems unlikely that Edna would miss a dog she's been neglecting for years, Meredith insists on telling her their plans. As she knocks on Edna's back door, she practises what she's going to say: that it's not just for Reggie's sake, but Edna's too; that she'll soon have a much happier, healthier dog.

As the door opens, Edna lurches into view like something from a ghost-train ride. 'Is this about God?' she says.

'No, I'm your *neighbour*.'

'I know that. I'm only old, not stupid.'

Meredith struggles to remember her lines. 'It's about Reggie ...'

'He's gone away to die.'

'No, he's—'

'He wanted me to let him out yesterday ... or maybe it was the day before, who knows? I knew then he was going to the doggie graveyard.'

'But he's not, you see. He's going to be fine.'

'I know, it's a comforting thought, but I don't like discussing religion.' She starts closing the door.

'But—'

'No, thank you. Not today.'

'How did it go?' says Jack, as Meredith joins him out on the driveway.

'It's probably best if we just make it a nice surprise for her.'
She peers at Reggie, already lying down in the back of her car.
Jack's papered the floor beneath him with pages from *GQ*: a
sea of articles on everything from Ryan Gosling's grooming to
this season's hottest fashion trends.

'It's too bad he can't see yet,' says Jack. 'He'd be very well
informed by the time we get there.'

Meredith cranes her neck to read the headline beside
Reggie's head. '"How to Make Her Orgasm Every Time".'

'He'll be needing tips like that soon enough.' He opens the
driver's door, starts to get in.

'Are you sure you're okay to drive?' says Meredith.

'What – you think the psychological burden of driving an
ageing Volvo may push me over the edge?'

'No. I just ...' Her words trail off as she realizes that this
is what she meant; that from now on she fears the slightest
nudge, the merest hint of a breeze, and her little brother will
be lost for ever. 'Ignore me,' she says.

'Melly, you're my sister. I've been ignoring you for years.'

It is, thinks Meredith, a good thing that Edna never pursued
a career in veterinary science: she'd have been telling all her
customers to euthanize their pets – 'Can't you see this cat is
almost dead?' However, the vet who inspects Reggie seems to
take everything in her stride. Reggie, too, is clearly undaunted
by the experience. Despite the thermometer sticking from his
rectum, he stands so proudly anyone would think he's being
worshipped rather than probed.

'I know it doesn't look like it,' says the vet, 'but he's actually not in bad shape.' She removes the thermometer, appears pleased with the result. 'Fingers crossed, once we've operated on the cataracts, there should be no issues with his vision. The skin will take a fair while to heal, but with the right medication and lots of love, you should have a very handsome dog.'

Meredith's eyes fill with tears. 'Don't mind me,' she says, blinking them away while she takes Reggie's head in her hands, wanting to bury her face in it but too worried about the mange. 'It's a new beginning, isn't it? A whole new lease on life.'

Evidently keen to move the situation forward, Jack turns to the vet. 'How soon can you take him?'

'If you leave him today, you should be able to pick him up tomorrow afternoon.'

Jack gives Reggie an affectionate rub. 'In that case, squire, we'll see you tomorrow.'

He pulls gently at Meredith, but still she lingers over the dog. 'If only it was always this easy to fix life's problems and start afresh ...' Aware that Jack and the vet are staring at her, she takes a step back. 'Sorry, it's just I hate goodbyes.'

Eager not to miss this window of self-control, the vet scoops up Reggie in her arms. 'Don't worry,' she says, already carrying him away. 'When you see him next, he'll be able to see you too.'

Meredith watches as they leave the room, the door swinging shut behind them. Although she'd never admit it, she's certain that in those last few seconds, Reggie looks right at her and smiles.

16

Charlotte has a migraine so Jemima's father announces that they'll just have a 'quiet afternoon', better known as doing nothing at all in total silence.

While Charlotte lies down in a darkened bedroom, Jemima's father commandeers the lounge and starts reading through a stack of academic journals, seemingly happy with the total, overwhelming absence of sound.

Not wanting to sit with him while, as usual, he gives more attention to his work than to her, Jemima drifts to the kitchen and watches from the window as Luke scours the garden for new things to collect. In the fields beyond, everything more than a few hundred feet away is lost in fog, yet another reminder of their profound isolation.

Standing here, it's obvious to Jemima she'll have to lie to her friends about this trip. To be frank, it was never a sexy proposition: staying on a French farm in winter can't compete with a holiday in Barbados, say, or skiing in Switzerland. Not to mention she's here with the social equivalent of a travelling circus: a man in his late forties who understands the density and mass of distant stars, but still can't fix his dandruff problem; his crazy girlfriend, a woman not just half his age but half his intellect too; not to mention an eleven-year-old boy whose holiday packing included a dead bird and two boxes of Ziploc bags.

So, no, the truth is not an option. Instead, despite all evidence to the contrary, she will tell her friends that the trip was actually the Most Amazing Experience of her Entire Life. As soon as they crossed the Channel, her father – a respected academic, let's not forget – revealed himself to be a much cooler man than she'd thought. Every night he encouraged her to drink expensive wine at dinner, wine so precious it was poured from bottles still covered with dust from the Second World War. And what dinners they were! Every meal was a ten-course, candlelit orgy of sophistication and glamour, served by handsome young Frenchmen with killer smiles. And when they weren't dining like kings, they were …

She gazes out the window for inspiration, but all she can see is a cow taking a dump. The rest of the herd is barely visible in the distance, not disappearing into the fog so much as being digested by it.

Only Tim will hear the real story. If he hasn't already been scared off by her honesty, she'll tell him the truth about this trip, will keep telling him the truth about everything. And if he's half the man she believes, he'll find a way to make everything okay.

Meanwhile, in Surrey
In leaving Reggie behind, it's as though a loose thread of Meredith's heart has been caught there too, and now she's

101

unravelling the further they drive; strand by strand she's slowly disappearing as they progress through the quiet, neatly groomed streets of suburban England.

'What do you want for dinner tonight?' says Jack, nothing about him suggesting that he shares her despair.

'I can't even think about food right now.'

'Can you think about plants?'

'Well ...' she says, a weak smile on her lips.

'When I checked the living room this morning, I counted eight trays of something or other.'

'Dahlias. They're just beginning to shoot.'

'And about ten pots of mud.'

'Oh, they're marigolds. I had this mad moment of inspiration and thought I could grow them from seed. Actually, I was growing them for Dad's grave.' She coughs. '*That* grave, I mean.' A moment of silence. 'Though I suppose I could still take them there. I mean, it's not like he's some evil impostor, is it? We're actually the ones who gatecrashed *his* life.'

'Melly, I think you should do whatever makes you happy. If there's one thing I've realized from my diagnosis it's that we have to do the things we love while we still can.'

'When you say it like that, you make it sound like you're dying. Your symptoms are still so minor. Even I wouldn't know if you hadn't told me.'

'Melly, ask yourself if you're saying that for my sake or yours.'

'I'm just telling you what I think.'

'I'm already at the stage where I can't do my job properly. I've got an office full of staff who think I'm just a burnt-out drunkard. And it's funny how even *that* seems preferable to the truth.'

'You could just tell them.'

'It took me over a year to tell you.'

'Well, let's at least try and focus on the positive. You might still have years of relatively good health ahead of you.' Jack doesn't respond. 'Unless there's something you're not telling me.' Still the same silence. Concerned now, Meredith twists in her seat to face him. '*Is* there something you're not telling me?'

'No, no,' he replies, the evasion in his voice clear to hear. 'Years of good health. I hope you're right.'

Twenty-five years earlier, 1987

It's Jack's eighteenth birthday, and after years in which it seemed there could be no escape from his family life, he now sees it disintegrating all around him. Where once there were walls and weight, he finally sees the universe beyond, a place of starlight and infinite possibilities.

The only problem is Meredith. It's not just that they're going to different universities, it's becoming more and more obvious that he's on a different trajectory through life: he's heading to a place she cannot go. No matter how many times he tries to inspire her, no matter how fired up she becomes to chase her dreams, she's soon talking again as though life is a mere exhibition, something to be observed rather than had.

He feels his plaything of the moment, Sally, rub up against him. A south-Londoner whose parents moved out to the suburbs a year ago, Sally's come to the party tonight with a bottle of her father's vodka and a clear intention to get laid.

'What are you thinking about?' she asks, the words sounding more like an indictment than a question.

'Life.'

'Well, better that than death, I suppose, but still a bit heavy for a birthday party. Here.' She pours him yet another shot. 'My great-grandmother was Russian.' She looks confused. 'Or maybe she just shagged a Russian, I can't remember. But if she was here, I'm sure she'd want you to get totally wasted.' She raises her glass, knocks it back in a single gulp. 'In Russia, they drink to forget.'

Sure enough, as Jack feels the vodka burn in his throat, his thoughts of Meredith do begin to fade. 'I've always imagined they drank to keep warm.'

'I wouldn't know. I have other ways of keeping warm.' And now the last of her inhibitions are gone, dissolved in the relentless flow of alcohol. 'The women in my family, we're very, very hot,' she says, snuggling into him. 'Even in winter, I'd be fine with just a fur coat and a pair of boots. I don't even need knickers.'

After eighteen years of doing so much together, Meredith can't decide if it's a good thing or not that she and Jack are apart this evening. If it had been up to her, they would have had a joint party: it would have made sense financially and her friends might have been a stabilizing influence on Jack and his circle.

Naturally, he'd been instantly dismissive of the idea. 'Melly, I sometimes worry you're eighteen going on thirty-three. It's supposed to be your big night. Just enjoy it.'

So here she is, at home, serving punch to her closest friends before they all head out for dinner. And it's only now, as she ladles out her insipid brew, that she wishes she was more like Jack, wishes she hadn't taken her eighteenth birthday and made it feel like a Tupperware party.

Her mother, who'd insisted on not being invited, nevertheless hovers in the background, plumping cushions and straightening curtains, so that it's hard to tell if she's trying to make Meredith's guests more comfortable or simply wants to monitor what's being said.

And yet by far the worst thing about the evening is Meredith's hair. It was supposed to be very Molly Ringwald, very *Pretty in Pink*, but, much like the night itself, it lacks the requisite volume and oomph. It's as though her follicles are somehow a barometer for life and she's now entering a difficult phase, this one awkward evening indicative of what she can expect for years to come.

In a few more weeks, her friends will scatter to universities across the country, and although they've promised to keep in touch, Meredith can see how it will work out: the way their lives will be covered with a fresh new layer of experience, so that these days won't just seem more and more distant, they'll vanish from sight.

This is the clarity that comes from being the one who stays behind. Her university is just thirty minutes away by bus – 'Think of all the money I'll save by living at home!' – yet now, as she prepares to watch everyone drain away, it seems the only real beneficiary is her mother, who no longer complains about being abandoned by her children, or at least being abandoned by her daughter …

The next morning, there are still balloons hanging in the living room when Meredith's mother joins her and Jack for breakfast, her mood as grey and overcast as the day.

She doesn't greet them as she enters the room; makes no effort to talk as she eats. Only after minutes of tense silence does she speak, her words directed at Meredith even while her gaze remains fixed on her plate. 'Your friends were laughing at me last night. Don't deny it.'

'Ignore her,' says Jack. 'She's just doing it for the attention.'

Their mother turns on him. 'And you! Who wouldn't even deign to invite your friends over.'

Jack stands up. 'Come on, Melly. We can have breakfast somewhere else.'

'Is it not enough that my husband died?' says their mother, as Meredith gets up too. 'Now my children are disappearing as well.'

Meredith hesitates.

'Melly, don't let her do this to you.'

'No, no, you must do as you wish,' says their mother, not even needing to look at Meredith as she says it, the whole room becoming web-like. 'Why would either of you care about *my* feelings?'

Meredith sits down again, gives Jack the lost, slightly hopeless smile that she does so well. 'There's some reading I should catch up on this morning. I think it's best I stay.'

It's only late that night, long after their mother has gone to bed, that Meredith hears Jack's soft footfall on the stairs. And then a gentle *tap, tap, tap* at her bedroom door.

As she opens it, he hands her a potted azalea, its pink flowers looking like fireworks frozen in mid-burst. 'Happy birthday.'

'You've already given me a present.'

'You can never have too many presents. As soon as I saw it, I knew you should have it.'

'It's beautiful.'

'It'll look good on your dressing-table, right by the window.'

Meredith carries it across the room and puts it in place. As she stands back to admire it, she can see that he's right. It does belong there.

'It's a way of remembering me,' says Jack. 'Once I've left for uni.'

'You make it sound like we'll never see you again.'

'Of course you will. It's just, you know ...' He looks at the plant, appears to find comfort in it. 'I wanted you to have something beautiful to remind you that life is full of good things. Even on a bad day, you can look at it and remember you're loved.'

Growing obsessions

17

Since being forced to surrender her computer, Jemima's relationship with the entire group has deteriorated significantly, but with nobody more so than Charlotte. There's such an uneasy silence between the two of them at breakfast this morning that Luke can only imagine it's the harbinger of a tsunami: all talk has recedèd to some far-off place and the seconds are now counting down until it returns as a devastating wave. And all the while Alastair sits at the table, his head buried in a newspaper, apparently unconcerned that something terrible is about to happen.

Luke is still pondering this when his father puts down the paper and goes to the kitchen. In his absence, Charlotte appears to disintegrate a little under Luke's steady gaze. If he had to live with her on a daily basis, he can imagine there'd soon be nothing left of her, like some cheap paperback that's been read once too many times and tossed aside, the cover in tatters, the binding ruined.

'What?' she snaps at him.

'Nothing,' he replies, his voice calm and steady. 'I just think you'd be happier if you learnt to relax.'

Seconds later Alastair returns with a plate of salami: tough, chewy discs of nitrates and animal fat. 'I thought this might be a nice addition to breakfast,' he says, offering Charlotte the plate.

'You know I can't eat that.' The words are less a reply than a shriek. Before anyone can react, she's rounding on Jemima. 'And as for you ... Don't deny you're thinking bad things about me.'

Jemima responds in a measured tone, her words addressed to Alastair: 'I would Google the symptoms of a midlife crisis –'

'I'm twenty-nine!' says Charlotte.

'– but, of course, I don't have my computer, and even if I did, we're in the middle of nowhere.' She finally looks at Charlotte. 'So I'll just have to go with my instincts that you're a crazy bitch.'

'Jemima,' says her father, already taking refuge behind his newspaper, 'don't use language like that at the table.'

Charlotte snatches the newspaper away, tosses it to the floor. 'So it would be okay to say it somewhere else in the house? How about we all go into the garden and I call you and your kids miserable bastards?'

Deciding that everyone could benefit from a distraction, Luke hurries to the back door, pulls it open.

'Where are you going?' calls his father.

'Nowhere,' he replies, reaching down behind one of the flowerpots to retrieve his most exciting find from the day before, a discovery he'd planned to keep secret, but this is an emergency.

Sure enough, the whole room does come to a standstill as he returns, holding a dead rodent by its tail.

'Is this a mouse or a rat?' he says. Unfortunately, in the commotion that follows, nobody hears his small voice. 'How do you think it died?'

Instead, it's Charlotte who dominates the room, her words coming out in a shrill torrent. 'I can't do this any more. I want to go home. Right now.'

18

Meredith occasionally speaks as they drive back to the vet, but it strikes Jack as a rhetorical bubbling rather than an invitation to dialogue, the geyser of her subconscious simply hissing to let off steam. 'I hope the kids are having better weather than this ... Goodness, seventy-four is for sale again ... Look at that, what a place to put a satellite dish ...'

The gaps between each statement become longer as they get closer to the vet's. By the time they're inside and are being taken to Reggie's cage, the silence is almost reverential.

When they first see him, he's lying down with his back to them: a mangy dog with a plastic cone where his head used to be. Even before the vet has opened the cage, Jack is crouching down beside it. 'Hello, Reggie.' The cone rises, turns towards them, the tip of a wet nose coming into view. 'Would you like to come home?'

And now he's standing, negotiating the confines of the cage to face them with eyes that sparkle, his coned head like a flower in full bloom.

The rest of the afternoon passes in an endless outpouring of love in which Reggie never seems to tire of gazing up at Jack and Meredith. He spends so long watching them, it's as though he's getting to know them all over again, intuiting things about them that were previously beyond his range.

Jack doesn't notice it at first, the way Reggie treats him differently from Meredith. It's only as the day wears on that it becomes more and more apparent. Whereas Reggie goes to Meredith for fun and affection, for colourful toys and pots of strange-smelling plants, it's obvious he considers Jack his ward, someone to be protected and watched over.

'He likes you,' says Meredith, Reggie lying slumped at Jack's feet.

'I'm sure the novelty will wear off soon enough.'

Jack glances at Reggie and immediately knows that's not true: the dog is staring at him with a gaze that seems diagnostic in its reach. 'You know what?' he says, getting up. 'I need a little stroll to sort through some of my thoughts. I might take him to the park.'

It's so difficult to imagine Edna as a dog walker that Jack thinks this could in fact be Reggie's first outing on a leash; his first exploration of the big wide world. Yet, rather than alarm or confusion at having Jack tethered to his neck, Reggie appears to take it as yet another aspect of his duty; indeed, he occasionally glances at Jack as they walk down the street, his slow pace seeming to be for Jack's benefit rather than his own.

'I don't mind you thinking I'm a total cripple,' says Jack, as they enter the park, 'but just for the record, that cone makes you look like a right plonker.'

Reggie ignores him, a dignified silence he continues to maintain for the next twenty minutes as he sniffs every tree, continually banging his cone against them. After claiming half the park with liberal sprayings of Eau de Reggie, he leads Jack to a bench and sits there at his feet while they both watch joggers run to and fro.

'I may not have told Melly the whole truth,' says Jack. 'About the prognosis, I mean.'

A lithe young woman in Lycra jogs by. Reggie watches her pass, his plastic cone momentarily catching the sun and making his whole head glow.

'It seems the younger you are when you become symptomatic, the faster you deteriorate.' Reggie turns to look at him now. 'It's a bit cruel, isn't it? It's the first time in years I've been considered young and suddenly I don't want to be.' More joggers pass by, but still Reggie looks only at him. 'I don't want to make Melly worry any more than she does, so for now it's just between you and me. Is that a deal?'

And still there's no reaction from his coned companion, just the same steady gaze of a dog that understands the real truth.

19

Following the fiery implosion of breakfast, Jemima's father had confirmed – in a loud voice, heavily peppered with swear words – that, yes, the holiday was over.

They've spent the rest of the day in the car, hammering through the French countryside in a desperate attempt to get back to England as soon as possible. Despite her mortal fears, Charlotte is up front again, this time with her eyes hidden behind a sleeping mask and her seat reclined so far back, it looks like Luke is about to wash her hair. Even though Charlotte doesn't speak, it's obvious that she's awake because tears occasionally creep out from beneath the mask and roll down her cheeks in fat ugly drops.

Jemima's father hasn't said a word the entire day. This, of course, is nothing out of the ordinary. It's only his body language that says this is more than the usual silence: the way he grips the steering wheel so tightly that his knuckles appear to be bursting through his skin; the rigid look about his jaw, as though he's been impaled by something thick and blunt but is determined not to admit it.

Jemima expects the worst as the car pulls onto their street.

117

She and Luke have only been away a few days, but when they left, their mother looked ill-prepared for the experience.

As they come to a stop, it's reassuring to see that the house is still there, everything as it should be, but still Jemima can't shake the thought that her mother may be hanging from some doorframe or other, a hopeless suicide victim in a Marks & Spencer cardigan and sensible shoes.

It's all the stranger, then, that when Meredith eventually opens the front door in her dressing-gown, she looks surprisingly well. She even manages a smile for Charlotte, a woman she'd presumably like to see face down in a shallow grave.

'I didn't expect you back so soon,' she says, to Alastair.

'Well,' he replies, 'the trip wasn't quite what we had in mind. We all felt it would be best to come home.'

'You look tired. Why don't you stay for a cup of tea? You've had such a long journey.'

Alastair glances at the car, Charlotte's scowling face barely visible in the darkness. 'No, we should really get going.' Still he lingers, obviously wants to stay. 'Actually, there's something I want to discuss with you. In private, I mean.'

In the fleeting silence that follows, Jemima is aware that something important is happening, a seismic shift that she can't yet understand.

'Of course,' says Meredith. 'I know a charming little café on the high street. Why don't we meet there tomorrow?'

Just like she did when they were still together, Meredith stays in the open doorway until Alastair is driving away, and even then she closes the front door reluctantly.

'Did you have a good time in France?' she asks Jemima.

'We came back four days early. What do you think?'

'Your father and Charlotte looked like they'd been arguing.'

'Twenty-four hours a day. Probably for months and months.'

It's clear Meredith is trying not to look excited. 'Do you know what they've been arguing about?'

'What if Dad plans to come back to us?' says Jemima, realizing as she utters the words that this is not only a possibility but something she no longer wants.

Meredith smiles to herself. 'We'll just have to wait and see, won't we?'

In the privacy of her room at last, Jemima does what she's longed to do for the last few days: she checks her mail. There are numerous messages from her harem, three alone from Brian. She skips all of them, goes straight to the one message she needs right now: Tim's name glowing on the screen like a homing beacon:

Thanks for being honest with me. The way I see it, the younger you are, the more you need me to protect you. I think we should meet soon.

Hands trembling, she types her reply:

How about Saturday afternoon? If you've got a car, you could pick me up near my house.

20

Even before he discovers the kids are back, Jack learns that he'll never find his father. Or that's what the private investigator says when he wakes Jack with a phone call at seven thirty in the morning.

'I'm going to tell you what I tell all my clients when the trail goes cold. The person you're looking for is dead.'

By now Reggie, who is sprawled across the bottom of Jack's bed, is also awake, lifting his coned head from the bedclothes with a weary groan.

'You've only been working on it for three days,' says Jack, his voice thick with sleep. 'Isn't it a bit soon to be coming to that conclusion?'

'I'm a detective, not a miracle worker. And you offered no leads for my enquiry.'

'I thought it was your job to find them.'

'Ah, I know where this is going. Just because I don't have a union to protect me, you think it's okay to take cheap shots.'

'No, that's not—'

'I risk my life doing this job. Every single day!' His voice becomes loud and insistent. Jack holds the phone at a distance, but can still hear him pontificating. 'Imagine the mental toll if I had a wife and family. How they'd fear for me every time I leave the house. For all you know, that's why I don't have a woman in my life. It's the emotional scars. And then you start *denigrating my profession.*'

Jack waits for him to say more, but now there's only silence. 'Look, it's fine. I'm sure you've done as much as you can.' He squints at his bedside clock. 'I'm just confused as to why you're calling at seven thirty in the morning.'

'I can't win, can I? If I called you at ten, you'd be all like "That man's such a lazy bastard", but, no, I get started early and still you just shoot me dow—'

Jack hangs up, certain that the man will continue shouting into his phone for some time before he realizes.

Under Reggie's watchful gaze, Jack calls Harry's mobile, knows he'll get voicemail at this time of day.

'Yeah, Harry, it's Jack. Look, you were right, I need that other detective you mentioned. Can you give me a call?'

The fear creeps up on him slowly: the nagging thought that the investigator is right, that his father, and the truth, will never be known.

Pancakes seem like the right response. Jack stands in the kitchen, still barefoot, finds himself wishing that everything in life could be this simple: mixing together flour, eggs, milk and water in the full knowledge of what to expect. Even Reggie appears to find the process soothing, wagging his tail in rhythm with Jack's whisking.

'You're up early,' says Meredith, breezing in with a carefree smile Jack's not seen in a long time.

'And you're looking suspiciously well rested,' he replies, as she lavishes affection on Reggie.

'The kids came back late last night.' She glances at the abandoned bags and dirty laundry piled in a corner. 'Though I suppose you've already figured that out.'

'Why are they back so soon?'

'It's a bit of a mystery. I'm meeting Alastair today to talk about it.' She blushes. 'I think he's going to ask to come home.'

Jack decides not to reply, focuses instead on whisking the batter, its lumps a fitting emblem of all life's disappointments: a father who remains unknowable; a sister who looks for love in all the wrong places.

'Perhaps you can take the kids out today,' she says. 'I'm sure they'd like to spend some time with you.' She stops to watch him work. 'Gosh, you're good at that.'

And still Jack says nothing, merely smiles to himself as the lumps begin to melt away.

Later that morning

It's hard to say whether Seeds & Leaves is a tea shop selling plants or a plant shop selling tea: there are so many plants that the tables all but disappear in the foliage. It's easy to imagine that customers regularly go missing in the rainforest tangle – old ladies found half digested by giant, triffid-like succulents.

Now that she's seated, Meredith is certain that this is the wrong place to meet Alastair. As much as she loves it, he's sure to disapprove of the tendrils and fronds that snake their way here and there; a riot of greenery that makes a mockery of his need for precision.

But then he's entering the café and it's too late for regrets. 'Alastair,' she calls, standing up as he advances across the room.

Watching him approach through the potted free-for-all, she imagines herself as an airport marshal, standing there with fluorescent wands, guiding him back to safety after a long solo flight. In a moment they will sit down together and he will tell her he's sorry, she will hold his hand, all will be forgiven.

She opens her arms to receive him, drawing him into an embrace and breathing in the— She lets go. 'You're wearing a different aftershave.'

'Do you like it?' He takes a step back, safely out of reach. 'Charlotte chose it for me.'

Meredith doesn't sit down so much as descend into her chair, her legs crumpling beneath her. Alastair either fails to notice or perhaps just takes for granted that this is how she always is – overwrought, but determined to put a brave face on it.

'Have the children said anything about France?' He doesn't wait for a response. 'I feel a little bad about the way it worked out. Charlotte has been having a terrible time of it recently. You see, we're expecting a baby.'

'Well … congratulations,' murmurs Meredith.

'But, good gracious, the hormones. I don't know, they've made her into some kind of monster. She'd be the first to admit it.'

'You could have explained that to the children.'

'The truth is we didn't want to tell anyone for a while, but France has sort of blown it into the open.' He shifts in his seat, appears self-conscious for a moment. 'And with a child on the way, we really need to talk.'

'Of course. The two of you have a lot to sort out.'

'No, Meredith, I mean you and me.'

In retrospect, Meredith will understand that he kept talking, but right now it seems as though time comes to a standstill. The room begins to wrap itself around her, so that she has the sense of staring at him down a long tunnel of green. With each passing moment Alastair appears to be getting further and further away, but still she hears his final words with perfect clarity.

'I want a divorce.'

21

After the disaster of their last outing with Jack, Jemima takes charge and demands they visit a shopping centre. No cold wet weather to deal with. Not a damp sheep in sight.

As soon as they arrive it becomes obvious that this is her natural habitat, that if shopping was considered a core business skill, she could be the CEO of a global conglomerate. She stands over the mall's illuminated map and explains her plans to Jack with all the authority of Eisenhower on the eve of D-Day.

'... and then I expect you to meet me in this shop here at twelve o'clock. Which means, one, you can pay for everything and, two, you can then take us to lunch –' she indicates her venue of choice, doubtless wishing she had a laser pointer to drive the message home '– at this restaurant here. And just so we're clear, you're not allowed to say anything bad about the food until we've finished eating.'

Although it's obvious that questions are not welcome, she nevertheless waits a few seconds before sending them on their way.

'Okay, then, see you at twelve,' she says, already disappearing into the throng of half-term shoppers.

Even at the best of times, Luke gets the feeling that either he or his sister must have been adopted. Now, as he accompanies Jack on a shameless spending spree in a bookshop, it strikes him that there are things about his relatives that he will never understand.

'Magazines are good,' explains Jack, perhaps feeling the need to justify picking up fifteen of them. 'Magazines are full of ideas, and ideas are the stuff of life.' He leads the way to the till, his arms full. 'What can we buy you today?'

'I don't need anything.'

'As I've explained to your mother on numerous occasions, life would be pretty dull if we only did the things we *need* to do.'

Luke waits while Jack taps in his credit card PIN, all the while the till operator standing over his haul of magazines with a radiant smile.

'I wanted to get a berry hat in France,' says Luke, 'but I couldn't.'

'Luke, I'm happy to buy you drugs when you're old enough, but I'm not buying you a beret. Everyone knows they're the sartorial equivalent of child porn.'

'But the only other things that interest me are free things. The kind of things other people just throw away.' He sees the look of alarm on Jack's face. 'Though I like watching people too. That's always fun.'

'And what is it you like about that?' says Jack, as they drift from the bookshop.

'I don't know,' replies Luke. 'I like trying to understand

people. To understand why they do the things they do.'

They watch as a middle-aged woman hurries past, her facial expression suggesting that her mind is far away, buried beneath an entire mountain range of stress.

'She was wearing too much makeup,' says Luke. 'I think she does it because she can't see how beautiful she really is.'

'I'm not sure you should be finding beauty in women who are old enough to be your mother.'

'I don't want to marry her. I just want her to feel better about herself.'

'How do you know she doesn't?'

Luke glances at him with an unintentional look of pity.

'Well, true …' says Jack.

'I think lots of people aren't as happy as they pretend to be. It's sad, when you think about it.'

Jack's phone starts to ring. 'Sorry,' he says, checking the screen. 'It's the office.' They come to a stop while he takes the call. 'Right, mate?' A pause. A frown. 'Why can't you just give me the number now?' Another pause. 'Harry, I've already been bouncing back and forth between here and London like a bloody yo-yo.' He glances at Luke, seems to regret his choice of words. 'Fine, but it'd better be worth it … Yeah, see you tomorrow.'

'You're going back to London?' says Luke, as Jack hangs up.

'Only for one night. My partner at work says he has a surprise for me.'

'What kind of surprise?'

'It's probably for the best I don't know.' He steers Luke in the direction of a cookware shop, its windows full of expensive pots and pans. 'This is what I'm in the mood for right now.'

He sweeps into the shop with such a purposeful stride that even some of the other customers turn to watch. Within seconds, a sales assistant is on hand, fawning and attentive, as if pheromones alone have announced that this man intends to spend a lot of money.

As the very latest range of cookware is introduced to them, it occurs to Luke that his uncle *needs* to shop, in the same way that Luke himself needs to collect: as a way of making sense of life; of finding solace in something that can be seen and touched and understood.

Before long, Jack has picked out enough pans for a life-time of solace and is once again handing over his credit card. Only now there's a difference in him. A subtle irritability in his manner.

'Are you okay?' says Luke. And then louder: 'Uncle Jack?'

'Excuse me,' calls the woman from the till. 'I just need you to enter your PIN.'

Jack approaches her, stares at the keypad.

The woman's smile becomes more measured. And still Jack just stares.

'Your PIN,' she says, louder and slower now.

'I don't know what to do,' says Jack. 'I don't know ...'

In the bewildered silence that follows, Luke reaches over and types Jack's PIN for him.

'It's a game we like to play,' he says, to the woman. 'In New Zealand they call this foreplay.'

He takes Jack's card and gathers up the bags.

'Oh, God ...' says Jack, rubbing his head.

'Don't worry, everything's fine.' He starts to lead Jack from the store.

'Luke, if I did or said anything strange ...'

'Are you feeling okay?'

'I'm fine. I ... just didn't get enough sleep last night, that's all.'

Luke glances at him, remembers that there's a time for questions and a time simply to observe. 'Yes,' he says. 'That's what I thought. But it's okay now. We can go and find somewhere to sit down.'

22

The day has worked out even better than Jemima antici-pated. When the others finally joined her in the clothing store, Jack didn't just look tired, he'd seemingly lost all inter-est in conversation. This rare silence continued through most of lunch, allowing Jemima to eat her junk food in peace: no remarks that her mayonnaise was chemical slop, for instance, or that her hamburger bun had the nutritional integrity of cardboard.

It's only towards the end of lunch that Jack begins to return to his usual self, slowly stirring into life with a few barbed comments about the décor and the other patrons.

Eager to get a rise out of him, Jemima delves into one of her shopping bags, pulls out a sky-blue beret. 'It's for you,' she says, handing it to Luke.

'Bloody hell,' says Jack, oblivious to Luke's delight. 'Did they not have anything in a more manly colour?'

'How is it?' asks Luke, the hat sinking over his head like molten plastic.

Jack reaches over and touches it, instantly pulls his hand away. 'And is it too much to expect that it be made of natural fibres?'

'I don't care,' says Luke. 'I love it.'

'Luke, this is like being happy that the Greeks have just left a big wooden horse at the city gates.' There's a moment of confused silence. 'What I mean is, Jem is your big sister. She's obviously only doing this to make you look stupid.'

'I am not,' she snaps. 'I'm just trying to make up for the nightmare of our trip to France.'

'A humanitarian gesture! In which case I'd like to point out that I was actually the one who paid for it.'

'Which just goes to prove that we have a healthy symbiotic relationship. You're like the parasite who feeds on us, and in return you buy us things. We're all just conforming to the laws of nature.'

On the drive home, Jemima inspects her purchases, bags full of clothes packed into the footwell around her.

'What do you think of this?' she asks Jack, holding up a sequined top she'd chosen for her first date with Tim. 'I have a – a party to attend on Saturday. I want to look mature.'

'Jem, there's a difference between mature and feral.'

'And I've got my exchange buddy arriving next weekend.'

'So she also dresses as a crack whore?'

'She's coming from *California*.'

'There's lots of California that's just as plain and suburban as this.' He evidently sees the look of panic on her face. 'That's not to say, of course, that plain and suburban is a bad thing.'

'Yes, it is.'

'Jem—'

'So what does that make *me*? She's going to arrive all – all paparazzi and spray tan, and I'm what? A victim of my upbringing.'

'All I meant was, you're probably very similar. Most of America is kind of like this.'

Luke pipes up from the back seat, his beret looking more like an acrylic helmet: 'I was reading some books about America the other day. It's actually *very* different. Everything is much bigger and nicer than here.'

'Did you hear that?' says Jemima.

'No, Luke, what I mean is they're the same kind of people. They have the same lives, the same problems. They're just ... different.'

'So it's the same,' says Jemima, 'but different? And *that's* supposed to be helpful?'

'The point is, there's nothing to worry about.'

But then they pull up at home and it's obvious that this, too, is not true: two men are carrying a giant potted plant into the house, their crimson faces and empty truck suggesting this is the last of many.

'Why am I feeling very afraid?' says Jemima.

'Your mother likes plants,' replies Jack. 'There's nothing wrong with that.' It was doubtless intended to sound reassuring, but even Jemima can hear the wariness in his voice.

They're still in the car when the two deliverymen leave, both looking pained as they hoist themselves into the truck and drive away.

'I would have got out ages ago,' says Luke. 'But I don't have a door.'

'He's right,' replies Jack. 'This is madness. How bad can it possibly be in there?'

'Post-apocalyptic' is the expression that springs to mind. As Jack leads the children into the house, he imagines this is how all of Surrey may look in millennia to come, after mankind has been wiped out and continental drift has taken Europe down to the tropics.

Meredith's voice wafts through the greenery. 'Jack? Is that you?'

'I presume you've had some bad news,' he calls to her.

'What makes you think that?'

He ducks past an oversized fern, its fronds hanging across his path like a beaded curtain. 'I hate to say you're transparent but—' He enters the kitchen, stops dead in his tracks.

In the centre of the room is an old armchair, its aged fabric now lying in shreds on the floor. Meredith stands over it, pushing cress seeds into its naked foam cushions.

'Meredith, are you quite all right?'

'It was Alastair's. The chair, I mean. It's supposed to be an allegory. Or is it a metaphor? I always get them mixed up.'

Jemima joins them. 'What the ...'

Meredith stops planting, her hands still full of seeds. 'Your father and Charlotte are having a baby,' she says. 'They're having a baby, so they're going to get married. And live together permanently. For ever and ever.'

'Well, screw them,' says Jemima. 'They deserve each other.'

'No, we should really be wishing them well,' replies Meredith, albeit in a voice that suggests she isn't capable of that yet.

'He isn't much of a dad to the two children he already has, I can't imagine why he wants another.'

'Oh, darling, your father's a good man. He's just ... he's an *academic*.'

'What's that supposed to mean?'

'That he's so clever and knowledgeable he's just not very good at anything else.'

Jemima rolls her eyes and leaves the room, disappearing into the dense foliage that is now their hallway. Moments later, she screams, 'My God, what have you done to the living room?'

Jack follows Meredith through to her and finds plants of all sizes hiding the furniture from view. Even the television sits beneath a thick wig of jungle creepers.

'Where are we supposed to sit?' says Jemima.

'Don't worry, it's all still here. Except your father's armchair, of course. That will have to be kept dark and wet until the seeds start to sprout.'

Jemima turns to her. 'How am I supposed to explain this to my American friend?'

'Plants help me relax.'

'There are pills for that.'

Luke speaks from the sofa, a disembodied voice from behind a giant aspidistra. 'I like it. I think it's nice.'

'And that,' says Jemima, turning to her mother, 'is all the proof you need that you have officially lost it.'

Shortly after

There's no reply from Tim yet, but Jemima knows there will be. It's obvious that he's as hooked on her as she is on him:

134

two fish who are slowly reeling one another in.

In the meantime, the anticipation of it casts a rosy glow over everyone else in her harem. A playful predator, she now takes some pleasure in toying with men she would otherwise choose to kill.

It's the perfect frame of mind for reading through the messages Brian has sent over the last few days.

My dear Lucy

Here is the picture you requested.

Respectfully yours,
Brian

Jemima opens the attachment, pores over its details: Brian doesn't just look self-conscious, he looks a good deal older than the photograph in his profile. He crouches on all fours in a vest and an ill-fitting pair of Y-fronts, the cotton looking to have yellowed with age, his cat-like pose suggestive of rheumatism.

His second message had been sent just moments later.

Dearest Lucy

I do hope my previous message didn't seem curt. The truth is I don't even like animals, but such is my affection for you, I am your humble servant! Please be assured I look forward to meeting you at the earliest opportunity.

Yours,
Brian

And a third message, sent yesterday afternoon.

My sweet Lucy

I find your silence distressing. This is how much meeting you has affected me!

I've also just noticed the heart-wrenching life story you've posted online. I can't imagine the anguish of being passed from foster family to foster family, but if there's anything I can do to help, anything at all, please let me know.

Love,
Brian

Anything. In Jemima's current mood, this seems such a careless thing to say.

Dear Brian

I'm sorry you've had to wait a few days for a response. I've been travelling internationally and have only just returned home. Between the hectic schedule and the jet lag

Even by the standards of Lucy's usual correspondence, it feels like a stretch of credulity to claim jet lag, but then she decides it adds a certain sophistication – certainly more than saying she's been stuck in France with her father.

the jet lag! My dear, THE JET LAG! I've been crossing so many time zones, my head is spinning.

Thank Heaven for my big black vibrator and a plentiful supply of batteries.

You're right that my childhood in those foster homes was very, very tragic. Utterly heart-breaking, actually. I'm fine now, but enclosed spaces and electric cattle prods still make me uneasy.

I know you're eager to meet, but I have to look after my mother (one of the nice ones). She's just started acting like a total retard and I think she may soon require twenty-four-hour care.

You asked if there's anything you can do … The truth is I am an old-fashioned lady, so I'm a little embarrassed to say this. BUT YOU DID ASK!

You see, I love the great outdoors. It's always been my dream that when I eventually meet my Prince Charming (that's you, I hope, my dear Brian!) he will help me get over a lifetime of intimacy issues by shagging me in the woods.

Please prove to me that you are the one. Send me a picture of you pleasuring yourself among the oak trees and bluebells. Then I'll know that you are mine, and I will be yours.

Big smudgy lipstick kisses,
Lucy

23

The next morning Jack comes downstairs to find that many of Meredith's plants are beginning to droop and wilt, as though he somehow slept through a massive meteor strike and has woken up just in time for the mass extinction that follows.

When Meredith joins him and Reggie in this theatre of death, her response is more visceral: she stands frozen on the stairs, mouth wide open in horror.

'You do know,' says Jack, 'the idea is to keep them alive?'

'I don't understand. I ...' She appears to flail for the right words, gives up. 'If I can't even tend a houseful of plants, it's no wonder my marriage failed.'

'Melly, I think you might be reading too much into the situation. They're only plants.' But still there's no response, just a woman in her early forties staring at a hallway full of wilting greenery.

There's a loud clunk as Reggie brings his leash from the kitchen and drops it at Jack's feet.

'I think,' says Jack, 'we should *all* go for a walk.'

Thanks to the weather – cold and grey, as though winter will never end – there are few other people in the park.

Jack and Meredith soon abandon the idea of walking Reggie and instead find a bench beside the lake, huddling there like animals sitting out a storm while Reggie sniffs from tree to tree, his cone presumably amplifying the experience.

Meredith watches as he cocks his leg against a trunk carved with hearts and initials, each of them an age-old declaration of eternal love. Looking at it on a day like this, she wonders whether any of those people are still together or if, like the graffiti, their passion has become distorted and unclear, a simple romantic notion that has long since outgrown itself.

'I don't think Alastair ever really loved me. Have I told you that?'

'Come on, Melly, I don't like the man but—'

'No, it's true. Even when we got married. I know he *liked* me. I know he wanted to *be* with me. But I don't think he really loved me.'

'And yet you still went through with it.'

'Yes, and I would again. Because it was good enough for me. Is that a bad thing to say? Does that make me sound totally useless?'

'I've never thought you're useless. Not once in my whole life.'

'It's funny, I always thought it was some limitation in Alastair. That he just wasn't capable of loving me as much as I loved him. Then he meets Charlotte and suddenly he's … Casanova.'

'Even if that's true, which I very much doubt, it's not your fault.'

'It's just not how I'd imagined life working out.'

'Well, trust me, I understand that one completely.'

139

'I can remember being in my twenties and thinking all things were possible. And look at me now.'

'You're only forty-three.'

'I know, but it's like life is made of concrete or something and I've already set. No one tells you when you're young that your life is going to harden and solidify. That you may wake up one morning and find it's turned to stone, and that you're not actually some architectural marvel, you're a – a pavement.' She opens her handbag, begins emptying it. 'I mean, look at me. A half-eaten tube of fruit pastilles, the keys to a very second-hand Volvo and some –' she suddenly regrets the honesty '– and some wart cream.' She puts it all away, closes her handbag. 'It's not exactly what I expected to become.'

'Melly, you have a nice life. I envy you. And even though you don't believe it yet, I think it's an even better life for Alastair not being in it any more.'

Out on the lake, a couple of male ducks start to fight, with loud quacks and self-important flapping of wings.

'Do you think ducks actually feel love?' she says. 'Or is it just some kind of genetic command to pair up like that? I mean, look at them. They're not much more than oven-ready meals, but they all have a mate.' She watches one of the males swimming along: a distinct swagger in his carriage, his feathers sparkling in elaborate blues and greens. And beside him a female, her drab brown feathers more redolent of a prison inmate's garb. 'I think for the men it's all about ownership, and the women simply conform to their demands because that's how it is.'

'Melly, are we really still talking about ducks?'

'Sorry,' she says, with a sigh. 'Ignore everything I've said. If you listened to me, you'd never want to settle down with someone.'

'It's a bit late for that, surely.'

'Did you really never want to?'

'Sure, there were times. I mean, let's face it, the only real advantage to living alone is being able to take a dump with the door open. I think I fell in love with one or two of them over the years.'

'But loving a person is generally considered the start of something rather than the end.'

'To be honest, I just couldn't face all the drama of sharing my life with a woman. All the mental agony that comes from trying to keep a relationship airborne.'

'Every couple hits turbulence now and then.'

'True, but when you see the wings snap off, you can forget about a soft landing.' He gazes out across the lake, the wind tugging at his hair. He has such a faraway look in his eyes, Meredith imagines he might turn to her at any second and ask her who she is. 'I heard from the investigator yesterday. He said it's impossible to find our father. He thinks he's dead.' He turns to her. 'Though I don't believe him, by the way. I'm going to get someone else onto it.'

'I don't know, maybe he's right. Maybe our father is dead.'

'In which case, I want to see a death certificate. I want to know something about him. So I can put a story to the man.'

'And you think the new investigator can get that?'

'I think anything we do is a step forward. Harry wants to meet for dinner tonight, so I'm going to take the train up—'

'Do you not feel able to drive?'

'Piss off! I'm not that bad yet. There'll be so much alcohol at dinner, I'll have to take a cab home anyway, so I may as well just leave the car here.'

'But it's going to happen one day, isn't it? I mean, not being able to drive any more. I know how much you love that car.'

'This is a cheerful conversation.'

'Sorry, I—'

'No, you're right. I'll have to cross that bridge sooner or later.' He pulls his coat tighter. 'When I first got the diagnosis last year, I was thinking I'd end it all before the symptoms got too bad. You know, take the car off for a *Thelma and Louise* moment ...'

'You'd tell me if you felt that way again, wouldn't you?'

'The truth is, I just hate the idea of being a quitter. I mean, there are two ways of reacting to the things that scare us, right? You can give up and seek oblivion, literal or otherwise. Or you can, I don't know ... *embrace* it. Charge at it like a rabid bull.' He turns back to her, a smile on his face. 'And I want it known right now that I plan to be the world's sexiest dementia patient. I expect my hair to be styled every day. *With the right products*. And I want it trimmed every two weeks. Including my chest hair.'

'Jack!'

'Just because I lose my mind, it doesn't mean I have to lose my standards too.'

24

It turns out Harry has chosen an expensive Japanese restaurant for their 'private' dinner. And if he really is planning to talk to Jack about something confidential, he evidently hasn't mentioned that to the other six people at the table.

Unnoticed, Jack observes them as he approaches; ponders how the evening feels like an archaeological dig, burrowing down through the various strata of his social life: Harry's a treasure but, quite frankly, some of the other people at the table are more akin to cheap pottery fragments in loose mud.

As he draws closer, he hears the buzz of coked-out camaraderie. On this occasion, free-flowing *sake* has added to the mix, temporarily convincing everyone they like each other far more than they really do.

'Jack!' they shout, as he finally appears on their radar.

'Fresh from the wilds of suburbia,' says Harry, standing up to give him a big hug.

Jack takes his seat opposite a married couple he's not seen in almost a year, and instantly he remembers why. The husband has a bullying manner he presumably considers self-confidence, and his wife – an athletic woman with impeccable highlights – is more an accomplice than a spouse. Watching the two of them across the table, Jack can easily believe their basement doubles as a mass grave, a place to discard the tortured remains of hitchhikers and prostitutes.

Jack gives them a polite smile, then turns his full attention to Harry. 'So much for a quiet chat.'

'Don't you worry about that, you're among friends now.'

'Look, have you got that other detective's number?'

'All in good time.' He says it with a sparkle in his eye, the promise of something momentous. 'Tonight, we're celebrating.'

'Celebrating what?'

'Life, my friend. Life.'

Over the next hour, Jack's fellow diners manage to surprise him with how much they can eat, these people whose standard diet is vodka martinis and the occasional canapé. Plate after plate of raw fish is hoovered up by people hungry for excess, everyone clamouring for more of the blue-fin tuna before it goes extinct.

'This stuff is all flown in fresh from Tokyo,' says Harry, clearly approving of the decadence. 'You've got to love the irony. Delicate little servings of fish with a carbon footprint the size of Belgium.' He leans close, his manner a tad drunken, his breath sharp with wasabi and ginger. 'Your rough patch. I understand it now.'

'What are you talking about?'

'Your problem at work. It's obvious, isn't it? Why didn't you say anything sooner?' He breaks into a broad smile, as though dementia is no match for one of London's top ad men. 'That's why I invited you here. My man's solved it for you. Though

Christ knows how he did it. It's probably all spy satellites and stuff. Best we don't know.'

Before Jack can say anything, Harry is tapping his *sake* cup with a chopstick and calling to the table: 'Excuse me, ladies and gentlemen ...' Evidently feeling a chopstick isn't up to the task, he stands and shouts, 'Oi, everyone, I want your attention.'

An expectant silence descends on the group.

'As you all know, Jack here isn't just my best mate, he's also a fucking genius.' He's distracted by an angry tut from a nearby table. 'Piss off,' he shouts at them, one finger pointing at Jack. 'If you knew who this man is, you'd be too busy genuflecting to worry about my language.'

He turns back to his own guests, takes a large mouthful of *sake* to compose himself.

'As you know, Jack's been taking a well-deserved break.'

Jack resists the urge to check for knowing smiles around the table.

'But I also happen to know he's had a lot on his mind recently.' He turns to Jack, begins to sound emotional. 'And I realize now maybe you were trying to tell me what the problem was for a long time, but you just didn't know how.'

For a moment it appears Harry might cry, but then he visibly rallies, starts speaking to the whole table: 'What none of us knew is that Jack has spent his whole life wanting a dad. And as for his mum, well, she was always a bit of a bitch really.' He turns to Jack again, looks worried. 'Am I allowed to say that about your mum?'

'Where's this going, Harry?'

'Well, I'm not going to sing you a Cliff Richard song because I hate that fucking music. But I'll go one better.'

He hands Jack a piece of paper. Nothing but a name and address scrawled in his pubescent handwriting.

'What's this?' says Jack.

'It's your dad, mate. He's not dead in the literal sense. He just lives in Scotland.'

25

Jemima's entering a sweetly domesticated stage in her relationship with Tim, or that's the way it seems after tonight's exchange of emails: the way he's offered to pick her up in his car on Saturday, and promised he'll take her somewhere pretty where they can talk in private.

She signs off her final message with a long row of kisses, then proceeds to float around her bedroom trying to choose what she should wear on the big day.

Her bed is covered with tops and skirts and shoes when a new email arrives, this time sent to her personal address; an address she hasn't even given to Tim, let alone her harem. And it's from a name she doesn't know.

Chelsea Hill.

Her first thought is that it's some kind of spam from a property developer, but then she reads the subject line: 'HI! WE'RE BUDDIES! (OR WE WILL BE NEXT WEEK!)'

As she opens the message, Chelsea's personality bursts from the screen like a thermonuclear blast.

Hi Jemima! I'm Chelsea and I just found out you're my exchange buddy. I hope you don't mind I wrote you first. I'm kind of competitive like that.

By the way, I LOVE LOVE LOVE the name Jemima. It's so English, like something off Harry Potter or something. Do you also have a porcelain cat? And drive a Mini? Is your mom like totally Emma Thompson? I'm not going to ask if your teeth are all crooked! That's just like some crazy urban myth, right?

Jemima peers at her teeth in the mirror, now seeing flaws where previously there had been none.

I'm attaching some pictures of my house (WHERE YOU'LL BE STAYING!!!!) My mom's already decided you're having the Chinese Room. We call it that because it has Chinese lamps, not because everything is made in China. If that was the case, we'd have to call the whole house Chinese. Hell, the whole country! Probably yours too. And what kind of exchange would that be, if we're both living in China?? (Actually, I'm real glad I don't live in China because even though I like some of the food, I don't think I'm capable of being authentically Chinese, do you know what I mean?)

I'm also sending you some pictures of my dogs and my cats and my parakeets. I was going to send you a picture of Marge and Homer, my two llamas, but they died a while back. (They had impacted colons. Don't ask me how that happened. I was like WTF??)

There's also a photo of me by our pool yesterday. I guess it's not warm enough to be by the pool where you are. Do you have a pool?? Hell, do you even have

sunshine? I've seen some pictures of London and I'm
beginning to wonder.

Don't you worry about me, Miss Jemima (I just said that
in a funny English accent. You totally crack me up, I love
it). I WILL BRING LOTS OF WARM CLOTHES (tho first I
need to go and buy some).

See you, MATEY!

xxx
Chelsea

Jemima stares at the pictures with a rising sense of horror:
frame after frame, drenched in sunshine, so much sunshine
that Chelsea even wears sunglasses indoors as she drapes
herself across the bed in the Chinese room, a vast swathe of
bed that makes her look miniaturized and doll-like: perfectly
manufactured and primed for action.

Jemima assumes the sound of her thundering downstairs will
garner some attention, but when she bursts into the living
room she finds her mother engrossed in her plants, fussing
over them as if they're special guests.

'I think we should cancel the exchange programme,'
says Jemima.

'Darling, we can't do that. Your friend arrives next week.'

'But that's the thing, maybe she won't be my friend. What
if we don't get on?'

'You're both teenagers. I'm sure you'll have lots in common.'

'Is this the same certainty that drives you to fill the house
with dying plants?'

'Darling, I spoke to the plant shop this afternoon and apparently they're not dying, they're adjusting. You see, it's just like you and your American friend. You simply need to give it time.'

Jemima glances around the room, at a tangle of withered leaves more suggestive of death than adjustment. And still it's clear that Meredith fails to see her alarm.

'Trust me, Jemima, everything will be fine.'

26

Tonight of all nights, when the only thing Jack wants is to get home, to close the door and be left alone with his thoughts, he has a cab driver determined to chat, a cheerful south-Londoner brimming with enthusiasm for small-talk, all the while driving through such a warren of side-streets, the journey begins to feel more like a fairground ride.

'So are you living here or just visiting?' shouts the driver, heading through yet another dark back way, the kind of route that in any other city would mean he plans to rob and kill Jack.

'Look, I'd rather not chat if you don't mind.'

'No, of course, that's no problem. It takes all sorts, doesn't it?' There's a brief silence. 'So, are you a banker or something?'

'Excuse me?'

'I mean, your friends back there looked like bankers. And you're obviously stressed. There are lots of stressed bankers around these days.'

'I'm actually a monk. In a *silent* order.'

The man scrutinizes him in the rear-view mirror. 'You don't look like a monk.'

'Jesus Christ—'

'And that's not the kind of thing a monk would say.'

'Look, piss off, okay?' He tries to close the glass partition between them, but it's wedged open.

'Well, there's no need to be like that. It's no wonder everyone hates bankers when you treat people like that.'

'I'm not a fucking banker!'

'You're not a monk either, not with a mouth like that.'

Jack wants to get out, would happily crawl home on his hands and knees just to get away from this man, but as he peers into the darkness, he has no clue where they are. It seems the ultimate testament to a London cabbie's dark arts: to take a city Jack has known for decades and leave him feeling dizzy and disoriented.

Despite Jack visibly brooding on the back seat, emitting vibes that are doubtless blowing out streetlamps and short-circuiting satellites, the driver returns to his cheerful small-talk. 'I've been watching a lot of *Downton Abbey* recently. Have you seen it?'

'That's it,' shouts Jack. 'Stop the car.'

'We're not there yet.'

'I don't care. I'll walk.'

The taxi pulls to a stop. 'I think a stroll might do you some good, to be honest. Help you relax.' Jack tosses the fare at him, starts walking away. 'I can see you're not a banker now,' the driver shouts after him. 'At least bankers know how to tip.'

Shortly after he gets home from dinner with Harry, Jack discovers that the evening still has some surprises in store.

It's a vague feeling at first, an abstract sensation that his stomach is taking on a life of its own. As the minutes tick by, he finds himself gravitating towards the bathroom, not out of any specific need but, rather, because it seems the right place to be. And that's where he stays, waiting, certain that something is about to happen, but unsure what.

Five hours later, Jack is still there, long since reduced to a shivering wreck huddled on the floor beside the toilet. He's thrown up so many times, he can only imagine that every retch is now the noisy disgorge of internal organs, his body tearing itself apart from the inside out.

By sunrise, he's familiar with every detail of his bathroom floor, and understands only too well why skid marks in the toilet bowl should never be left for another time.

He still needs to tell Meredith about their father, but when he finally crawls to the sofa, he's hollow, unable to do anything except lie there, staring out across the roofs of London, at this city of ambition, hope and despair coming to life beneath a grey and stormy sky.

Meredith's morning
Even though Luke insists on wearing his beret, and Jemima spends the whole time texting her friends, breakfast is a reassuring taste of normality: Meredith and the children eating food so highly manufactured that unpredictability is out of the question. Comforted by the eternal sameness of her sliced bread, Meredith spreads her toast with more than the usual smear of strawberry jam, its contents suggestive of fruit only in the same way that her fabric conditioner is suggestive of flower meadows.

'What are you planning to do today?' she says, throwing the words out to anyone willing to answer.

'I think we should get rid of Dad's yogurt,' says Luke.

'Yeah, it's gross,' adds Jemima, not even looking up from her phone. 'It's like a symptom of autism or something.'

'Yes, you're probably right,' replies Meredith, taking care to direct her words at Luke rather than Jemima. 'I've been keeping it there as a reminder, but it's all a bit late for that now, isn't it?'

Luke nods sagely. 'Some things are better forgotten.'

Like your hat, thinks Meredith, choosing instead to take another bite of toast.

Luke speaks again: 'It's an important occasion. We should have a ceremony.'

'The Vikings would have set fire to it and pushed it out to sea,' says Jemima, eyes still down. 'We learnt that at school.'

'Well, I don't think we need to do anything too elaborate,' replies Meredith.

A moment of silence.

'Though I suppose we *could* do something special.' And now that the words are out, she can see that simply to discard it would be a profoundly anti-climactic moment; that she would, in fact, blast it into space if only she knew how. 'Perhaps I'll think of something and we can all do it tomorrow. How about that?'

'Can't,' says Jemima. 'I'll be at a – a party tomorrow afternoon.'

'You didn't mention anything about a party.'

'I was supposed to be in France, wasn't I?'

'Well, do you need to take anything with you? I'm not sure what we have in the cupboards.'

'No, it's not that kind of party.' For the first time that morning, she looks up. 'It's, er, not even a party, really. We're just going to, you know, spend the afternoon sitting around and chatting. Girly stuff.'

An hour later, Meredith is driving home from an impromptu shopping trip, her desire to despatch Alastair's pot of yogurt now verging on an obsession.

She glances in the rear-view mirror, her entire view blocked by helium balloons – the same colourful balloons that will soon lift the yogurt from her life and carry it away. It is, she decides, fitting that she can't see the road behind her. 'There's no looking back,' she says to herself. 'Not any more. What's gone is gone.'

The moment feels less profound, though, when she finally gets home and has to corral the balloons indoors. Jemima stands at the top of the stairs and watches as Meredith pulls the last of them into the house.

'They're for your father's yogurt,' she says, suddenly aware of how preposterous this sounds.

'Today was supposed to be the end of your madness, not an escalation.' Jemima raises her voice as Meredith herds the balloons towards the kitchen. 'And why do they all say "Happy birthday"?'

'Because they were the only ones I could find.'

Leaving them to float around the kitchen ceiling, she takes the yogurt from the refrigerator, shouts through to Jemima, 'I want you and Luke to join me. This is a family occasion.'

She's barely finished speaking when Luke thunders

downstairs, still wearing his beret. 'I think you bought too many balloons,' he says, the words nevertheless sounding like a compliment.

'To be honest, I wasn't sure how many we might need, and it's not like I could ask the girl in the shop.' She glances up at them, bobbing about aimlessly. 'It's better to have too many than too few. This is no time for skimping.'

She starts tying the balloons together, knotting their strings into a cradle around the pot of yogurt.

'Maybe they'll end up in China,' says Luke.

'Well, that sounds a little far, but who knows?' She ties a few more knots, the pot already looking snug. 'You could always ask your father,' she adds, no trace of irony in her voice.

Jemima slinks into the kitchen, her expression making it clear that she's a reluctant participant.

'Perfect,' says Meredith, standing back to admire her handiwork. 'I think we're all set.'

In her mind's eye, Meredith had imagined the yogurt drifting over the rooftops of suburbia, climbing skyward in a poetic, meditative ascent. In reality it shoots straight up like a Harrier jump jet, almost snatched from her hands by the law of physics.

'Maybe I did use too many balloons,' she says, squinting upwards as it grows smaller and smaller.

'Wait until it gets sucked into the engine of a jumbo jet,' says Jemima. 'You'll probably kill everyone.'

Meredith turns to her, alarmed. 'I wish you'd said that

before I let go.' She glances upwards again; nothing to see now but a distant pinprick of black against an overcast sky.

'Too late,' replies Jemima, heading indoors.

Luke and Meredith stand in silence for a few moments, both of them still staring heavenwards. 'Did it feel good?' he says.

'I was hoping we'd be able to see it for a while longer.' She turns to face him. 'But maybe that's the point. It's gone, isn't it?' She smiles to herself, suddenly aware that she feels lighter and freer than before. 'How would you feel if I got a job?'

'What kind of job?'

'In a shop. It would just be for a few days a week, while you and Jemima are at school.' Her smile grows. 'I saw an ad in that lovely little shop in town, the one that always smells so nice.'

Luke appears to consider her words. 'It's a great idea,' he says. 'You should go and apply for it right now.'

'Really, darling, it's not that urgent.'

'Me and Jemima will be fine here without you.' He glances up at the sky again, speaks with a gravitas worthy of a much more serious occasion: 'The past has gone. Now you need to get on with your future.'

As soon as she enters Scents of Romance, Meredith finds herself enveloped in the shop's dense aromatic cloud, its cinnamon candles, bags of pot-pourri and entire shelf of handmade soap making every breath a fragrant sensory overload.

Heart pounding, she approaches the woman behind the till. 'I'm here about the sign in the window,' she says, eager to avoid anything as *déclassé* as 'I want a job'.

157

'Do you mean the two-for-one bath bombs or the new tri-ple-pack Bitter Orange Room Spritz?'

'I mean the job,' replies Meredith. 'I want a job.'

'Oh, thank God.' It's only now they're standing face to face that Meredith sees the woman's eyes are watering slightly. 'It's only for twelve hours a week, but I do need someone urgently. Do you have any experience?'

Meredith is still wondering how to make 'no' sound like 'yes' when the woman waves dismissively. 'It doesn't really matter, does it?' She takes a couple of puffs on an inhaler, continues speaking while trying to hold her breath: 'You're alive. You speak English. I think that's enough.'

'And I do love the shop. You sell so many gorgeous things.'

'Thank you, that's very kind of you. Though we probably won't be saying that when we all get cancer from this bloody smell.' She puts her inhaler away, blows her nose. 'The hours are ten to two, Monday, Tuesday and Wednesday. Can you start next week?'

Meredith is so happy that the words come late, long after the smile has lit her face. 'Yes. I'd love to.'

'Oh, perfect, you've made my day. A girl called Agnes will be here on Monday. She'll talk you through everything.' She hesitates, obviously unsure how much she should say about Agnes. 'She's from *Ukraine*,' she adds, making the word sound like a communicable disease. 'She can be a bit strange, but she's a lovely girl. For a foreigner, I mean.'

'Do I need to fill in any forms?' says Meredith. 'Perhaps sign something?'

'Lord, no, life is already complicated enough. Why don't

we just seal the deal by giving you something? As a sort of welcome gift.'

'Really? That's very kind of you.'

'The truth is I'm scared you'll change your mind over the weekend, but of course I'm not supposed to admit that.'

Meredith feels the woman's eyes on her as she wanders around the shop trying to choose something. Eventually she picks up a small bag of pot-pourri.

'You know what?' says the woman. 'Why don't you take a big one? You can sleep with it next to your bed for a few nights. It'll help you acclimatize.'

27

Saturday morning, and during the final hours in the count-down to meeting Tim, Jemima devotes herself to quiet meditation over her hair, makeup and outfit. She naturally spares a few moments from this monastic routine to check her messages. There's nothing new from him, which on this occasion is a good thing. Her heart sinks at the sight of Chelsea's name in her mailbox, but she passes over that in favour of Brian's latest correspondence.

Dear Lucy

I'm writing to assure you I'm working hard to procure *that picture* you requested. I did make an attempt yesterday, but there was a bitterly cold wind, not to mention a couple of dog walkers who almost caught me in the act, so to speak.

I fear the weekend will be a bad time to try again, but Monday approaches on angel's wings. Please don't give up on me, Lucy. I will never give up on you!

Much love,
Brian

Seeing no point in a reply, Jemima deletes his message and moves on to Chelsea's.

Good day to you, Miss Jemima! LOL! Does everyone talk like that? I can't wait to find out. AND USE AN UMBRELLA.

I forgot to say in my last mail, I'm not a lesbian, but I'm totally cool if you are (or your mom or whatever). I believe in diversity.

I was going to send you some pictures from our last trip to Hawaii (if you're a lesbian, you'd love me in my bikini LOL) but I'm sending you some pictures of our ski trip to Aspen instead, including a picture of my mom when she broke her leg. It was so cool, she was in hospital for like two weeks and my dad ordered sushi for dinner EVERY DAY. And after those two weeks, I swear I could swim WAY better. (I'm surprised scientists don't spend more time researching that.)

I'm going to spend the whole weekend by the pool so I look my best for all those cute English boys.

Cheerio and God save the Queen (though I hear Prince Charles wants her dead. Is that true? It's all so Hamlet).

xxx
Chelz

At breakfast that morning, Jemima doesn't initiate conversation until her mother's had a restorative sip of tea.

'What would happen if we burnt the house down?' She glances around the table, notices that both her mother and

Luke appear alarmed. 'I just mean, *if* the house burnt down, I presume we'd be put in a hotel or something while we found somewhere else to live.' Still no response. 'Don't you think that would be nice for a while? Living in a hotel?'

'No,' says Meredith. 'It sounds ghastly. Why even think it?'

'But we'd be given lots of money for new clothes, which would be a nice extra. And, let's face it, it could only do good things for your image.'

'Darling, I wouldn't need any new clothes because I'd be spending the next few years in prison. Insurance companies generally take a dim view of people burning down their own houses.'

'But maybe it happens because I leave a candle burning in my bedroom or something. I'm a teenager. I'm forgetful. The insurance company would understand that.'

'And presumably you want us to do all this before your friend arrives next weekend?'

'She can't stay here! I mean, look at everything. Look at *us*.'

'Darling, she lives in America. For all you know she has to sleep with a gun under her pillow.'

'She has a swimming pool! And even the *bed* in their spare room – *one* of their spare rooms – is bigger than – bigger than this whole house.'

'Then imagine how charming she'll find this place. So cosy and so … English.'

Later that morning
Jack has explained to Luke that the supermarket is an ocean on which to drift at leisure, but Meredith clearly sees it as

more of a *Titanic* moment. In fact, to look at her now, surrounded by the crowds of a busy Saturday, one would think the ship's already hit the iceberg and now they're all just waiting to die.

'I think we should stock up in case Uncle Jack's not back for a while,' says Meredith. 'He hasn't returned my calls.'

Luke, who's trying to steer a trolley that's considerably bigger than him, naturally assumes that her worried tone is because of the supermarket. 'I think,' he says, pausing to adjust his hat, 'you'd enjoy this experience much more if you weren't so tense.'

'Darling, we're in a windowless space with five hundred other people. Under these circumstances, a little tension is a healthy response.' She picks up a box of cereal and stares at it as though the lettering on the package is hieroglyphic and unintelligible, then puts it in the trolley anyway. 'The quicker we choose things, the sooner we can leave.'

'Uncle Jack wouldn't say that.'

'That's because your uncle savours every opportunity to spend money.'

'But he's your twin brother. You're supposed to be the same.'

'But we're not identical twins, darling. We were born at the same time, but we were two different babies, just like you and Jemima.'

'So is there nothing you have in common?'

'I wouldn't say that.' She's clearly struggling to think of something. 'We have a shared history, which is often the closest connection of all.'

They enter the frozen-food aisle. Faced with weeks' worth

163

of dinners almost ready for the table, Meredith appears to cheer up.

Luke watches her load the trolley with fish in breadcrumbs, fish in batter, fish in sauce – a deep-frozen maritime haul.

'What was Uncle Jack like when he was my age?'

Meredith smiles at the recollection. 'A miniature version of what he is now, actually. I used to think nothing could touch him. Like he could walk through fire unscathed.'

'And don't you think that any more?'

She smiles again, but there's sadness in it. 'We all change, Luke, and life is sometimes … It can be full of surprises.'

They ride home in a comfortable silence, Luke imagining that his mother needs this quietude to recover from the supermarket. He sits in the front passenger seat, marvels at how the streets appear so different from this perspective: seen from the safety of a car, in the company of an adult.

He's so enjoying the ride, he almost misses it: the sight of Jemima standing on the roadside, obviously waiting for something, her sequined top sparkling in the daylight, her legs looking twice as long in a very minimal pair of shorts.

'There's Jem,' he says, as his mother sails past.

Meredith slams on the brakes.

In that instant of recognition, it's clear that Jemima considers running away, but then decides against it.

Meredith reverses the car back to her, shouts through Luke's open window, 'Jemima, what on earth are you doing here?'

'I'm, er, waiting for, um, Jenny's mum to pick me up.' She scowls at Luke, an unspoken warning to keep his mouth shut.

'But you left home before we did. Do you mean to say you've been waiting here all this time? And why didn't she want to pick you up from home?'

Jemima shrugs, always a sign that she can't think of any new lies to tell.

'Well, get in,' says Meredith. 'I'll drive you there now.'

'Actually, I'd rather just go home,' replies Jemima, bringing a hint of perfume to the car as she clambers in. 'I don't really want to see them after all.'

The car makes an unhappy noise as it pulls away; the arthritic creaks and groans of old age. Meredith doesn't seem to notice, is too busy glancing at Jemima in the rear-view mirror. 'And what were you all supposed to be doing dressed like that?'

'It was a ... you know ...'

Luke jumps in. 'Did you never have a party with your friends when you were young?'

The question appears to distract Meredith. After a long silence, her words come softly: 'Well, not very often, no ...'

28

It's dark by the time Jack reaches Meredith's, the well-lit rooms giving the whole house a celebratory appearance; something festive to brighten the long winter nights.

In those final seconds before he goes inside, he quietly gives thanks to be back here among people who understand and accept him. Or, at least, that's how he feels standing on the doorstep. As soon as he enters the house, he can hear Jemima shouting something at someone: a brief, unintelligible blast of teenage angst followed by the loud slamming of a bedroom door. Even the jungle of the hallway appears more boisterous than he remembers, as though, having narrowly escaped death, it's now determined to live with wild abandon.

Meredith bustles from the kitchen, her apron looking like she's been in a particularly savage food fight. 'Gosh,' she says, as she gives him a hug. 'You've lost weight.'

'Yes, I call it the sushi and puke diet.'

'Is that a new celebrity thing?'

'No, Melly, it's called food poisoning.'

'Oh, you poor thing. Do you think you can eat some dinner?'

'What are you cooking? Tinned or frozen?'

166

'Neither,' she replies, evidently taking it as a serious question. 'I'm doing a roast.'

Jack knows that in his sister's hands the meat will more likely taste as though it's been through a kiln than an oven, but with memories of raw fish still fresh in his mind, the idea of food that's been baked to extinction sounds oddly reassuring.

'It should be ready in about an hour,' says Meredith. She takes a long look at him, appears worried now. 'I think you should have a rest.'

'Melly, we need to talk.'

From the kitchen, an alarm clock bursts into life. 'Go and lie down,' she says, already hurrying away. 'We can talk later.'

Upstairs ...

Since getting home this afternoon, Jemima has sent fifty-three messages to Tim and still there's no response. When she started, she thought each message should be an escalation of the one before – riper, more colourful swear words, that kind of thing – but, frankly, she didn't want the pressure of having constantly to excel herself, so instead she just keeps sending the same message again and again, the wait between each becoming shorter and shorter.

WHERE WERE YOU???? I WAITED FOR THREE HOURS!!! No one treats me like this, YOU TOTAL SHIT BAG.

She considers venting some of her anger at Brian, who would at least respond with a heartfelt apology even if he didn't understand what he was apologizing for, but there's just no point. She wants a response from Tim, and until she has it, nothing will make her happy.

From downstairs, she hears the clatter of pots and pans, a reminder that her mother is cooking tonight, taking perfectly good ingredients and rendering them nigh-inedible in a perverse act of love.

It's such a depressing thought that Jemima does the only thing that brings her comfort right now: she sends message number fifty-four.

An hour later

Jack looks so peaceful sleeping on the sofa that Meredith doesn't have the heart to rouse him for dinner. He's already slept through Jemima playing loud music, not to mention the smoke alarm going off in the kitchen, so it seems wrong to Meredith that he should be woken for something as mundane as her cooking.

She stands in the living-room doorway and watches him sleep, his baby-like face so disengaged from the pressures of being brilliant that she can almost believe they're children again.

Inevitably still wearing his hat, Luke comes downstairs, as silent as coastal fog, only alerting Meredith to his presence when he's standing beside her. 'Isn't it a bit creepy to watch someone sleep?'

'I was just making sure he's all right.' She starts to close the door. 'Now that I know he's okay, we can let him rest.' Yet still she peers in at him as the door swings shut and the shadows envelop him, so that for a brief moment all that remains is a shaft of light on his angelic face, and then that, too, is lost to darkness.

Despite the whole house smelling of roasted meat for at least two hours before dinner, Jemima waits until the food is actually on the table to announce that she's now a vegetarian.

'Meat is murder,' she says, staring at the joint of beef. 'That animal died a slow and painful death.'

'Then surely the least we can do is eat it,' replies Meredith. 'Otherwise its suffering was in vain.'

'I'll just have vegetables, thank you.'

Meredith offers her a bowl of Brussels sprouts. 'I'm afraid these may have died a slow and painful death too.'

'I'm only eating the potatoes,' says Jemima.

'Which have been roasted in goose fat,' replies Meredith.

'Then I'll just have to pretend I didn't hear you say that.' She fills her entire plate with potatoes and starts to eat, her eyes still firmly on the beef.

Even Meredith has to admit it looks more like a small burnt log, the last remnant of a devastating forest fire. By now she's attempting to carve it, the dense dry meat requiring more of a vigorous sawing action.

Jemima drops her half-eaten potato, pushes back her chair. 'I can't eat any of this. Not in the same room as that ... dead animal.'

'I can bring you a cheese sandwich,' says Meredith, as Jemima heads for the door.

'Dairy is slavery.'

'Then how about some buttered toast?'

Ignoring her now, Jemima storms away.

'It's funny,' says Meredith, as she serves Luke a few chunks of desiccated meat, 'I'd love to invite Grandma to dinner, but she doesn't even know who we are any more. I'm beginning to know the feeling ...'

'Don't worry about Jemima,' says Luke. 'She's a teenager. You have to make allowances.'

'Yes, you're right,' replies Meredith, already starting to rally. 'And I think she's a bit nervous about the arrival of her American friend.'

A moment of silence, Luke's face suggesting he's about to ask a difficult question.

'Is Uncle Jack going to be okay?'

'Of course he is. He's just tired.' Eager to change the subject, she shovels some Brussels sprouts onto his plate, their flesh yielding a little too much to the spoon. 'Are you all ready for school on Monday?'

This does the trick. The very mention of school seems to wipe all other thoughts from his mind. 'I suppose so ...'

'You're not going to wear the hat, are you?'

'What difference does it make? I'll get picked on no matter what I do.'

Unsure what to say now, Meredith stares at her dinner, a meal she no longer wants to eat. Much like her emotions in recent days, everything about this food has been taken to extremes and now it sits there, damaged and unappealing.

On the other side of the table, Luke also appears over-cooked, burdened by fears and stresses that no young child should have to bear.

'Perhaps you need a project,' she says. 'Something to take your mind off the nasty things.'

He sits up a little straighter. 'Like what?'

'I don't know. You like to collect things ...'

'But it only makes other people angry.'

'Maybe you just need to collect different sorts of things.'

'I like things that tell a story.'

'Well, there you go. Maybe you can collect other people's stories. Learn more about them and write it all down.'

'Won't people think me a bit strange?'

'We can't keep everyone happy,' she says, as much for her own sake as his. And now her mind drifts to Alastair's armchair in the back garden, its damp foam cushions wrapped in a burka of black rubbish sacks. 'Sometimes the things that make us happy don't always seem sensible to other people. But as long as we're not hurting anyone, I think it's fine.'

Luke's eyes begin to sparkle with possibilities. 'I could take photos. That would be a good way of saving people's stories.'

'That's a lovely idea. As long as you treat people with kindness and respect, and it doesn't involve bringing dead animals into the house, you should do whatever makes you happy.'

29

Jack wakes up to a darkened room, a silent house. He's still fully clothed on the sofa, but now there's a blanket tucked over him and a pillow beneath his head. In those first few seconds, drowsy and disoriented, he can't recall where he is. The plants only add to the confusion: a blackened, nightmarish chaos threatening to swallow the entire room.

It's only as he feels Reggie wake up beside him that the panic subsides.

'Hello, boy,' he whispers, gently stroking Reggie's head, his hand squeezed between a hairless ear and a plastic cone. 'Did you miss me?' Reggie responds by nuzzling him, wiping his wet nose along Jack's wrist.

Everything about the house seems different in the absence of light and sound. Even Meredith and the kids feel far away now, not just upstairs but in a totally separate reality.

'Do you think this is what it will feel like? You know, when the time comes ...' He blinks into the darkness: eyes open, eyes closed, it doesn't make much of a difference. 'Will you stay with me once it's happened? Even when I'm no longer such scintillating company?'

Reggie moves closer, rests his coned head on Jack's stomach.

'I could have had a six-pack if I'd wanted to. Abs of steel.' Even in the gloom, Reggie appears doubtful. He stares at Jack as though he knows all about those years when he talked of running a marathon or taking up water polo. 'None of that's going to happen now, is it? Not that I care, by the way. Truth be told, most sports fanatics are total wankers.'

Reggie closes his eyes. And still Jack strokes him, speaks more gently.

'It's not been a bad life, has it? All things considered, I mean. I've been a lucky man. I wouldn't mind that on my gravestone, actually. "It wasn't a long life, but he lived it well."'

It's Luke who wakes him the second time, the room drenched in sunlight.

'Welcome home,' says Luke, his beret so lopsided that one eye appears to be drooping.

'Thank you,' Jack replies, his mouth dry, his eyes gritty.

'Smile.' He holds up one of the disposable cameras, takes a picture. 'I'm going to start collecting people.'

'Alive, I hope.'

'Of course. It's just their stories, really. The things that make them happy and the things that make them sad.' He seems to scrutinize Jack as he speaks: a young child who sees things that others don't. 'What's your story?'

'My story is, I'm very glad to be back here. It makes me very happy.'

'Are you going to stay for a long time?'

'I hope so, yes.'

Out in the hallway, Meredith calls something to Jemima

upstairs. Moments later there's the unmistakable sound of sensible shoes padding their way back to the kitchen.

Jack heaves himself upright, his head beginning to throb. 'Okay, little man, I need to go and talk to my sister.'

Wrapped in his blanket, he wanders through to the kitchen, sits down opposite her, nothing between them but a breakfast table strewn with breadcrumbs and splashes of jam.

She smiles at him. 'Good morning, sleepyhead. How are you feeling today?'

'Look, Melly, it's about our father ...'

Suddenly this room and this house seem ill-suited to the enormity of what he's about to tell her.

He stares at her for one second, two, three. And then he begins to speak.

Thirty years earlier, 1982

She used to be ashamed of living on this street. This little pocket of council houses in an otherwise prosperous town.

Until Margaret Thatcher came to power a few years ago, living here felt like having a facial scar: it was an address that singled her out as a woman who'd got life wrong. But now it seems half her neighbours are buying their houses from the government, and even though she can't afford to buy hers, there's still a reflected glory – indeed, who's to know that she doesn't own hers too? In a few more years, this street will be no different from all the others in town and she need never again feel self-conscious about telling people where she lives. It's as though, after years of rejection, life is finally admitting her to the cocoon of the middle classes, finally allowing her to become something new.

'Why does it matter whether we own our house?' says Meredith, her hair tied back in a style that is not and never will be fashionable.

'What a stupid question,' snaps her mother. 'You say such ridiculous things, and then you wonder why I like your brother more.'

Even this passing reference to Jack makes her feel better

about motherhood. Now thirteen, Jack is beginning to reveal the man he will become: a proud bearing, a decisive spirit. Under her guidance, he'll surely become a doctor or a lawyer, the final stage of her assimilation to polite society.

As for Meredith, it would be enough if she just learnt to be seen rather than heard.

'If you stay like this, how do you think you'll ever get a good husband?' she says. 'Men don't want a woman like you. Always saying the wrong things. Making them feel bad.'

'I wasn't trying to make you feel bad.'

'And yet you do. I sometimes feel like I can't even bear to be in the same room as you. Imagine how that makes me feel. Having to say that to my own daughter.'

Meredith often wonders whether family life would be this unkind if her father hadn't died. In the early days, she'd barely understood his absence. It's only now as she gets older that she ponders what he was like, not just who he was as a man but how he might have made her feel as a woman.

Her mother never speaks of him by choice, and when she's asked it always provokes the same brusque response: 'Your father's dead. Talking won't bring him back.'

The closest Meredith can get to understanding her father is by observing Jack. This naturally creates awkward moments: the politics of wanting to be a bossy sister now clashing with her need to know more about a man she'll never meet.

It feels as though their mother uses Jack in much the same way, raising him to be the husband she lost. Indeed, when she watches them together, it sometimes seems to Meredith that she's witnessing the earliest days of her parents' marriage, like seeing the light from a distant star long after the star itself has died.

'What are you thinking?' says her mother, the tone suggesting that private thoughts are a bad thing, a subversive trait.

'Nothing,' Meredith replies, such a knee-jerk reaction, she forgets that it's a word rather than an act of capitulation. 'I was just thinking about Jack.'

'You should spend more time trying to *be* like him,' her mother says. 'He's going to be extraordinary. The first good thing that's ever happened to this family.'

Although she never taught Jack to believe in Santa Claus – life is much too harsh for nonsense like that – it's becoming obvious to him that his mother traffics in a different kind of deception: an insular fantasy of what their lives should be; what their lives *will* be when everything starts going their way.

Until recently, Jack had never questioned her decisions: for better and for worse, they were all in this together. Yet now he sees she has such a narrow, suffocating vision of the future that, if he doesn't want what she wants, there's nothing left.

These thoughts keep him occupied during today's science class: an interminable lesson about things he will never need to know; chemical reactions and atomic structures that he's determined to forget in years to come.

It's only towards the end of the lesson that it gets more interesting. Grouped into pairs, they're each given a lit candle and a glass beaker, the mood in the room lifting with the prospect of something to do.

'We're going to learn what it is that keeps a flame alive,' explains his teacher to the class. 'Is it the candle's inherent properties? The wax, for instance? Or is it something in the environment? On the count of three, I want you to invert your glass beakers and place them over the flame.' Excitable murmuring ripples around the room: the possibility of an explosion, perhaps. 'All right? One, two, three ...'

Jack covers his candle and watches as the flame keeps burning in its own little world, cosseted and insulated from reality.

Then it starts to flicker, its certainty wavering.

Mesmerized now, Jack leans closer. Within seconds the flame snuffs out, choked to death by walls so transparent one would barely even know they were there.

Desperation sets in

30

Meredith had imagined it would be a moment of jubilation. Of dancing on tabletops and cracking open a bottle of champagne. *Her father is alive!* Yet as she sits there, listening to Jack, she can think only of what's been lost: all the years that have been sacrificed to her mother's lies.

'... so which option would you prefer?' says Jack.

Meredith stares at him, aware that her mind's been wandering. 'Could you say it again?'

'We either write a letter or we just go straight up there and break the news to him face to face.'

'Can we not just call?'

From his expression, it's obvious Jack's already explained this too. 'He doesn't have a telephone.'

'Who doesn't have a telephone in this day and age?'

'I don't know, Melly. He lives in some village way out in the Highlands. Maybe they're all like that up there.'

'But the kids go back to school tomorrow. And the girl from America arrives on Saturday.'

'And she's here for – what? Two weeks? That means it'll be another three weeks or more before we can get up there.'

'Jack, I'm aching to meet him as much as you are, but you

surely see how impractical it is just to drop everything and go up there unannounced? He might not even be there.'

Silence.

'Come on, Jack, be reasonable.'

'You're probably right,' he says, at length. 'We'll send a letter and take it from there.'

They try to write it together, a blank sheet of paper on the table between them, but how does one start a letter like this? And the longer they stare at the blank page, the more complex the task seems to become.

'You're the one who works in advertising,' says Meredith.

'Melly, we create TV commercials for soap powder and chocolate bars, not long-lost children.'

A mug of tea soothes the stress, the two of them standing in the kitchen window while Reggie amuses himself in the garden, his coned head peering this way and that, like a satellite dish scanning the universe.

'I think it should just be simple and straight to the point,' says Jack. 'Something like "This is who we are. This is who we believe you are. If we're right, and if you want it, let's arrange to meet."'

'Sounds like a letter from the bank, doesn't it?'

'Better that than nothing.'

Meredith holds her mug in both hands, treats it more like a comforter than a drink. 'You're probably right. Better to just send something than waste another forty years trying to work out what to say.'

Upstairs

Jemima's had almost twenty-four hours to imagine the many different ways she'd like to see Tim die, the myriad layers of Hell she'd like him to experience during his eternal damnation.

It comes as a surprise, then, that one simple message from him makes her think she's falling in love.

Dear Jemima

I'm really, really, really sorry. My car's been having some engine trouble recently and it took me ages to get started.

The truth is I did turn up. I was forty minutes late, but I did arrive. But when I saw you, you looked so beautiful, so perfect, I didn't have the courage to stop. You're too good for me. That's what I felt.

I know, I'm a total dick. I just panicked.

And now I've made everything a hundred times worse (maybe that should be a hundred and eighty-nine times worse, since that's how many messages you sent yesterday).

Can you forgive me? If I get another chance, I won't let you down, I promise with all my heart.

xx
Tim

PS That sparkly top looked amazing. Will you wear it next time too?

PPS Did I say how beautiful you are?

*

Jemima doesn't walk downstairs, she floats. Even the sight of the hallway doesn't rile her. For the first time in days, she no longer feels like she's crash landing in a remote corner of the Amazon. *They're just plants.* And, yes, she still has to stoop to avoid the fern, but it's not enough to spoil the moment.

The atmosphere in the kitchen is a little sullen – Jack and Meredith sitting at the table staring at a sealed envelope – but she knows these people well enough to ignore it. They're inclined to moodiness. The good news is, they have her.

'I'm hungry,' she says, to no one in particular. She opens the refrigerator, tears a shard of meat from the remains of the roast beef.

'I thought you were a vegetarian,' says Meredith.

'Not any more. It was just last night. You know, a trial run.'

Luke enters the room, hat on and camera in hand. He immediately gravitates to the envelope. 'What's that?'

Meredith appears to steel herself. 'We've just found out that our father, your grandfather, is alive. He's living in Scotland. So we've written a letter and asked to meet him.'

Everyone stares at the envelope.

'What if he wants to come and live with us?' says Jemima.

'Darling, you may be jumping the gun just a little.'

'Well, I think it's exciting,' says Luke. He takes a picture of it, the flash only adding to the dazed look on Meredith's face. 'What do you think he'll be like? I hope he has a beard. And smokes a pipe.'

Within seconds the silence feels bated, everyone wondering if they dare confess their private dreams.

'I just hope he has a kindly face,' says Meredith. She

begins to smile. 'And big, strong hands. A man who likes to build things.'

'Model railways,' says Jack. 'He likes to build model railways.'

'Isn't that a bit nerdy?' replies Meredith. 'I was thinking really big, useful things.'

'Like boats!' says Luke. 'Real boats.'

'Exactly,' continues Meredith. 'He once built a boat and sailed around the world. And he still writes to all the friends he made along the way.'

'And he has a jolly wife,' says Jack. 'She loves to bake, so the house always smells of cakes and biscuits fresh from the oven.'

'Yes! And they have a huge garden! The kitchen is always full of home-grown herbs and vegetables.' Meredith looks happy at the thought, as though this alone would make him worthy of unconditional love. 'Oh, and at night they sit by a roaring log fire and remember all the places they've visited.'

'Maybe they have kids,' says Luke.

Neither Jack nor Meredith seems troubled by this.

'Maybe even grandchildren too,' adds Meredith. 'Maybe we're part of a big family we never knew about.'

'I want him to have a big dog,' says Luke. 'Called Bessie.'

'Definitely,' says Meredith. 'And three cats.'

Jack looks unimpressed. 'For Christ's sake, Melly. This is our father we're talking about, not some ageing spinster. It'll be a big dog called Bessie, *one* cat, and maybe a parrot.'

Meredith claps her hands. 'No, a mynah bird! And it talks all day about the weather.'

'I'm hoping he's a handbag designer,' says Jemima, eager to join the conversation, but unsure what else to say.

The momentum takes a few moments to recover.

'He would probably have been a young man in the sixties,' says Jack. 'Who knows? He might be the last of the hippies. All free love and let's have another joint.'

'I'm sure he won't be like that,' says Meredith, stiffening. 'After all, he's one of us. We can't be so very different from each other.'

This immediately kills the mood. Until seconds ago they were a dysfunctional family dreaming of redemption, but if the mystery man really is just like them, even Jemima knows he's more likely to be a liability than a saviour.

After a long silence, Jack speaks, his voice low, his gaze fixed on the envelope. 'All I really hope is that he never knew about us.'

31

The next day, Meredith wakes up to find her subconscious has made some progress on the knotted Rubik's Cube of her fears, reducing it from a nightmare to a mere challenge. She can't yet look at it and *like* what she sees, but neither does she want to pick it up and throw it into the nearest bin.

It helps that the sun is shining, a rare winter's day on which the whole world seems to sparkle beneath a sky of perfect blue. Standing at her bedroom window, she vows to send Luke to school with renewed optimism; to post The Letter with a heart full of hope; and then head off to work with a skip in her step.

In many ways the morning proceeds according to plan. 'Optimistic' is not quite the right word for Luke's expression as he leaves the house with Jemima, though at least his beret appears to bring him some comfort. And the effect of posting The Letter is much how Meredith imagines smoking weed: she suddenly finds herself smiling at strangers in the street, is desperate to mention her father in conversation with anyone, everyone. 'I had a wonderful weekend, thank you ... I wrote to my father ... He lives in a pretty little village up in the Highlands ... We'll be visiting him in a few weeks ...'

It's only as she arrives at the shop that her enthusiasm for the day begins to flounder. Now that she's here as an employee, rather than a customer, she wonders if the smell of soap and pot-pourri is a tad *too* strong for a four-hour shift. By the time she leaves this afternoon, it seems feasible that she'll be stumbling away with blurry vision, her neural processes addled by patchouli and cedar.

That would certainly account for the manner of Agnes, the twenty-something girl who's supposed to be showing her the ropes, but who appears too dulled by the vapours to go into specifics.

'This is the till,' she says, her thick Ukrainian accent making it sound more intriguing than it actually is; an assassin's gadget, perhaps, or some clumsy piece of Soviet surveillance technology. 'The money comes in, the money goes out. Though if they try to pay with a fifty-pound note, tell them to … How do you say in this country? Get fucked.'

'Unless, presumably, they're actually buying something that costs close to fifty pounds?'

Agnes evidently thinks this is unlikely. 'For expensive purchases, most people use the credit card. Your people, they love the credit card. Debt, debt, debt. So much debt, I think they begin to bleed through the eyes.' She glances around the shop as though she'd like to see it all burn. 'The truth is they only buy this stuff because they hate themselves. They need the smell for the distraction.'

The conversation drifts into an awkward silence, the heavy scent of vanilla candles doing nothing to calm Meredith's rising sense of panic. 'Could you possibly show me how any of these things work? The till, perhaps, or the credit-card machine?'

'What does it matter? There are no customers.' Before Meredith can respond, Agnes fixes her with a prying look. 'How old are you?'

Aware that Agnes is probably not the kind of woman to pay compliments, Meredith assumes this is going to end badly. 'I'm forty-three,' she says, mentally bracing herself for a high-speed crash.

'You look good. Where I come from, the men begin to die at your age.' Deciding this is probably the closest Agnes ever comes to saying something nice, Meredith is just about to thank her when she continues: 'But I also find it depressing that a forty-three-year-old woman needs a job like this. For me, it's the ...' She appears to rack her brain for the right expression, her internal computer doubtless running through a vast data-bank of merciless Slavic epithets. 'For me, it is the death of hope. It sickens me to look at you. But, really, it's nothing personal.'

The next couple of hours pass in relative silence, Meredith seizing the lack of customers as an opportunity to make her way round the shop adjusting bars of soap a millimetre here, a millimetre there.

'The boss wants you to take a few bath bombs home,' says Agnes. 'She wants you to try them so you can help sell them to customers.'

'Oh, lovely.'

'No, they're shit. The first time I tried one, I was expect-ing an explosion, like a real bomb. But it's just coloured water. In my country, I could feed an entire family for the same money.'

Meredith's mobile phone begins to ring. Glad for the distraction, she wanders away from Agnes and answers the call while inspecting a range of edible massage oils. 'Hello?'

'Mrs Thomson, I'm calling from the secondary school. It's about your son, Luke.'

'Is everything all right?'

'Don't worry, Luke's fine. It's just there's been an *incident* and we'd appreciate it if you could come in for a little chat. Right now, if at all possible.'

Forty-three minutes later

For the last six months Meredith has tried to reassure Luke that senior school is a wonderful place full of exciting opportunities, but now that she's walking up to the building, she can see she may have overstated the case. It doesn't help that the school looks penal: a failed attempt by the architects to diversify from their usual portfolio of death camps and high-security prisons. And it's obvious that what little good the designers did achieve has been lost to decades of bad weather and disenchanted youth.

As she nears the main entrance, Meredith begins worrying that the secretary was speaking in relative terms. *There's been an* incident ... *Luke's fine* ... Perhaps everyone who works here takes it for granted that Luke will have a rough time for the next few years. Perhaps their idea of him being fine is that he lost only one eye, or maybe just the fingers on his left hand.

It comes as some consolation, then, to find Luke in one piece, appearing perfectly happy to sit outside the headmistress's office.

'Luke, darling, what happened?'

'Nothing.'

She decides that this is not the moment to push him and so they sit in stillness, the bath bombs scenting the air around them even from the depths of Meredith's handbag.

One of the secretaries approaches, her clothes looking much like her personality: buttoned down, drip-dry. 'Miss Hardy is sorry to keep you waiting. She'll be ready to see you in a few minutes.'

Meredith notices her sniff the air as she drifts away.

'Miss Hardy is a very unhappy woman,' says Luke. 'The other kids call her names.'

'Really, like what?'

He takes a few moments to consider his response. 'Fat cunt.'

'Luke, that's a terrible thing to say.'

'You asked!'

Just then, the door swings open and Miss Hardy comes out to meet them. 'Mrs Thomson,' she says. 'Thank you for coming at such short notice.'

As they follow her into the office, Meredith can see why the children call her names. It's not just her weight. Even though she has the top job, there's a tangible air of despair about her, as though she despises herself more thoroughly than the children ever could.

She takes refuge behind her desk, beckons for Meredith

and Luke to sit down. 'I'm sure you're aware why I've called you in today,' she says.

'Not really,' replies Meredith, her eyes flitting between Miss Hardy and a row of diet books behind her.

'I suppose you could liken me to the captain of a ship. A ship full of precious little boys and girls.' She smiles to herself as she says it, a fleeting moment of happiness. 'In the early days I thought that meant I could steer the ship wherever I wanted. I had real ambition, I can tell you.' The smile fades. 'What I understand now is that if I can just keep this place afloat I will have done my job. And I have to tell you, Mrs Thomson, the bilge pumps stopped working some time ago and the weather forecast is grim.' She leans back in her seat, appears to be enjoying the litany of misery. 'I know what you're thinking. They all look like harmless children. But I know the truth. They're future gang leaders and rioters—'

'But not Luke.'

There's a moment of silence, both women staring at Luke as he counts the books on the shelves, his lips moving in unspoken computations.

'Well, no,' she concedes. 'Not Luke. But there are another twelve hundred children here. Our only hope for survival *as a community* is to maintain order in this place. And when an eleven-year-old boy wears a sky-blue hat—'

'I did advise against it.'

'It's not just the rumpus it caused among the children. It's entirely blocked one of the ground-floor lavatories and the plumber can't come until tomorrow.' She sighs. 'Then there are the photographs …'

'Photographs?'

'I was under the impression this was some kind of family project.'

'I'm sorry, I have no idea what you're talking about.'

She takes a disposable camera from one of her drawers, puts it on the desk in front of her. 'It's not *having* a camera that's the problem. It's using it to take pictures of people when they're not expecting it.'

Luke turns to his mother. 'I saw my English teacher kissing one of the other boys.'

'Now, now,' says Miss Hardy, her smile a little too wide, a little too forced. 'As I told you, Miss Harper has spent some time in France. That's how people say hello there.'

'Using their tongues?' asks Luke.

Miss Hardy looks away, seems to hope that a few seconds without eye contact will somehow reboot the conversation. 'And as I've already explained to your son, I wasn't crying in my car, I simply have allergies.'

'I can assure you,' says Meredith, 'Luke won't be wearing a hat or bringing a camera to school again. Though while I'm here I would like to talk about the bullying that Luke's experiencing. It's been almost every day since he started.'

'Mrs Thomson, these aren't children we're talking about, they're animals. I think you should be grateful they just bully your son rather than eat him.' A bell rings out in the corridor, the beginning of a break period. Miss Hardy shudders. 'That sound always makes me think of nightfall in the jungle. A time when predators walk among us. I think it's best if Luke takes the rest of the day off.'

'Will he not miss something important?'

For the first time, Miss Hardy actually looks amused. 'Most of our students don't pay any attention in class anyway. It really doesn't matter if he's here or not.'

32

It's not where Meredith had expected to be today. And it's clear from Luke's facial expression that this is not what he'd had in mind either: a young boy trying to figure out if he will ever fit into this mad, unpredictable world, and where does his mother bring him? A graveyard.

'George Cooper,' says Luke, running his finger across the weathered headstone. 'Died 1968.'

'I dare say he knew a thing or two about not fitting in,' replies Meredith. 'Being an immigrant back in the fifties and sixties probably wasn't much fun.' She stands further from the grave than usual, as though the truth of his identity requires them to get to know one another all over again. 'When your uncle told me this wasn't our father's grave, I thought I wouldn't come here any more. But in a funny way I feel like we have a relationship of sorts. When I think of all the things I've sat here and told him ...'

Luke scans their surroundings through the viewfinder of his camera. 'Even though he's not your dad, he's been like a dad, hasn't he? Someone to talk to, I mean. Being here whenever you need him.'

'Yes,' says Meredith, smiling at the idea. 'I hadn't thought of it like that.' She steps closer to the grave, already feeling the formality of the occasion ebbing away. 'There were times when I was young, I used to sit here and shout at him for dying. If the dead really are with us, he must think I'm mad.'

She hears a shutter click; turns to find Luke taking a photo of an old bench a short distance away.

'That's where our mother used to sit when we were young ...' For an instant, she can picture her sitting there, always with the same sad look on her face, a look that Meredith used to imagine was grief.

'Could she talk back then?' says Luke.

'What's that, darling?'

'Grandma. Could she talk back then?'

'Yes. She was still talking even when you were born.'

'Then why did she never tell you that this wasn't really his grave?'

Meredith glances at the empty bench again, all its secrets lost to the passage of time. 'I don't know,' she says softly. 'I really don't know.'

Later that afternoon

It's not a mere dinner that Jack's preparing, it's a culinary statement: a reminder that unless one has standards, all life is stripped of meaning.

He stands over bubbling pots, their contents surrendering to his will in clouds of fragrant steam. As he stirs and tends them, he quietly gives thanks for these simple pleasures; gives thanks that he's still capable of doing the things he loves.

He hears the front door opening, and the sound of footsteps. 'Piss off,' he shouts. 'Dinner's a surprise.'

But then Meredith is entering the kitchen looking like she secretly carries the cares of the world on her shoulders. Luke trails behind her.

'What are you two doing back so early?' says Jack, still trying to block his cooking from view. 'And where's your hat?'

Luke doesn't answer, simply takes a can of cola from the refrigerator and drifts from the room. Whether out of concern or solidarity, Reggie follows.

'It's not been the best of days,' says Meredith.

'How about I go and have a chat with him?'

'Would you? He'd like that.' She touches his arm, appears to draw strength from him. 'Like the rest of us, he thinks the world of you.'

'Who is it?' says Luke, as Jack knocks at his door.

'I'll give you three guesses. Can I come in?'

'Okay,' he replies, his tone making it sound more like surrender than an invitation.

Jack opens the door to find Luke sorting through his archive of Ziplocked discoveries: crumpled supermarket receipts and well-chewed gobs of bubblegum. Reggie sits beside him, a loyal companion.

'I was thinking we should do something together one of these days,' says Jack. 'Just you and me.' Silence. 'Maybe we could go to the park. I went there with your mother last week. Had a good time.' He cringes at his choice of words. 'God, listen to me. I make it sound like I shagged her.' And still Luke only stares back, his expression blank. 'Look, forget I said that too. Forget I said anything. I just thought we could go there because it's a nice place to talk.'

'What do you want to talk about?'

'I want to make sure you're okay.'

'Don't worry. I only have another four and a half years of school.'

'It's not just that. You live with two women, one of whom's a roaring mess of teenage hormones and the other ... God, the other is my sister. I know exactly what living with her can be like. And your dad's not around. That must be hard.'

'Why?'

'Well, because dads are supposed to be around.'

'I don't think he wants to be.'

'Look, I'm sure he does. I'm sure your dad loves you very much.' He can see that Luke doesn't believe it; that Luke recognizes in Jack's voice the same tone of wishful thinking that Meredith uses when she talks about the kids at school: how they don't really hate him, no matter how many times they call him a cocksucker or flush his lunch down the toilet.

'Tell you what,' says Jack. 'How about we go camping? Tomorrow night in the garden. You and me on a *Boy's Own* adventure.'

'It's cold out.'

'It's cold on Everest, but it doesn't stop all those daft sods trying to climb it.'

'We don't have a tent.'

'You leave that to me. Tomorrow night we're going to camp in style.'

That evening

For reasons that Tim won't explain, he doesn't want to meet on a mid-week evening, and Chelsea's imminent arrival means the next two weekends are impossible for Jemima. 'It just sucks,' she writes to him. 'I feel like Anne Frank. But let's look on the bright side: at least that means there'll be a happy ending.'

She's still a little irritated that he won't agree to chat on the phone, won't even agree to chat online, but at the same time it feels courtly, this old-fashioned back and forth, waiting for ever for the next email to arrive.

It's while she's pondering the olde-worlde pleasures of dating a man in his twenties that a new mail arrives from him, its contents a single line, a single question ...

Jemima's mind is elsewhere when she goes downstairs for dinner, but even she notices the difference: family mealtimes are normally mundane affairs – mere buffer zones between more important things – but tonight the lights are dimmed, the dining table glowing with six candles.

'Isn't it a bit weird for a family to have a romantic dinner together?' she says.

'It says a lot about you,' replies Jack, 'that you consider elegance a prelude to incest.' He guides her to her seat, waits for Luke and Meredith to get settled too. After a long, expectant silence, he speaks with a flourish that's pure Gordon Ramsay: 'Ladies and gentleman, we begin with an *amuse-bouche* ...'

He puts a plate in front of Jemima that's entirely empty except for two small scallops drizzled in herb oil.

'Is that it?' she says. 'That's dinner?'

'It's the *amuse-bouche*,' replies Jack, a hint of irritation in his voice. 'After this, we have celeriac bouillon ...'

Jemima turns to her mother. 'What language is he speaking?'

'Soup, darling. Your uncle has cooked vegetable soup.'

'Then a mere *soupçon* of sorbet to cleanse the palate before an intermediate course of porcini ravioli. Followed by roast venison with—'

Meredith looks concerned. 'Jack, don't you think this is a little elaborate for a school night?'

Jack ignores her. 'With *pommes dauphinoise* and a wild berry *jus*. And for dessert we have crêpes Suzette flambéed with Grand Marnier.'

'Potatoes,' says Meredith, clearly anticipating Jemima's confusion. 'And then pancakes.'

'And,' Jack continues, 'we finish with a cheese course.'

'Dear God, Jack, is this your usual standard for a Monday night?'

'What was I supposed to do with my day? If I'd had my way, we'd be in Scotland, you know that.'

Too hungry for this argument, Jemima stabs both her scallops on a single fork, talks though a full mouth. 'Do you think it's wrong for a girl to send naked pictures to her boyfriend?' The table suddenly seems much quieter. 'I mean, I'm talking about a girl at school, obviously. Her boyfriend has asked for, you know ... *those* kinds of pictures.'

'That's appalling,' says Meredith.

'But they're in love!'

'Love is about respect.'

200

'What's so disrespectful about a little nudity?'

'Nothing, just not when you're still children.'

'But it's obvious they're going to get married one day, so what's the difference? He'll see it all sooner or later.' She assumes the silence that follows is proof that everyone agrees with her. 'Anyway, I was just asking for the sake of it, really. She's already done it.'

33

The next morning, Luke chooses to ride to school in the safety of Jack's car, an experience that offers just as much protection as Jemima's hormones, but with none of the hierarchical abuse.

'What are you going to do today?' he asks Jack, as they cruise through the streets. 'Jemima says you do nothing all day.'

'Did dinner last night seem like nothing?'

And now Luke's worried: 'Is that how dinner's going to be every night?'

'As a matter of fact, tonight's dinner will be very simple. I'm dedicating most of my day to our camping trip.'

'We're only going to the back garden.'

'But it still requires thought and careful planning.'

Luke merely nods, unable to generate enthusiasm for an event that seems so distant, a wide expanse of difficult territory to traverse in the meantime.

'Just because yesterday was tough for you,' says Jack, 'it doesn't mean today will be too.'

'But it makes it quite likely, doesn't it?' His heart sinks as the school appears up ahead, the pavement crowded with uniformed kids.

'I know it can be tough.'

'Were you bullied at school too?' replies Luke, hopeful for a moment of kinship.

'Er, no, actually.' Luke deflates. 'But I empathize.' As they pull to a stop, Jack clearly flails for something more encouraging to say. 'Remember, it's you and me tonight.'

Too burdened by the prospect of the day ahead, Luke simply gives him a weary smile and opens his door.

As he heaves himself from the car, Jack speaks again: 'It's true I never got bullied at school, but I've been through some tough experiences.'

'Like what?'

'When I first started work in London, I had some colleagues who went out of their way to make my life difficult. Sometimes it felt like a real struggle to get up in the morning and go back to work.' He appears distracted for a moment: an army general remembering some of the battles he lost. 'You've just got to remember, all the mean things those other kids say and do, it's about them, not you. They want to see you break.' He leans closer, his words becoming more impassioned. 'Do you remember when we were at the mall together and you could understand things about the people around you just by looking at them? That's a real talent, Luke. That's one of the many, many things that makes you special. I promise you, things will get better one day. You've just got to keep being you.'

Luke's father had once described school as an asteroid belt: a million chunks of rock forced by planetary gravity into some semblance of order. It wasn't a useful observation, but as Luke pushes through the school's hectic corridors, he can see there are certain similarities – not least of which is that a few stray fragments are sure to come loose at some point during the day, inevitably bringing fear and destruction to someone's life.

He's nearing his first class when he sees Miss Hardy standing to one side, not watching the flow of pupils so much as stranded by it, as though this is merely the beginning of death by drowning.

'Good morning,' he says, pausing beside her as the other kids brush by in an endless stream of heavy bags and untucked shirts.

'Oh, good morning, Luke.' She barely looks at him as she speaks, her attention clearly on the other children, doubtless on all the frightening possibilities of anarchy and mob brutality.

'You look very pretty today.'

She turns to him, appears confused. 'I beg your pardon?'

'Your hair looks lovely today. And the colour of your jumper, it suits you.'

He watches as she begins to blush, all her other fears momentarily forgotten. 'Thank you,' she says.

He gives her a big smile and continues on his way, already feeling a little taller amid the jostle and scrum of school life.

34

With the kids at school and Meredith working, Jack's had the freedom to create pure magic. Yes, the grass will be dead in a matter of days, the slabs of turf stranded on a bed of solid concrete, but right now – the only moment that's ever mattered to Jack – it looks like a real garden. It's true that the turf hasn't lined up properly in a number of places, so that on closer inspection the lawn has the appearance of an accident victim patched together by a hapless surgeon, but on the whole it's a triumph.

Sitting squarely in the centre of this impromptu lawn is a tent worthy of Everest base camp, its sleek, shell-like form yearning for Himalayan storms and white-out conditions, its interior a den of thick sleeping bags and soft feather pillows.

Elsewhere in the garden, hidden from view, speakers play the sound of a howling gale.

Meredith looks so tired when she gets home from work, it takes her some time to say anything, the air around her scented with pot-pourri. 'Had you ever considered,' she says, 'that Luke might just want to spend some time with *you*?'

'Of course,' replies Jack, 'but I don't see why we can't also give the occasion a little oomph.'

'He'd probably be happy if the two of you just hung a blanket over a broom handle.'

'And what about me?'

'Well, maybe it's not about you on this occasion.' The words come out harshly, the sound of an approaching hurricane doing nothing to ease the atmosphere. 'It just seems to me that you think money can fix everything.'

'There's nothing wrong with money.'

'That's not what I meant. I just sometimes wonder if it isn't a form of self-medication. That the solution to every problem is gilt-edged oblivion.'

'Ouch.'

She sighs. 'Sorry, it's been a long day. And I don't know why I'm attacking you when it seems my answer to everything is to buy another plant.'

Jack notices her glance in at the kitchen, the greenery in the hallway visible even from here, creeping towards them as though it's slowly consuming the whole house. 'Melly, life is scary for both of us right now. I can think of far worse ways to cope than tents and potted plants.'

'I don't suppose the letter arrived today, but maybe tomorrow …'

'I keep imagining the phone ringing. Hearing his voice …'

They stand in silence for a few moments, the background storm growing louder and stronger, an urgent warning to seek refuge.

'Well, as much as I disapprove of the expense,' she says, 'it does look rather lovely out here.' She manages a slight smile as she says it, her tone confirming that she's much more impressed than she's willing to admit. 'You could give Peter Pan a run for his money, do you know that?'

'Pfft,' replies Jack. 'As soon as I've learnt to fly, Peter Pan can blow me.'

That night
It's a new experience to be so close to Jack. To be so close to any man, for that matter. In the eleven years that he's walked the planet, Luke's never shared such a small space with another man. He finds himself watching Jack with the same fascination that people might view rare game in the wilds of Africa, his every movement different from the species that normally predominates in this house. 'Will you stay with us for ever?' says Luke. 'I'd like you to stay for ever.'

'Trust me, I would if I could.'

'Then why don't you? Mum says you can do anything. She says you're a genius.' A repentant pause. 'Though she also said we're never supposed to tell you.'

'Well, don't worry,' Jack replies, with a smile. 'It can be our secret.'

Between them, Reggie sighs in his sleep, his cone appearing to roll across the floor as he shifts his head.

Jack starts packing away empty crisps bags and chocolate wrappers, the remains of their tented feast. 'I can't believe I'm about to say this, but how about we get some sleep?'

'Okay,' replies Luke, certain that anything this man suggests would be all right.

With the lights out, the night feels bigger: that's the first thing Luke notices. It's not even half past nine yet it feels like the dead of night, everyone else in the neighbourhood huddled in front of their televisions, thankful for their radiators and gas fires.

In darkness now, Luke wills himself to stay awake, to commit every detail of this experience to memory.

Eventually Jack speaks: 'Why aren't you sleeping?'

'Why aren't you?'

'Because I have a lot on my mind.'

'Are you frightened?'

'Luke, we're in Surrey, not the Masai Mara.'

'I mean about your dad. Are you frightened of meeting him?'

'No,' Jack replies. But then there's a long pause, as though he's reconsidering the statement. 'When I was young, I used to dream that he was still alive. That he'd come walking up to our house one day ...'

Luke waits for him to say more, but there's nothing. 'Did you want him to take you away?' he asks.

'I wanted him to love me. I didn't know what that might mean, or what it might involve. I just knew I wanted it.'

'Did your mummy not love you?'

Again, hesitation. 'Sometimes even a grown-up needs someone to teach them how to love. And if they never find that person, they spend their whole life never really knowing how.'

Jack's words are softer and quieter now, and for a moment Luke feels that he's a submariner, diving deeper and deeper into his uncle's past, into a place of long-kept secrets, everything around them dark and still.

'What about you?' says Luke, almost a whisper. 'Who taught *you* how to love?'

On the other side of the tent, a slight gasp, a muffled sigh. Even in the absence of light, Luke knows what's happened: the way Jack's silence has relaxed into thick, soft folds; the gentle breathing of a man now fast asleep.

35

The letter might arrive in Scotland today, and now there's no amount of cooking or shopping that can soothe Jack's mind. He's alone in the house again, Meredith and the children sucked away by the demands of the real world, the bubble of Jack's leisured life only magnifying his fears.

Taking Reggie to the park doesn't help. Its pathways are full of people going about the stuff of everyday life, none of them needing to question their parentage, their identity.

It's only when Jack returns home and starts dismantling the tent that he realizes what he wants to do today.

He kicks at some turf to reveal what lies beneath. 'Do you know what?' he says to Reggie. 'This concrete represents everything I hate about this town. And Melly's marriage. And life in general.' Reggie stares at him, appears concerned. 'I'm going to get a bloody great sledgehammer and smash it to bits.'

He glances across at Edna's garden: a derelict tangle that has no place alongside his vision of perfection.

'How about we go and have a little chat with your former mistress?'

Reggie immediately goes back inside the house, watches Jack from the safety of his basket.

'I'll take that as a no …'

Unescorted, he crosses to Edna's back door and knocks loudly. He's barely finished his *rat-a-tat-tat* when Edna is there, a grimy lace nightcap sitting askew on her head, her face framed by lank white hair. 'I've got nothing for your swine today,' she says. 'Not even egg shells.'

'I'm here to discuss your garden,' Jack replies, in the loud, slow voice that comes so naturally when talking to her.

'What of it?'

'We need it for the war effort. I want to clear it all and—'

'What do I want a garden for anyway? It's an air-raid shelter I need. A proper Anderson one. You give me that, you can do as you please with the garden.' She peers up at the clouds suspiciously. 'The sooner the better, I say.'

'Fine. I'll get started today.' He turns to leave, but then stops. 'Would you like to see Reggie?'

'He's dead.'

'No, he's with us.'

'It's a comforting thought, isn't it? I feel his presence too.' As she glances up at the sky again, Jack assumes she's about to start her usual tirade. Instead she smiles. 'I just hope he's up there with a big juicy bone.'

That afternoon

When Meredith gets home, her first reaction is not shock that Jack is tearing up her garden but, rather, the overwhelming sensation that Alastair has gone. He's gone from her life and he's never coming back.

'You might have asked,' she says, standing on the back

211

doorstep as Jack lifts his sledgehammer and strikes the ground yet again.

'Why?' he replies, the concrete breaking beneath him. 'We both know it's the right thing to do.' He takes a pickaxe, pries away a large chunk. 'Nine times out of ten, the best thing to do in life is just get on with it.'

'Are you okay? You look a little tired.'

'On the contrary, it's good exercise. Physical and mental.'

'Well, I can make dinner if you like.'

'If it involves fish fingers, no, thank you.' He stops working, looks confused.

Meredith waits, expects this to be the opening volley of some cruel joke, but he just stands there, his face blank.

'Jack?' she says.

No response.

'Jack?'

He looks at her, still appears confused. 'What did you say?'

'Perhaps you should come inside for a little while. Have a cup of tea.'

'Why?' he replies, returning to his usual self. 'I'm fine. I'd rather be doing this than sitting around waiting for the phone to ring.' He raises the sledgehammer, brings it down with a heavy thud. 'I'm not going to waste my days just waiting and waiting ...'

Even after she's gone back indoors with Reggie, Meredith lingers by the kitchen sink and watches him. He works like a man possessed now, taking swipe after swipe at the concrete spall of the garden.

With each blow, the ground fractures more and more so

212

that, as she stands there, it seems as if their lives are really just resting on a sheet of ice, a frozen crust over dark, unfathomable depths.

Thirty-five years earlier, 1977

It's the Queen's Silver Jubilee and the street is alive with bunting, the red, white and blue of the British flag fluttering in the wind. There'll be a street party almost right outside their front door, but Jack and Meredith's mother has already announced they won't be going.

'Our neighbours aren't the kind of people we want to be socializing with,' she says. 'And I'm not going to give them an excuse to start whispering to each other about my cooking, laughing with each other behind my back.'

'There'll be bonfires the length of the country,' says Meredith. 'Maybe we could go and look at one of those instead.'

'Oh, why not?' replies her mother. 'If I dust off the magic carpet, we could *fly* there. Perhaps stop off for tea with the Queen herself while we're at it.'

A statement like this, as eight-year-old Meredith has only recently learnt, is not an actual suggestion but, rather, a *conversation killer*. And it's her mother's forte. She rarely misses an opportunity, in fact, to kill dialogue, in the same way that other people's mothers kill every spider and insect they find in the house, relishing the moment of execution a little too much.

Jack sits sprawled on the sofa, his attention fixed on the

bulbous hulk of their black-and-white television, a noisy game show rendered in monochrome. 'I'm happy to stay at home,' he says. 'I like it here.'

Even in the absence of a smile, it's obvious their mother approves of the comment. 'You see?' she says, to Meredith. '*That* was the right thing to say.'

The street party that afternoon was a washout, the rain falling so heavily it was hard even to *see* the street, let alone imagine people wanting to be out there.

Jack's mother clearly believes it's more than just a turn in the weather. It's a sign. It's a preordained smiting of people who need to be put in their place.

She looks less happy later that night when it becomes obvious that everyone has squeezed into the house two doors down, the sound of their merrymaking now drifting through the neighbourhood. 'Listen to them,' she says. 'They're like animals.'

Singing, laughing animals, thinks Jack, though he says nothing.

'This is why we don't want to be with them,' his mother adds. 'Normal people don't behave like that.'

'So Dad wasn't like that?' he says, instantly catching his breath, unsure whether she's in the mood to talk about the past. He flashes a glance at Meredith on the other side of the room: she sits frozen and wide-eyed, clearly longing for an answer.

At length, their mother replies: 'Of course he wasn't.'

'So what was he like?' says Jack.

Another long silence. 'He's gone. There's no point talking about him. No point even thinking about him.' She stares at her hands, and for a moment Jack thinks she might cry. 'When I was young, I wanted to travel. I wanted to see the world ...'

'You could marry someone new,' says Jack.

'Who would want this? Us? *Me?* Money only marries money. That's just the way the world works.' While she stares at the floor, the sound of laughter and music drift from the neighbour's house. 'Some people are born to have an easy life, for everything to go their way. And for the rest of us it's just ... it's like the rest of us were born to struggle.'

Life explodes

36

Chelsea arrives with all the subtlety of a low-flying helicopter. After everything Jemima had prophesied about her, she's not quite the beauty Meredith had expected, but she nevertheless has a sun-kissed quality, a glow that in later years may well look leathery and cancerous, but right now singles her out as a fine specimen of youth.

It's clear from the outset that Jemima is cowed by Chelsea's presence, is mentally unprepared not only for the cultural difference but also the inevitable competition of having another teenage girl in the house.

Contrary to expectations, Chelsea doesn't say how 'quaint' everything is, as she's shown around. At first it seems a good thing, this absence of cliché, but then doubt begins to set in and Meredith wonders if Jemima's predictions were right: that perhaps their visitor actually finds the house – and, by logical extension, the entire experience, including them – disappointing.

'You like plants,' is all she says, as she's forced to duck beneath the massive fern at the foot of the stairs – less an observation than the verbal equivalent of drooling.

Despite the vegetation, the tour of the house takes only

a few minutes, every non-quaint room greeted with a polite 'oh'. They spend the longest time outside, standing around in the fractured concrete and muddy no man's land of the back garden.

'We're going to clear the land over there too and open the garden right up,' says Meredith, forced to lead the tour now that Jemima has lost all powers of speech.

'Is that where you're going to put the pool?' says Chelsea.

'Gracious, no. In fact, it's not even our garden. The old lady who owns it wants us to put in an air-raid shelter.'

'What – like, in case Iran gets the bomb?'

'No, it's not for *nuclear* war. It's actually going to be a very traditional shelter, designed for protection from German bombs.'

'Jeez, are they still doing that?' She looks up at the sky, appears troubled.

For a moment, Meredith wonders what Alastair might say if he was here. Buoyed by the fact that he's not, she simply smiles. 'I'm sure you're tired from your journey. Why don't you go and rest?'

By the time dinner is ready, Chelsea comes downstairs like the Duracell Bunny with a fresh set of batteries. In fact, to look at her, Meredith finds it hard to believe that this is the restorative value of a mere nap: there must surely have been some kind of medication involved too.

They take their seats at the kitchen table, Jack busying himself in the background with steaming pots and pans.

'I thought you lived in London,' says Chelsea, apropos of nothing.

'Officially this is still London,' replies Meredith. She hears Jack snort. 'We're on the edge of Greater London. Or maybe just off the edge.'

'Are we near Big Ben?'

'Well, relative to California, very.'

'Can we go tonight? Can we go and feed those birds in Trafalgar Square?'

'I think the school has arranged some sightseeing.' She glances at Jemima, hopes this will be seen as her cue to start talking, but no, she still sits there, dumbstruck. Before Meredith can think of something to push the conversation along, Jack drops one of his pans.

'Bollocks,' he yells.

'Jack, you should remember we have a guest.'

'Oh, don't mind me,' says Chelsea. 'I like that word. It's very ... What's that really old English guy called, the one in all the movies?'

'Peter O'Toole?' suggests Meredith.

'No,' says Chelsea, 'Hugh Grant!'

Jack approaches them, his clothes covered with flecks of cream sauce. 'Most of dinner will be served in a couple of minutes, but first I need to get changed.'

Chelsea waits until he's left the room. 'Your uncle is very cute,' she says to Jemima.

'Don't tell him that,' replies Meredith, now officially her daughter's spokesperson.

'Trust me, I won't. In my experience, when you tell a guy he's cute, from that moment on he just wants, you know ...' She appears to acknowledge Luke's presence for the first time.

221

'S-E-X. In big flashing letters.' A rare pause. 'Am I allowed to say that? My mom says Brits are totally uptight about stuff like that.' She turns back to Jemima. 'Are the boys in your school hot?'

Even to a direct question like this, Jemima just shrugs, yet still Chelsea seems unfazed, possibly even sees it as a social advantage; an opportunity to use someone else's quota of airtime too.

'Do you like Justin Bieber?' Her face flushes crimson at the mention of his name. 'I *so* like Justin Bieber. If you have any boys like Justin, but with a cute One Direction accent, I will totally die.' She fans herself a little too urgently, so that for a moment it's hard to tell if she's just excited or perhaps having some kind of turn. 'When I'm driving—'

Finally, Jemima speaks: 'You can drive?'

'Sure, I just got my permit.'

Jemima visibly slumps, looks as if she will never say anything ever again.

'Anyway, when I'm driving with my mom, I love listening to Justin on full volume, the whole way just grinding in my seat like "Oh, baby, baby" ...'

Overall, dinner was a success. Faced with Chelsea's near-incessant monologue, Meredith decided the wisest response was to act as though she'd fallen into a flooded river: rather than fighting the current, she just surrendered to the experience; found herself carried through the evening on a torrent of words, drifting past the verbal equivalent of submerged houses and the bloated carcasses of drowned livestock.

It's now late and Meredith's in bed, staring at the ceiling

and wondering if it's true that she's uptight. And if she is, is that one of the reasons why Alastair left? One of the reasons why he never really loved her in the first place?

In retrospect she can see that his pot of yogurt was a sign. Their humdrum family life was no place for a man who liked passion fruit. *A taste of the tropics with real fruit chunks.* At best, Meredith would consider herself a vanilla yogurt, and there've been many days in the last year or two when she's felt decidedly plain and unsweetened, the kind of thing that couldn't bring honest pleasure to anyone.

She isn't ready to admit it, but in the mind-numbing wait for their father to reply she's been looking at some dating websites, has already dedicated an inappropriate amount of time to thinking of the words she might use in her own profile.

'Ordinary suburban mother seeks Prince Charming,' she whispers to herself. As soon as she's said it, she knows it's wrong, like asking a man to trade in his sports car for a second-hand wreck with engine trouble. And surely she should make it clear that she's a *single* woman rather than merely a frustrated wife looking for an occasional distraction.

'Divorced woman—' Again she stops because technically she's not divorced yet.

'Soon-to-be-divorced . . .' But somehow that sounds even worse.

'Middle-aged woman. Now unattached. Looking for marriage with the kind of man who prefers it in the missionary position with the lights off.'

And as she hears the words, her voice so soft they're barely audible even to her, she realizes Chelsea is right. She is uptight.

37

Participating in an exchange programme had sounded fun to Jemima in the same way, say, that getting a pet monkey sounds fun: it was going to be something cool and different that would transform her dull life. But now that Chelsea's here, she knows it was a mistake. Metaphorically speaking, the first day or two were just irritating – Chelsea climbing all over the furniture, swinging from the light fittings, that kind of thing – but now the problem is becoming more acute: by Jemima's estimation, Chelsea is becoming territorial, even predatory. She doesn't stand in the middle of the room and thump her chest – not yet, anyway – but Jemima gets the clear feeling that they're inching inexorably towards some kind of confrontation; that she's essentially at the mercy of a disease-carrying primate with a nasty bite.

Her bedroom is a case in point: over the last few days, Chelsea's belongings have slowly taken over more and more of the room. At the same time, Chelsea announced that the inflatable bed on Jemima's floor was aggravating an old back injury – 'I was waterskiing this one time in Hawaii ...' – so now Jemima finds herself sleeping on the floor of her own room while Chelsea luxuriates nightly in her bed.

She's tried airing these concerns with her mother, but Meredith – much like everyone at school and seemingly everyone in the whole town – has fallen under the spell of this invasive species. Their wholesome all-American manners. Their beautiful teeth.

'Darling, I don't know what you expect,' says Meredith. 'Of course her stuff is all over your room. The wardrobes and drawers are almost completely full of your things. And as for swapping beds, I'm sure she'd do the same for you.'

Jemima snorts: she can sooner imagine Chelsea putting an axe through the back of her head. Maybe even doing it repeatedly, hacking away to vent some unrelated frustration, then leaving the whole bloody mess for some put-upon Mexican immigrant to clean up.

She glances into the hallway, then speaks quickly to fit in everything she wants to say while Chelsea is still upstairs. 'She calls you "Mrs T".'

'I know – it's quite cute, don't you think?'

'No!' She can see from her mother's expression that she's getting nowhere. 'At the very least I think you should tell her she can't have her friends over.'

'But they're nice.'

'You wouldn't say that if they were ... I don't know, vampires or Satan worshippers.'

Meredith looks confused. 'No, darling, you're right. But since they're just normal teenagers ...'

Before Jemima can sort through the wreckage of her argument, the front-door bell rings. Moments later there's the sound of Chelsea thundering down the staircase. 'I'll get it,' she yells.

And now her perfect friends are spilling into the house, the air filling with the sound of excited chatter.

Chelsea leads the group into the kitchen, a bottle of nail varnish in her hands. 'Mrs T,' she says, 'we're setting up a nail salon and you're our first customer.'

Luke's day
For Luke, it's been the best of times and the worst of times, though not in that order. He once again had his lunch confiscated by Elliott, his arch-bully, but this time his sandwiches were rubbed through his hair before they were flushed down the toilet. Then his shoes and socks were tossed up into the branches of a large oak tree, so that most of his afternoon has been spent going from class to class barefoot.

While in previous months this would have been enough to send him running home, or at least given him sufficient reason to cry in the toilets for an hour or two, today he's chosen quiet resistance, not just for his sake but for everyone who's frightened of Elliott and his ilk. If he acts as though rinsing whole-grain mustard from his hair was a humiliating experience, Elliott will have won. If he admits he's been famished all afternoon, Elliott will have won. So instead he's walked with quiet dignity, his only thought that the floors feel surprisingly gritty in bare feet.

It's at the very end of the afternoon that Miss Hardy intercepts him, the two of them standing in the middle of the corridor at home-time, an island in a fast-flowing stream of kids.

'Luke, I'm sorry it's taking so long to get your shoes back.'

A voice echoes down the corridor. 'Fat cow.'

Luke sees Miss Hardy flinch. She talks faster now, appears to need the refuge of words. 'I just wanted to let you know that the caretaker has found a longer ladder. I think he should be able to reach them soon.'

From elsewhere in the crowd, a loud mooing sound. And now it's obvious that no amount of words will make her feel better.

'It's not about you,' says Luke. 'It's about them. They just want to see you break.'

She smiles at the encouragement, at this unexpected moment of empathy and kindness. 'Tell you what,' she says. 'Why don't you come and wait for your shoes in my office?'

In addition to a carpeted floor, Miss Hardy's room also reveals itself to have a secret stash of chocolate. 'I just keep them for social occasions,' she explains, as she opens one of her desk drawers and pulls out a family-size box of milk chocolates. 'I wouldn't eat them alone,' she adds, even though she smiles at the very sight of the box, like returning to the embrace of a dear friend.

As she lifts the lid, it's obvious that she's been doing a lot of socializing recently.

'Don't be shy. Take as many as you like,' she says, offering them to him. 'I have two more boxes in there.'

They sit in silence at first, the two of them sharing in a holy communion, the transubstantiation of mere chocolate into feelings of love and security.

After eating several with a broad smile, Miss Hardy leans

back in her seat. 'I think that's probably enough for me,' she says, though Luke notices that she looks longingly at the box as she says it. 'I have my diet to consider.'

'I think you're perfect just the way you are.'

She glances at him, blushing. 'Such a sweet thing to say. I wish it were true.'

'But I mean it.'

She looks down, appears to blink away some tears. 'I've had a rather disappointing week. Things haven't quite worked out the way I'd hoped.'

'My uncle says life is full of unexpected things, but what matters is being happy.'

'It's good advice but, you see, I was hoping to meet someone this week. A *man*.'

'What happened to him?'

'Well, just between you and me …' She eats another chocolate, perhaps needing it to fortify her for the confession. 'It's the teachers who came over with the American children.' She lowers her voice. 'I was hoping one of them might be *available*. Someone who appreciates curves on a woman, if you know what I mean.' She pops another chocolate into her mouth, doesn't even seem to be aware that she's done it. 'I thought it might be the start of a whole new chapter in my life, but it hasn't worked out that way …'

Luke watches as she takes yet another chocolate, her mind clearly elsewhere. He thinks of what a great photograph it would make.

'Perhaps if I just lost a little more weight …' she says, still distracted.

'Maybe you don't need to change *what* you are, just how you *feel* about what you are.'

He watches her ponder the words, a smile appearing on her face.

'Where did you learn to be so wise, young man?' She offers him the box of chocolates. 'I think you deserve a few more.'

'Only if you have some too.'

'Well,' she says, blushing. 'If you insist ...'

38

At first, Jack considers his headache to be Chelsea's fault, but within hours he's shivering too, his joints feeling leaden. Although it's possible that this is also symptomatic of Chelsea's presence in the house – even bleeding gums and hair loss seem feasible – he decides to quarantine himself in his bedroom.

Within minutes, Meredith is taking his temperature, her face a billboard for familial anxiety.

'Don't worry,' says Jack. 'It's just flu.'

'I know,' she replies, her tone giving the lie to the words. 'I'm just worried about you.' She takes his temperature with an ear thermometer, so that for a moment Jack feels like a cow being tagged for the slaughterhouse. 'You're running a bit of a temperature,' she says, checking the reading. 'You should probably stay in bed for a while.'

'I couldn't do anything else if I tried.' He notices her glance at the thermometer again, as though a second look may improve his prognosis. 'Why do you look so worried? Is this how Mother tipped off into the great unknown?'

'No, it's not.' She puts the thermometer down, evidently wanting to look stern, but unable to. 'You're feeling poorly. That's surely enough to elicit my sympathy.'

'Why do you think we've still not heard from him?' Meredith looks confused at the change of subject. 'I mean, he must have had the letter for over a week by now.'

'Maybe he's on holiday,' she replies. 'Or maybe he needs some time to get his head around it all. Who knows? Maybe his reply is in the post already.' Despite her words, Jack can see the same fear in her eyes: that their father doesn't care; has never cared. And yet still she forces a cheery tone: 'It will all work itself out in its own time. Right now, we just need to focus on you getting better.'

Over the next few days Jack stays in bed, feverish and exhausted, the rumblings of the children bookending his waking hours: the frantic to and fro of the mornings, and the more leisurely chaos of the evenings. It's during the day that he sleeps, the house silent, the sunlight having an oddly soporific effect.

Every night he lies awake, the passing hours seeming to slow to a crawl, nothing to break the monotony but Reggie's fitful snores or occasional whining in his sleep, sometimes so excitable that Jack can only imagine he's dreaming of a mirrored kennel and a bitch on heat.

Meredith quickly adapts to this rhythm, greeting him in the late afternoon as though it's the start to a bright and beautiful new day, and always managing an unruffled tone as she breaks the news that, no, there's still nothing from Scotland.

It's on the Thursday that he decides he's had enough.

'As soon as I'm feeling well enough, Melly, I'm going up there. I have to. I know we should do it together but—'

'It's fine,' says Meredith, her voice calm, soothing.

'I just can't wait any longer. It's worse than being sick.'

Meredith strokes the hair away from his forehead, her touch so gentle it could almost be a caress. 'I think it's a good idea,' she says. 'But for now, just rest.'

39

Meredith's grown so accustomed to Jack doing all the shopping that it doesn't register at first that the kitchen cupboards have been stripped of food; that the locusts will soon return from school for yet another feeding.

She hurries out to her car, already worried she may have left it too late: one traffic jam, one slow queue at the supermarket, and she can imagine the kids would have started on her plants by the time she gets back.

Which is when she learns that, after months of geriatric grumbling, her car has chosen this moment to die.

She goes back indoors, hurries straight up to Jack's room. Despite a sickness that's drained all the life from his face, he nevertheless looks alarmed when Meredith asks to borrow his car.

'Can't you call a cab?' he says, his voice smaller and weaker than normal.

'And ask the driver to wait while I do my shopping?'

'The car park at the supermarket is a bit tricky.'

'Jack, I'm not a complete invalid. I do know how to drive.' He appears to doubt this statement. 'Look, the kids will be back soon. All I'm asking—'

'Do you promise to drive slowly?'

'That's all I ever do.'

'But you're not allowed to drive too slowly. That kind of thing causes even more accidents.'

'Jack, either say yes or no, but spare me the inquisition.'

He nods at his dressing-table. 'The keys are over there. I expect *both* of you to come back in one piece.'

Meredith's always refused to believe a car could have sex appeal, but now that she finds herself behind the wheel of Jack's – aware that even young men are turning to watch her pass – she's forced to admit that this car not only has sex appeal, it has a good deal more than she has. And yet it also reveals itself to be an attentive and generous companion, glossing over her erratic driving with gentlemanly discretion. By the time she nears the supermarket, it's channelling her inner Sophia Loren, and Meredith is unsure which is more surprising: that she has one or that it comes so naturally.

Thanks to the car's deep, throaty exhaust, a sound that can doubtless be heard even in neighbouring towns, there was no chance of Chelsea missing her. She's still a hundred yards off when Chelsea steps into the road and flags her down.

As she pulls to a stop, Meredith notices Chelsea's clique milling about in the background, Jemima hovering to one side, looking much like a kidnap victim.

'Hey, Mrs T,' says Chelsea, her trademark enthusiasm in full flow. 'How's Jack today?'

'Still a little poorly, I'm afraid.' She considers adding that he has the look of a zombie, but then decides against it: there's no knowing how literally Chelsea might take a comment like that. 'I'm sure he'll be okay in a day or two.'

A handsome young man emerges from the group. As he angles to get a better look at the car, he catches Meredith's eye.

'Hey, meet Rob,' says Chelsea. 'He had his passport stolen, so he only arrived last night.' She stands to one side, gestures for him to say hello. Moments later he's bending down, filling the open window with his broad, athletic frame and a smile so charming that Meredith feels her heart skip a beat.

'It's very nice to meet you,' he says, reaching over and shaking her hand, holding it a second too long. 'I love your car.'

'Oh ... thank you ... It's ... well ... it's my brother's, actually. I'm just ... you know ...' He doesn't reply, doesn't move, just keeps watching her with his bright, disarming smile. 'It's terrible that someone would steal your passport.'

'Yeah, tell me about it. They took the car my passport was in, too.'

'Oh, no!'

'But it was nothing like this.' He strokes the bodywork with large, strong hands. 'I bet it feels great to drive.'

'Well ...' She blushes, looks away.

From behind, the sound of Chelsea's voice: 'Hey, Mrs T. We're going to hang out at the mall for a while.'

'So ...' says Rob, with a smile that could have melted steel. 'Until next time.'

She watches him saunter away, is certain he knows. For months she's claimed that she has no interest in these things, as though sexual desire is something one grows out of, and yet here she is, ogling a fifteen-year-old, her mind full of graphic thoughts.

As she pulls away, with a head-turning growl of engine and exhaust, she decides she will place her personal ad today: she will fast-track the process and fill her life with a whirl-wind of age-appropriate men – anything, in fact, to distract her from the image of Rob and that impossible smile.

When she gets home, Jack is up, shuffling around the kitchen wrapped in a blanket. Despite his pale skin and days-old bed head, he looks more troubled by *her* appearance.

'What happened?' he says. 'Is it the car?'

'What are you talking about?'

'You just look, I don't know, stressed.'

Meredith takes a deep breath, tries to think of sombre things: the price of milk; the death of her marriage. 'I'm fine. Everything's fine.' It's obvious he still doesn't believe her. 'You shouldn't be up.'

'I have to be up eventually.'

'How about when you're no longer sick?'

'I'm hungry. That's surely a good sign.'

'The kids will be back soon. Even if you are feeling better, I doubt you're ready for Chelsea.'

Jack rummages through her shopping bags, takes out a can of vegetable soup, peels back the lid right there at the table.

'Would you like me to heat that up for you?' says Meredith.

'I want it like this,' he replies, already eating straight from the can, every spoonful a quivering, gelatinous mass. And still he watches her, his eyes trying to discern what she's unwilling to say.

'Unless you need me for anything, I'll go and work in the garden for a little while. Dig some soil or something.' She starts gathering up her gardening gear, not even bothering to change.

'You seem awfully keen to get out there,' he replies, his mouth full.

'It's a beautiful day, don't you think?' They both look out at the leaden grey sky, a day that might be beautiful at forty thousand feet, but not down here, not right now. 'What I mean is, it's such an English day ...'

'Are you sure you're okay?'

'Of course. I'll start dinner soon, but I don't want to miss this ... dampness.' She opens the back door, steps out into the beginnings of a cool drizzle. 'As soon as you've finished eating, you should really go back to bed and rest.'

Contrary to expectations, tinkering in the garden offers no distraction from her thoughts of Rob. In fact, it makes them worse. It seems as though everything in nature is a reminder of him: the thought that this garden will soon be bursting with young buds and tender shoots; with flowers yearning for pollination, their phallic stamens standing proud; the air buzzing with honeybees seduced by the promise of sweet nectar.

Confident that Jack has retreated to his room by now, she goes back indoors and turns on her computer. As it hums into life, she promises herself that not only will she post her ad right away she will meet anyone and everyone who responds. She will immerse herself in a world of middle-aged men. Coffee dates, lunches, whatever: as long as they're old enough to understand the ravages of time and gravity, she will say yes.

40

Jemima had assumed that the turning point in her week would be when Chelsea finally cut to the chase by dumping her body in a shallow grave, then spending the next few days on national television tearfully begging her to 'just come home, we miss you'.

Instead, Chelsea looks Jemima in the eye and says, 'I think Rob likes you.'

Jemima feels the ground sway beneath her feet. She can easily believe this is a freak oscillation in the planet's axis, surely more likely than Rob finding her attractive. 'And what makes you think that?' she says, unconsciously flicking her hair and trying not to blush.

'He just seems, like, really keen to hang out at your place.'

Days of hating this girl evaporate in an instant. 'What do you think he sees in me?'

'Are you kidding? You've got that whole Brit thing going. And his parents are, like, totally Republican, so they'll love you. The wedding will be *very* Winston Churchill.' She throws her arms around Jemima, pulls her into the kind of asphyxiating hug that could give Meredith a run for her money. 'Isn't this so cool? Maybe you'll end up living in California and we can be, like, best friends for ever and ever.'

*

It's Friday night and Jemima's too busy hanging out at home with Rob, Chelsea and the gang – her new crew, her entourage, her posse – to notice that her mother looks more flustered than normal. At some point in the evening she sees Rob watching Meredith, but it's at the same moment that Chelsea speaks, evidently putting words to his thoughts.

'Is everything okay, Mrs T? You look a little stressed. Kind of like my mom when she's out of Xanax.'

'Oh, I'm fine. Just a little, you know ...' Everyone nods in clueless solidarity. 'I have a – a few things on my mind, the least of which is that it cost a small fortune to get my car fixed, and then there's the garden, of course. Still so much to do.'

'We can help with that,' says Rob.

'Nonsense, you're on holiday.'

'We're here to experience Great Britain. And what better way to do that than helping a real English lady with her garden? Give us a few hours out there tomorrow and we'll have it all fixed up.'

The bass of his voice is so melodic, so persuasive, even Jemima finds herself agreeing.

'Well, that's very kind of you all,' says Meredith, 'but, really, you're under no obligation. If you wake up in the morning and don't feel like it, that's fine.'

'No, I'd love to help,' says Rob.

'And I think it's a brilliant idea,' adds Jemima.

That night, while Chelsea is in the shower, Jemima visits her harem, sees them all from a new perspective. This isn't a group of men, it's an evolutionary slag heap.

She hammers out a simple redundancy notice and sends it to each of them in turn. Only Tim merits preferential treatment. 'You have competition,' she writes. 'You'd better work hard to prove you're worthy of my attention.'

The next morning
Under any other circumstances, this would have been a morning of bitter regret. As far as Jemima is concerned, the promise to spend a precious Saturday helping clear the garden of rubble wasn't an *actual* promise so much as a string of syllables that sounded appropriate at the time; to consider them contractual is to misinterpret the birdsong of human dialogue.

But then Rob arrives and it becomes apparent that his idea of gardening is that everyone else merely spectates while he does lots of heavy lifting.

Before long, both Meredith's and Edna's gardens are bare earth and Rob starts digging the trench for the air-raid shelter. Despite it being a cold day, he works bare-chested, saying he prefers not to get his shirt dirty.

Watching him, Jemima decides she may have completely overrated the value of feminism. Would it really be such a bad thing to dedicate her life to this man, spending her days cooking for him and ironing his clothes, spending long nights in the selfless act of procreation? On several occasions, as her mind dances through their married life together, she catches herself staring at him open-mouthed. Fortunately Rob seems to expect this kind of attention, just gives her a cheeky wink or a brilliant white smile and keeps working.

After an hour of digging, he's up to his striated pectorals in mud, nothing to see of him now but massive shoulders and the head of a god.

Meredith, who's spent much of the morning watching from the kitchen window, finally comes out of the house. As she approaches, Rob stops digging. 'What do you think, Mrs T?' He gives her a broad smile – surely proof of how special this boy really is that he makes an effort to win over his girlfriend's mother too. 'How deep do you want me to push it? I'll give you whatever you need.'

As ever, Meredith appears overwhelmed. 'Well, gosh, er, this is fine. The idea is to just bury it partially, so it creates a sort of hillock.'

'Hillock. I like that. It's cute.' He stretches his stiff arms and back: a sinuous mass of muscles Jemima's only ever seen in movies. 'If you don't mind, I'd like to take a break.'

For the first time in days, Jack is beginning to feel human. He can finally look in the mirror and see a shadow of his former self: a man who looks good for his age; a man who can still get attention.

Then he comes downstairs to find Adonis sitting at the kitchen table, dried mud smeared across his broad, bare chest, his six-pack flexing as he rocks back and forth.

The young man jumps up, shakes his hand with a firm grip. 'Pleased to meet you, sir.'

Jack slumps into a chair. 'I wasn't aware it's so warm out.'

Unlike Jemima, whose eyes follow the boy wherever he moves, Meredith busies herself making sandwiches, seeming reluctant even to look up.

'I suggested Rob keep his shirt off while we have lunch,' she says. 'I mean, there's no point getting his clothes dirty just for the sake of a sandwich.'

'I'd like to take a shower when I'm finished,' says Rob. 'If that's okay with you?'

'Of course, I'd love you to,' she replies, a little too quickly for Jack's comfort. Perhaps aware of how it sounded, she focuses on the sandwiches again, huddled over them now as if they're her only sanctuary.

Thirty minutes later, the kids are back in the garden, this time watching Rob demonstrate how many press-ups he can do with one hand.

Jack and Meredith watch him from the kitchen window.

'Don't you hate youth?' says Jack. 'The one thing money can't buy. Unless it's someone else's, of course, but even then it's only by the hour.'

'I have mixed feelings on the subject.'

'That's not how it seemed to me. Whenever you spoke to him, your voice was two octaves higher.'

'What rubbish.'

'See? You're doing it again.'

Meredith coughs, lowers her voice. 'He'll only be around for another week.' She turns her back to the window, leans against the sink. 'What's the worst that can happen in seven days?'

'It's okay to look, Melly.'

'No, it's not. It will only encourage him.'

Jack watches as Rob moves to the fence, hanging from it backwards while he raises his knees and crunches his abs. 'I think you'll find he needs no encouragement.'

'I've placed an ad,' says Meredith, her tense body language suggesting she wants this to be the answer to all her problems: earplugs against the siren call of youth. 'I've already had three replies.'

She looks so desperate for his encouragement, he just smiles. 'Good for you. May they be the first of many.'

41

Although he's barely well enough, Jack leaves for Scotland on Monday morning, heading into London on a train crowded with commuters, the air thick with the pre-battle tension of a workday. It's such an electrifying atmosphere that he spends most of the journey having to remind himself he's not heading into town for back-to-back meetings: there aren't any pitches to brainstorm or clients to woo. Unlike these people, who will slam into the day with varying degrees of success, he will simply pass through the mass of London, continuing his long journey north.

The taxi ride from Victoria to King's Cross is suitably silent, the cabbie barely even acknowledging Jack's presence. He drives at a measured pace, Jack gazing from the window as though watching a documentary about the past.

Before long, he's boarding the express at King's Cross, this time with passengers who have the manner of truant school-children: grown men and women who are free to nap on office time.

As he sits waiting for the train to leave, it occurs to him that there should be more to the moment than this: at the age of forty-three he is finally on the way to meet his father; it surely deserves liveried trumpeters on the platform, or a twenty-one-gun salute at the moment of departure. Instead, the train pulls away with such stealth, he doesn't even notice it's moving at first. As it picks up speed, the last of the platform rushes by in a flourish of abandoned luggage trolleys, and then it's out into the grey morning, the train moving faster and faster behind the Victorian terraces and suburban semis of north London; a blur of neat little lives not his own.

Meanwhile

Meredith is back in the days of videotape recorders, or that's how it feels. Meeting Rob has filled her head with things she doesn't want to see and now she must tape over it all, replace it with something else, anything else. Preferably the emotional equivalent of a David Attenborough documentary: chaste, tasteful, interesting to a point, but not at all the kind of thing that will leave her lying in bed at night touching herself.

It doesn't take long to decide that Brian is the one. He'd responded to her ad within hours of it appearing online, and already, in the space of a brief back-and-forth, they've agreed to meet for coffee.

She tries to pretend that his enthusiasm is sweet – the cyber equivalent of being courted by an attentive man – but it's obvious from everything about him that he's just sad and lonely.

As she prepares to leave the house, she takes another look at his picture; stares at it and asks herself how much she would be willing to do with this man. He smiles awkwardly for the camera, the edges of a comb-over visible atop his high forehead.

He isn't handsome, it's true, but she's not doing this for love: she's doing it to remind herself how completely overrated sexual intercourse is. And as Brian is a man of legal age and clearly desperate, he already ticks the most important boxes.

She meets him in a small café off the high street, a place that turns out to be much like Brian himself: past its prime, but eager to please.

It's immediately obvious that the photo on his profile, which wasn't especially flattering, had been taken in an earlier decade, and that the intervening years have not been kind to him.

Perhaps sensing this, Brian insists that coffee is his treat and tells Meredith that she must order whatever she likes. The offer might mean more if the most expensive thing on the menu was something nicer than a large latte with two scoops of vanilla ice-cream, but still she orders it, if only to communicate that she's a woman who demands the best.

'So is this one of your usual haunts?' asks Brian.

Meredith hesitates, wanting to consider the politics of her response. Surely if she says no, it would be tantamount to admitting she's only looking for a quick shag. That this is a date with such sordid intentions, it's best kept to the shadows.

'I come here whenever I can,' she replies, surprised at how easy it is to lie. 'It's a nice place.'

Moments later the waitress brings their drinks and Meredith finds that her coffee comes with two sparklers and a paper parasol. She decides to take it in her stride, her aloof manner suggesting this is how she always orders her coffee.

Brian waits until the sparklers fizzle out, their gaiety now reduced to two blackened sticks. 'I must say, Meredith, I like your style. A woman of your age, it's good to see you still have some life in you.'

Meredith wants to point out that she's only in her forties. That a mere twenty summers ago she was certifiably young, with beautiful skin and a belief that all things were possible.

'My wife always used to say you're as young as you feel,' says Brian. 'May she rest in peace.'

'I'm sorry for your loss. Was it very long ago?'

'A few years ...' He stares at his drink, his face draining of emotion. 'I want to say it gets easier, but that's not entirely true.'

For the first time, Meredith actually feels something for this man: a desire to save him from his sorrow and make him happy again. 'I would like to think our loved ones are never very far from us, even in death.'

Brian appears to take comfort in her words. 'Well, let's hope she's not too close right now. I'm not sure what she'd say about me sitting here having coffee with a beautiful woman.'

And in that instant, against all her better judgement, Meredith can feel herself blush.

Although they stay in the café for more than thirty minutes, Meredith spends most of that time working out how she can invite Brian home without sounding like a slut. As it happens, she needn't have worried. They've barely left when Brian offers to give her a lift home 'or wherever you're going next'.

'Home would be lovely, thank you.'

'It seems only right to take you to your door.' He smiles as

248

he says it, his face creasing into a leathery mass. 'You must forgive me if my ways are a little old-fashioned. I suspect they don't make them like me any more, and probably for good reason.'

'Not at all,' she replies, deciding she must avoid looking at his face lest it dampen her resolve for the task ahead. 'It's encouraging to know there are still gentlemen out there.'

This somewhat formal back and forth continues all the way home, by which time Meredith feels more like a character from an Austen novel: a prim spinster who's about to reveal herself as a desperate harlot.

When they pull up outside her house, Brian turns the engine off.

They sit in silence.

Finally, Meredith speaks. 'If you'd like a cup of—'

'I'd be honoured.'

A few minutes later

Never having done this kind of thing before, Meredith's unsure what happens next. Deciding it's best to keep up the pretence of making tea, she starts to fill the kettle. Before she even has enough water for one, Brian is standing close behind her, his cold bony hands on her shoulders. 'My darling, you don't need to do that.'

It's the touch that does it. It's the hands that tell her she can't go through with this. Even if she can avoid looking at Brian during sex, she can't avoid his corpse-like fingers, as though the dead are rising from their graves to partake in the pleasures of online dating.

While she's pondering how to let him down, Brian starts to cry, gripping her shoulders even tighter. 'You must forgive me,' he says. 'It's just you're the first. Since my wife passed away.'

He retreats to a chair, which, moments ago, would have seemed like a blessing, but now Meredith feels a need to go to him. 'Brian, I can't imagine how hard it must be for you.'

'And some of the women on that website, I can't tell you.' He shakes his head at the cruelty of it. 'There was one young lady, we were chatting for, gosh, weeks! And the things she asked me to do! I'd be ashamed to tell you. And then one day she just writes and says, "You're old and ugly. Piss off."' Revisiting the memory brings fresh tears. 'And you've seen that picture, Meredith. That was me in my prime.'

Wanting only to console him, she takes his hand in hers, gives it a squeeze that she hopes is more maternal than romantic. For a few seconds they sit like this, two people finding comfort in a harsh and unpredictable world.

'I want you to know I'm here for you, Brian. We can talk as long as you want.'

He looks at her through rheumy eyes. 'You must forgive me for my honesty, Meredith, but it's not talk I need right now ...'

42

Edna hadn't planned to leave the tap running, but she hadn't planned to drop dead either. These things just happen.

One moment she was filling the bathtub, an eighty-odd-year-old woman preparing for her weekly scrub. The next she was tumbling into it, her corpse beginning to stiffen even as the warm water lapped against her skin.

By the time the bath overflowed, Edna's long white hair was floating above her face like moonlit grass. Thanks to years of neglect, it wasn't long before the small gap beneath the bathroom door was blocked with old newspaper and dog hair, the water slowly rising.

Several hours have passed and now the water's finding new ways from the room, pressing itself down through the cracks of a building that's older than Edna herself.

Downstairs, the walls are beginning to weep, like a Catholic miracle.

Ceilings bulge and buckle in foreboding ways.

And then it happens. Less a structural failure than a massive existential crisis: decades of quietly rotting floorboards and walls deciding they no longer want to be a house; no longer want to be anything recognizable.

It's ironic that Edna had spent decades telling people she didn't want to be cremated, because as the ceiling collapses in the living room, it ruptures a gas pipe and a rush of methane begins to fill the air, the whole house becoming ever more flammable even as the walls drip and the detritus of a spinster's life floats across the floor.

Back at Meredith's

It's the damned dog's fault. Just as Brian is about to seal the deal with Meredith, the dog starts going berserk in the garden, barking like a madman.

At first Brian just tells her to ignore it, tries to move her hand down to his crotch, but then she pulls free and says she has to find out what the problem is.

The problem, of course, is that it's a dog and no amount of attention will remedy that, but Meredith still goes outside, starts talking to it as if it has the vocabulary of a well-read teenager. 'Reggie, I can't imagine what the commotion is. There's really no excuse for this reproachable behaviour.'

Brian watches as the dog runs rings around her in every sense, all the while barking shrilly, a sound better suited to something smaller and easier to kick.

He's just about to tell her they need to get a move on before the Viagra wears off when Meredith turns to him, looking concerned. 'I can smell gas.'

He joins her, sniffs the air.

Now acting more like a dog than he'd care to admit, he keeps sniffing as he follows his nose, each step taking him closer to Edna's house. 'I think you need to call the Gas Board.'

'We have to go in there. It's an old lady, she lives alone.'

'Leave it to me, Meredith. You go and make the call. Hurry!'

As she runs into her own home, the dog trotting behind her, Brian finds himself wondering what value Meredith might place on his chivalry. How one old woman rescued from a gas leak may be worth any amount of screwing, perhaps even a few blow jobs too.

Spurred by the thought, he tries the back door. It swings open to reveal a room inches deep in dirty water, the air thick with the smell of gas. Undeterred, he steps inside.

'Hello?' he shouts, the water soaking through his shoes. 'Hello?'

He's barely made it into the hallway when he hears the grandfather clock prepare to chime.

As the age-old mechanism creaks into life, it doesn't occur to him that this is a problem: metal striking metal.

He's still thinking of all the things he'll do to Meredith when it happens: before he's even heard the chime, the air ignites all around him and the whole house explodes in a fireball.

43

To anyone who doubts the scale of the destruction, Chelsea has just one word: YouTube.

While Jemima copes with the realization that she could have lost her home and even her mother, Chelsea is doing what any good friend would do in the same situation, she's filming it all on her phone: the way Edna's house has been cordoned off, its blackened ruins making the neighbourhood feel like a war zone. And then the sombre moment when Edna is carried from the house in a body bag. She uploads it all to YouTube with the brief message, 'Total drama in the Old World. PEOPLE DIED!!'

It's hard to say when Luke turned up. One moment he wasn't there, the next he was, his face wet with tears. Meredith and Jemima look so traumatized themselves that they seem to take his distress in their stride.

Chelsea leans close to him, decides this is her moment to be a big sister. 'It's okay,' she says. 'The old woman would have died in an instant. Like being microwaved, but way faster.'

'It's not that,' he replies. Reggie nuzzles into him, the only living thing that understands his pain. 'It's this boy at school ...'

'Boys! Tell me about it. Count yourself lucky you don't have tits. It's like having catnip strapped to your body.'

Luke stares up at her through big, wet eyes and for a moment Chelsea imagines that the two of them will now share an eternal bond.

'He beat me up. While everyone else just watched. He punched me!' says Luke, his voice suggesting he would now like to do the same to Chelsea.

Moments later, his anger dissolves into yet more tears.

'If it's any consolation,' she says, 'people will probably think you're pretty cool in a few years' time. You're just way ahead of your— Jesus!' She scrambles for her phone as the paramedics bring out a second body bag, much bigger and heavier than the first. 'Who the hell is that?'

She notices that Meredith winces at the sight of it, appears overwhelmed now. 'Mrs T,' she says, still filming it all on her phone, 'are you doing okay?'

'It's been rather a long day ...'

'Don't worry. After an experience like this, you can legitimately ask your doctor for some seriously amazing meds.'

Despite having stood on a cold street for several hours as first-hand witnesses to the tragedy, they still watch it on the news that night when they're finally allowed home.

'Police have released the name of the second person to die in the explosion,' explains the reporter. 'A Brian Evans of Guildford.'

As Brian's picture appears on screen, Jemima chokes on her cup of tea and hurries from the room.

Chelsea follows her to the kitchen. 'Do you need the Heimlich Manoeuvre? We learnt it at school.'

'I knew that man!'

'No way! He looked really creepy.'

'I think he came here looking for me.'

'Like a stalker or something?'

'What if people find out I knew him?'

'But I don't get it. How did you—' She sees the horror in Jemima's face. 'Ew, that is so gross.'

'I didn't know him *that* well. I met him online.'

'Oh, my God, like he was some weird old perv sending you dirty pictures and stuff?'

'Er, something like that, yes.'

'I love it. A sexual predator.'

'I told him to get lost a couple of days ago.'

'So he came here looking for you! Jesus! It's like he was planning revenge or something. This is so cool. First, we're all like "Oh, no, some dude died," and now we're like "Yeah, the creep got fried."'

'You can't tell anyone. You have to promise.'

Jemima holds out her pinkie, looks desperate for this pledge of secrecy. As Chelsea locks fingers with her, she tells herself these promises only have continental jurisdiction: as soon as she's back in the States, she's going to milk this story like a cow.

After a day like this, loud banging on the front door is the last thing Meredith, Luke and Jemima need. As the caller pounds away, simultaneously ringing the bell too, the three of them are visibly scared: Meredith probably waiting for the next death, Jemima possibly having yet more creepy stalkers out there, and Luke doubtless expecting another round of violence.

Then comes the voice, shouting through the door: 'It's me, Rob. Is anyone there?'

It's Luke who gets to the door first, throwing himself at Rob, clinging to him as though he's the world's last place of safety. Rob appears to take this in his stride, simply scooping Luke up as he advances into the house. He goes straight to Meredith's side. 'I saw what happened, are you okay?'

'I'm afraid we're all still a bit dazed.' She gives him a brave smile. 'Luke, darling, I'm sure Rob doesn't want to carry you around like that.'

'No, no, it's fine,' replies Rob. 'Actually, it's good for my biceps.' As if to demonstrate, he lifts Luke up and down a few times. 'I even feel that in my traps. You make a great dumbbell, little guy.' Getting no reaction, he rubs Luke's hair, surprisingly tender. 'Hey, it's okay. No one important died.'

'It's not just that,' says Meredith, in a loud whisper, as though Luke won't hear her this way. 'He's had a rough day at school. One of the other boys … You know how it is.'

'Is that so?' He turns to Luke again. 'We might have to see about that, what do you think?'

'He's a really nasty boy,' says Luke.

'Well, you know what? Bad things happen to bad people. It's like some law of physics or something.' Chelsea and Jemima glance at one another, today having proven how true those words are. 'What do you say you and me have a word with him tomorrow?'

257

Luke nods happily, but now Meredith appears concerned. 'You don't need to do that, really.'

'It's no trouble,' he says. 'I have a black belt in like ... a whole bunch of things.'

'No, you see, Rob, this is what worries me. I don't want you to use violence.'

Rob nods, though it's impossible to tell if he's actually agreeing with her or simply acknowledging her alien point of view. 'You don't need to worry about anything, Mrs T. I'll take care of it.'

44

The next morning, Meredith's first reaction is to ignore the telephone and avoid the possibility of hearing yet more bad news. She only gives in when the ringing stops for a moment, then starts all over again.

'Hello?' she says.

'For Christ's sake, Melly, where were you?'

'Jack!'

'My hotel's a shit-hole.'

'Edna's dead. Her house blew up.'

'What? Are you and the kids okay? Is the house damaged?'

'We're fine.' She sighs. 'God, listen to me. The house next door is in ruins, two people are dead, and I say everything's fine.'

'*Two* people?'

'Oh, don't. It's … complicated.'

'But everything's all right? I mean, relatively speaking.'

'Well, the kids have gone to school as usual. I'm here all day just in case the workmen next door need me. How are you feeling?'

'I'm also fine,' he replies, a hint of evasion in his voice.

'Are you sure you're well enough to drive?'

A moment of silence. 'I've arranged for a driver.'

'Then you're obviously not fine.'

'There's nothing to worry about.'

'Jack, I know you better than that. You love driving.'

'Look, the guy's waiting for me outside. I was just calling to find out if there's been any post. You know, for *us*.'

'Still nothing, I'm afraid.'

She glances around the room, wishes she was there with him, about to meet her father, rather than sitting next door to the ruins of a house amid the ruins of a marriage.

'Have a safe journey,' is all she says.

'I've brought a picture of you and the kids. You're here with me too.'

'Thank you,' she replies, her voice breaking. 'Please tell him how much I look forward to meeting him.'

45

It's late morning by the time Meredith remembers that two weeks have passed since Reggie's operation.

'It's your big day,' she tells him, as she removes his plastic cone.

It's a simple act, but today of all days it seems as though hope and redemption are made of such tiny things; that if Meredith is lucky, a lifetime of these small kindnesses will knit together into a happy ending for her and everyone she loves.

Reggie looks confused at first, as though he'd imagined the cone was an unavoidable part of himself, the canine equivalent of an ugly nose, perhaps. Then he sees his tail and the fun begins: chasing it around and around in circles; stopping to catch his breath, only to find its provocative wag sets him off again.

He and Meredith only venture into the back garden once the workmen at Edna's house have wandered off for a tea break. They're standing side by side, Meredith struggling to grasp the scale of the devastation, when Reggie saunters under the police cordon and disappears inside.

Having seen two people die in there in the last twenty-four

hours, Meredith rushes closer, calls into the wreckage, 'Reggie! Reggie!'

Silence.

Suddenly worried that noise may somehow destabilize the structure, she lowers her voice, hisses his name: 'Reggie! It's ... it's lunchtime!' Still nothing. 'Please come out. I'll buy you a steak. A big juicy steak. Or a bone! Would you like that?'

She's so busy trying to coax him from the house, so busy being ignored by her dog, she doesn't notice a woman coming down the driveway, her clothes black, her eyes puffy and tearful.

The woman speaks only when she's a few feet away. 'Excuse me.'

Meredith turns, startled.

'I'm sorry,' says the woman, beginning to cry. 'I didn't mean to scare you ...' She pulls a ragged piece of tissue from her pocket and blows her nose. In the seconds that follow, she gasps through her tears and struggles to catch her breath. 'I'm here to see where Brian died. I'm Angela. His wife.'

After mentioning 'Brian' and 'wife' in consecutive sentences, Angela crumbles into hopeless sobbing, the kind of inconsolable grief that makes Meredith wonder what kind of marriage they had: this apparently harmless woman, mourning the memory of a man who used to pretend she was dead.

It helps that she's incapable of talking right now because Meredith needs this time to craft the perfect lie. Not just something watertight, but uplifting too, the kind of lie from which a grief-stricken widow might be able to take some comfort in the weeks and months to come.

After shepherding her into the kitchen, Meredith makes a pot of tea while Angela sits at the table, leaning against it as though she no longer has the strength to support her own body.

Reggie still hasn't reappeared, but by now Meredith assumes that a dog who managed to navigate Edna's house blind can surely manoeuvre around its ruins with 20:20 vision.

She hands Angela a steaming mug of tea. 'Your husband was a good man.'

'I just don't understand why he was there. Why he was even in this part of town.'

'I met him in the high street.' She pauses, wishes she could just leave it there, at a statement of pure, undiluted truth. But Angela is looking at her now, clearly needs to hear more. 'I was crossing the road when one of my shopping bags broke. I tried to pick everything up, but there was no way I could carry it all in my arms. And people were just driving past like they didn't care. That was when Brian pulled over and offered to help.' Angela's tears start to slow. Buoyed by the therapeutic effect of her words, Meredith relaxes a little, begins to embrace the possibilities of medicinal fibbing. 'He very kindly offered to drive me home. And we had a lovely conversation on the way back here. He was telling me how he'd been out looking for a gift to buy you.'

'Really?'

'Yes, he was telling me … telling me that he felt he'd been neglecting you recently. That he somehow might have given

263

you the impression he didn't care. And he said he wanted to make it up to you because he loved you very, very much.'

As Angela starts to howl, Meredith decides she may have overdone it.

'Being the gentleman that he was, he naturally helped me carry the shopping into the house. Which was when we smelt the gas leak.'

'It was very strong?'

'Oh, yes, very. When I told him an old lady lived there, he insisted on going inside.' She notices the look of surprise at the unexpected news of her husband's valour. 'It's true, Angela. Your husband wasn't just a gentleman, he was a *hero*.'

This naturally pushes her back over the edge, but Meredith consoles herself that the story is over now, so she can cry for as long as she likes.

While Meredith gently rubs Angela's arm, Reggie nudges open the back door and crosses to his basket with something between his teeth. Meredith tries to get a better view, but Angela is in the way, her shoulders heaving like a pneumatic pump on a wellspring of tears. Unsure what else to do, Meredith pulls her into a tight embrace and is finally able to see Reggie clearly.

He sits in his basket with the blackened remains of Edna's lace nightcap, nudging it gently with his nose. Unable to bring it back to life, he lies down and rests his head on it; such a mournful scene that, before Meredith is even aware of what's happening, a tear is rolling down her cheek.

46

Jack's young driver, Callum, occasionally glances at him in the rear-view mirror, evidently torn between curiosity and his desire to be a paragon of discretion, the perfect chauffeur.

It's only as they near their destination that the words burst from him: 'Are you here for business or pleasure, sir?'

'I, er . . . There's someone I need to see.'

Now that Callum's started talking, it's hard to believe he'll ever stop. 'And will you be staying long in Scotland?'

'That depends. A day or two, perhaps.'

'Your business is in London?'

'Yes. Or at least it was . . . I'm taking some time off.'

This is clearly the news Callum was waiting for: that Jack is no mere customer, he's a man of leisure, a man so successful he doesn't even deign to drive himself. 'Most of my work is for weddings, so it's a pleasure to be driving a real businessman.' He beams at this turn of fortune. 'And for a good run, too.'

'I do drive myself,' says Jack. 'I have a very nice car, actually.' This only seems to confirm Callum's suspicions. 'What I mean is, I like driving. I'm just . . . I don't want to be driving right now.'

'And why would you when you can sit back and enjoy this magnificent scenery?'

His head beginning to hurt, Jack peers out of the window, wishing he still had a full day's driving ahead of him; that his father's life lay in some far-off, unknown location. Perhaps it's just the overcast sky, but there's nothing about this landscape that invites intimacy. It's harsh and weather-beaten; the houses scattered here and there, hunkered down as if expecting trouble.

The car could be a spaceship and it wouldn't look more out of place as it enters the village: a gleaming chauffeur-driven Mercedes at odds with this grey, windblown place.

Jack spies a small shop, instantly wants to delay the inevitable. 'I'd like to stop for a moment,' he says. 'There are some things I need to buy.' He resists the urge to tell Callum that he should also fill up on petrol, check the tyres, do anything, in fact, to stall their arrival at his father's house.

No sooner have they pulled up in front of the shop than Callum is rushing round to open his door.

'You don't need to do that,' says Jack, as he steps out into the cold wind. Callum gently closes the door behind him, remains standing there. 'And you certainly don't need to wait for me.'

'No, it's my pleasure, sir. It's all part of the five-star service.'

Despite the chill weather, not to mention the theatricality of Jack's arrival, the woman in the shop greets him with a relaxed smile. 'Can I help you?' she asks.

'Just looking, thanks.' He starts browsing the aisles, desperately trying to drown his thoughts in the shop's eclectic inventory: dusty bottles of shampoo jostling for space alongside kerosene lamps and packets of iced buns.

He settles on some mints, something he has no intention of eating, but now more than ever he needs the pain relief of some mindless retail.

As he approaches the till, the woman smiles at him, a look so direct that for a moment he imagines she's seen some family resemblance. Any second she'll mention his father's name and say what a fine man he is, a pillar of the community. Instead she gestures at a heated cabinet next to the till. 'Would you like a sausage roll?'

'Oh, um … did you make them?'

'Lord, no! We have a delivery once a week. They've been in there for a few days now, so they're sure to be lovely and hot.'

Outside, Callum still stands beside the car, the wind tugging at his uniform and peaked cap.

'Perhaps I'll take a couple for my young friend out there.'

It's the faint air of abandon that makes his father's plain grey bungalow different from all the others in the village: paint-work that's beginning to peel; curtains that are drawn shut in every window.

If Callum is disappointed that their destination is not a castle or a grand hunting lodge, he hides it well. Indeed, now that the whole car smells of pastry and pork sausage, he has the radiant smile of a lottery winner.

'I want you to stay in your seat,' says Jack. 'I may be a long time.'

'As you wish, sir,' replies Callum, already reaching for the greasy paper bag.

Jack follows the cracked garden path up to the house. Finding the bell doesn't work, he knocks instead, a *bang, bang, bang* that leaves him feeling like a bailiff come to settle old debts.

Moments later, a man appears from around the side of the building. 'Can I help you?'

Jack scrutinizes him, looks for something he can recognize in himself. This man is gaunt, his hair thinning and his clothes redolent of jumble sales at draughty church socials, but he has a gentle face.

His heart pounding, Jack steps closer. He can feel the word 'Dad' in his mouth, is suddenly longing to say it while he clings to this man, a lifetime of dreaming come to an end.

'I'm afraid John is away at the moment,' the man says. 'I can tell him you came.'

Jack stares at him, so disappointed, the words tumble out. 'I think he's my father.'

After an awkward silence, the man speaks: 'I'm his neighbour, Patrick. Why don't you come over to my place for a cup of tea?'

47

You learn a thing or two on hunting trips: how to stalk your prey, the need to wait for exactly the right moment and, when the time comes, knowing that you don't make the kill by asking the animal to lie down and die. The only way to get the job done is to put the thing in your sights and blow its brains out.

Rob would have shared this philosophy with Meredith last night, but she seemed a bit spooked by any talk of man-stuff, acting like the kind of woman Rob's father would call a 'Communist tree-hugging lesbian'. Which, now Rob comes to think of it, could make family get-togethers awkward if he and Meredith ever settle down together.

Rob waits in a quiet corner of the playground with Luke.

'Are you going to hit him?' says Luke.

'Do you want me to?'

'Not really. I just want him to be a nicer person.'

'Do you know how I got such a great body?' says Rob. Luke stares up at him with all the rapt attention of a cult follower. 'Because I know how to be tough when I need to be.' He taps his head. 'It's all up here. I can switch it on and I can switch it off. Mr Nice Guy or Tough Motherfucker, it's up to me.'

Luke points at a boy crossing the playground. 'That's him. That's Elliott.'

Older and taller than Luke, the boy walks with the swagger of an unchallenged predator.

'Hey,' shouts Rob, waving the kid over. For a moment, he just stares back, looks confused. 'We need to talk. Get over here.'

The boy approaches slowly, clearly unsure whether to stay or make a run for it.

As he gets closer, Rob puts his arm around Luke. 'I hear you have a problem with my friend.'

Rob's discussed this phenomenon with his coach: the way he gets so into the zone, he only knows what's happening when he crosses the finishing line in first place. At first his coach thought this was great, but the more Rob explained the sensation, the more insistent he became that Rob should see a doctor.

This is one of those moments.

The last thing Rob can remember, he was talking to the kid, just the two of them having a calm, civilized conversation, but now here he is, holding the boy in a brutal headlock, bellowing at him: 'I will decapitate your mother, do you hear me?'

Rob hears a collective gasp, realizes he's surrounded by a crowd of onlookers. He lets the kid fall to the ground in a tearful, snot-nosed pile. Lest his audience think it a gesture of weakness, he shouts at them too: 'That goes for all of you, is that clear? Your friends, your friends of friends.' He points at Luke. 'From now on, this boy is your messiah. If anyone even *thinks* about touching him, I will fly back to this country and do bad things to you.' Stunned silence. 'Is. That. Clear?'

While everyone nods, pale and terrified, Miss Hardy steps out from behind a clump of bushes. Has obviously been waiting for the right moment to approach.

'I don't want to know what's been going on,' she says, twisting her neck to avoid looking at the kid on the ground. 'Whatever our American friend here was saying, I'm sure what he basically means is that from now on we all have to be nice to each other.' Everyone stares in disbelief. 'In the spirit of Anglo-American friendship, I think we should give him a round of applause.'

She starts to clap. The only person who does.

From behind her, one of the boys mutters, 'Fat bitch.' She spins round. 'You're in detention for the rest of the week.'

'What the fuck?'

'Two weeks.' She turns back to the group. 'Like I said, from now on, we're *all* going to be nicer to each other. And, as our American friend has just explained, if you can't manage that, *bad things will happen.*' She starts to clap again. 'So, come along, everyone. A round of applause, please.'

And one by one, though obviously confused by life's unexpected twists and turns, they begin to clap.

48

The carpet in Patrick's living room is so thick, it reminds Jack of walking on mossy pathways deep in the woods.

'I'll put the kettle on,' says Patrick, appearing grateful that he can escape to the kitchen for a few minutes.

While he's gone, Jack wanders over to a sideboard full of framed photographs and starts checking each one in the hope of seeing his father.

Most are of Patrick and a rotund woman, both of them smiling for the camera somewhere sunny and Mediterranean. In a few, they're dining with other couples, everyone looking sunburnt and tipsy, their sombreros askew.

'That's my late wife,' says Patrick, finally returning with two mugs of pale, milky tea. 'She died ten years ago.'

'I'm sorry.'

'We had thirty-six years together. The happiest years of my life.' He smiles at the photos. 'She may be gone, but no one can take away the memories. So many happy memories ...'

They sit down, Jack perching himself on the edge of the sofa while Patrick sips his tea, neither of them knowing what to say.

'Are you staying nearby?' says Patrick eventually.

'On the road to Inverness.'

'Oh, aye? Well, you've had quite a drive, then.'

More silence.

Finally, Jack speaks: 'How long have you known ... John?'

'Oh, must be twenty years or more now. When he moved in, we thought he'd be gone in a year or two. That's how it generally goes with outsiders. They think how nice it'd be to get away from it all, and a year or two later they can't take it any more.'

'So he's not from around here?'

'No, no, a southerner, like yourself. Kept himself to himself for a long time. Still does, I suppose ...' He looks away, appears uneasy with the topic.

'Do you know where he is at the moment?'

'He often pops off with his camper van, but he's never gone for more than a few weeks. Perhaps if you came again next week or the week after ...'

'Does he go with anyone?'

'Well, he's a solitary sort.'

The roof creaks in a loud gust of wind. Patrick glances upwards, seeming relieved by the change of subject. 'You should come during one of the big storms,' he says. 'You'd think the roof was about to be torn clean off.'

'Has John ever mentioned having kids?'

Patrick looks back at his cup of tea. 'He's not a man to talk about the past.'

'It's a simple yes or no question,' says Jack. 'Did he ever mention having a family?'

'Well, no.' He shifts in his seat, appears uncomfortable. 'No, I can't say he ever did.'

'I suppose that's something, at least.' He looks away, all the emotion of the trip bubbling up from somewhere deep, deep inside. 'I just wanted to meet him so much. So, so much...'

He closes his eyes, feels the whole world become still.

At length, Patrick speaks again, his voice echoey and distant: 'Is everything all right?'

Jack's eyes open. 'What have you done with the kids?'

'Excuse me?'

'Where are Luke and Jemima?' He stands up, storms towards the bedrooms. 'Luke? Jem? Where are you?'

Patrick chases after him, reaches for his arm.

'Don't touch me!' yells Jack, slamming him into the wall. 'Luke? Jem? We're leaving.'

Patrick stands to one side now while Jack continues his search. It's only after checking every room that he starts to slow down, his aggression fading into fear. 'Where are they? We have to go.'

'Why don't you come and sit for a while?' says Patrick, his voice gentle, soothing. 'We can look for the children in a moment.'

He guides Jack back towards the living room, even as he continues calling through the house. 'Luke? Jem?'

'You've had a long journey. But everything's okay. You're safe here.'

'But we're leaving. We're going home ...'

'Not to worry about that. Everything will be fine.' He watches as Jack collapses onto the sofa. 'You can rest here for as long as you need to.'

It's impossible to know how long Jack remains there staring at the floor. When he eventually looks up, Patrick is sitting opposite, his concern clear to see.

'What happened?' says Jack.

'I was about to ask you the same thing.'

Over the next twenty minutes or so, Patrick proves himself to be a good listener and a generous host, but still he seems relieved when Jack says he needs to get going.

'Yes,' he says, 'you're probably best getting back on the road. There might be rain soon. You don't want to get caught in that.'

He follows Jack out to the doorstep, the wind feeling colder than before.

'I'll be sure to tell John you came,' says Patrick. 'And I wish you all the best with your health, I really do.'

Jack's barely taken two steps from the house when he hears the front door shut behind him.

Down in the car, Callum is fast asleep, his seat reclined and his cap pulled down over his eyes.

The wind tugging at his clothes, Jack crosses Patrick's front garden, returns to his father's house. Crouching down, he peers through the letterbox. Even in the gloom, he can see the place is sparsely furnished, the empty walls appearing dirty in this light. A pile of unopened mail sits on the doormat. And there, mixed in with it all, the letter from Jack and Meredith, still waiting to be read.

Callum wakes with a start as Jack gets into the car, slamming the door behind him. 'Get me away from this bloody place as quickly as possible.'

'Yes, sir,' he replies, his voice thick with sleep.

As the engine purrs into life, Patrick comes hurrying towards them, almost running down the garden path. 'I know your father wouldn't want me to say it,' he says, straining to catch his breath, 'but after what you've told me, I can't lie to you. It's your family, you see ...' Another gulp of air, his face flushed with the exertion. 'He has mentioned you once or twice over the years. He said there were two of you. Twins.'

49

Jemima and Chelsea sit wedged in a sunny nook beside the school sports hall, conjoined in all but physiology.

'This week will go down in history as the strangest week ever,' says Jemima.

'The. Strangest. Week. Ever,' corrects Chelsea. She passes Jemima the can of Coke they're sharing. 'Though look on the bright side. If you become famous, at least now you have something interesting to put in your autobiography. Hell, me too. "My crazy-ass trip to Mother England".'

'I mean, a house blowing up!'

'Blowing up with some creepy rapist inside. A creepy rapist looking for *you*.'

Jemima thinks of the last photo Brian sent: crouching on all fours, trying his best to be a sex kitten. This doesn't seem like the kind of thing she can admit to Chelsea, especially since she's decided to keep the picture. In the last day or two, it's struck her that she and Brian had had more in common than she'd thought: both looking for something that necessitated a lie. And when she thinks of it in that way, she just hopes that, wherever he is now, he's found the happiness he was looking for.

'Yeah, he was a total creep,' she says, wanting to maintain her cover. 'I'm glad he's dead.'

Chelsea reaches for the can of Coke. 'Do you think I'll see Jack before I leave on Saturday?'

'I don't know. My mum says he's staying in London for a few days.'

'Avoiding me.'

'No, he's seeing a doctor or something.'

'Nah, it's a cover. I can feel it. I have, like, this sixth sense. Except I don't see dead people, I just know when guys are totally sex-obsessed.'

'I wish Rob was.'

'Are you kidding? He's been asking me about your garden all day. He said he might go over this evening and "till the soil". If that's not a euphemism, I don't know what is.'

'But he doesn't even look at me.'

'It's totes a Republican thing. When you meet his mom, you'll understand. It's like she was born vacuum-packed or something.' She takes a long, ponderous sip of Coke. 'If you and Rob could just hang out at a shooting range for a while – you know, let off some rounds – he'd probably do you right there.'

Jemima watches as Luke wanders across the playground, doubtless enjoying the novelty of moving around in safety. 'My brother's so weird.'

'I know, right? Transformed from, like, Super Geek to …' She appears unsure of what he is now, eventually chooses to inspect her hair instead, long, golden strands that catch the sun.

'It's obvious everyone just tolerates him,' says Jemima. 'It's not like anyone actually likes him.'

They both watch as Luke studies a leaf on the ground, finally picking it up and putting it into a Ziploc bag.

'You should be happy for him,' says Chelsea. 'Being tolerated is probably the closest he'll ever get to having friends.' She holds up her hands and frowns at her nails as though they've just said something offensive. 'What are you going to do once I'm gone? Isn't your life going to be, like, totally empty without me?'

'Well, something like that.' She decides not to mention her date with Tim on Sunday, a date she's not even sure she wants to keep any more. He's now insisting on a picnic out in the woods, and has even arranged for his older brother to pick her up so he has more time to make everything perfect. 'He's a bit of a fat old bastard,' he'd explained in his last message, 'but he's a nice guy and he's promised to sod off once we're together.'

'Do you think I should date other guys before I come to America?'

'Sure, why not? I mean, you're not coming over for … what? It's, like, three months, which is officially *for ever*. Is there someone you're interested in?'

'Kind of, but it's complicated. He – he doesn't go to this school.'

'What the hell? I say do it.'

'But what about Rob? Isn't it like cheating or something?'

'My mom's always telling me, you shouldn't wish for The One. You should wish for the stamina to have As Many As Possible.'

Meanwhile

Meredith gets home from work to find Rob sitting on her front doorstep, his legs spread wide apart, as though his genitals need more space than most people's. 'Rob, shouldn't you be in school?'

'What's the point of an education if I never learn to follow my heart?'

She tries to sound stern. 'I think you need to get back there right away, before anyone misses you.'

'But I need to tell you something. I repeated my sophomore year in high school.'

'And why would I want to know that?'

'Because I'm a year older than the others. I'm not a kid like them, I'm a man.'

'Look, Rob—'

'Teach me how to make love to you.'

'I'm not even sure a teenager should be trying to "make love". You'd be much better off just having sex.'

'Then let's do that.'

'No, that's not what I meant.' She sighs. 'I just think you'd be better off doing it with someone your own age.'

'I'm not good enough for you, am I?'

'Dear God, that has nothing to do with it. You're ...' She sighs again, and in that moment of utter speechlessness, Rob rallies.

'I leave in a couple of days. If it's not now, it's never.'

She steels herself, tries to think of pruning back a thing of beauty: a cruel but necessary act. 'I'm sorry, Rob, in that case it's never.'

50

It's oddly reassuring to be back at the specialist's office. Jack's made four or five visits in the last couple of years and yet it seems that not a single detail has changed in all that time. It's as though this space, with its Nordic furniture and minimal-ist aesthetic, is the point around which the entire universe pivots. Life and London and Jack himself are all changing from one thing to another, but this place remains in a state of perfect stasis.

'It could just be stress,' the specialist is saying. 'By the sound of it, you've been under a lot of stress recently.'

They stare at one another, both aware that he's obliged to say this; that they must dismiss the benign possibilities before they can move on to the really bad news.

'It's not stress,' replies Jack. 'I've spent the last twenty years in advertising. I understand stress.'

'But the *emotional* stress ... The search for your father ...'

'It's definitely nothing to do with that,' he says, his tone souring.

'Tell me about this sickness last week. Any fever?'

'For a day or two, yes.'

'But you didn't see a doctor?'

'It was just flu.'

'Bad enough to keep you in bed?'

'For three or four days. Why do you ask?'

The specialist appears to draw breath. 'There is some anecdotal evidence that suggests, in people who are already showing some symptoms of dementia –'

'People like me?'

The specialist nods. '– that even a simple infection can accelerate the onset of further symptoms. It's all to do with the body's inflammatory response, which in a healthy person would be a good thing, but for someone in your position ...'

'How long do I have?'

'It really doesn't work like that. It could be a very gradual process. It could take months, maybe even longer. Though it's true that this form of dementia tends to progress very quickly, especially in a patient as young as you.'

Jack smiles, desperate for some light relief. 'I don't feel very young right now.'

The specialist smiles too, but his eyes suggest only pity.

'What's the worst-case scenario?' says Jack.

'I can't—'

'I won't quote you on it. I just need to know.'

'I'm not saying it will happen this way, but it's *feasible* you may see a significant deterioration in the coming weeks.' He looks away, appears burdened by the honesty. 'The best you can do is just monitor your symptoms.'

'There's really nothing else?'

'There is one thing. Probably the most important thing you can do right now. You can make sure your affairs are in order.'

An hour later

It still feels like yesterday. Jack's first day on the job, a young sprat in a shark tank, and there was Harry in the same position, somehow managing to look both cocksure and terrified.

Twenty years have passed. Half a lifetime. And here's Jack once again, with his heart in his mouth as he walks into the office – their office, their agency – but this time it's to say goodbye.

Harry sees him from some way off. 'Jack!'

He hurries into his room, has already taken a bottle of champagne from his well-chilled stash by the time Jack joins him. 'We need to celebrate!'

'Celebrate what?'

'Well, for starters, it's a fucking Thursday. Isn't that reason enough? More importantly, my friend, you're back where you belong.' The cork comes out with such a pop that the main office momentarily becomes a sea of heads, everyone peering into the goldfish bowl of Harry's domain. 'Did you meet your dad?'

'I went up there, but no … not exactly.'

'Then I say, fuck him.' He hands Jack a generous glassful. 'If he doesn't appreciate you, you're best back here where people do.' He raises his glass, knocks back a hefty amount.

Jack doesn't share the toast. 'Look, Harry, we need to talk.'

'Not about your dad, I hope. He sounds a right wanker.'

'Mate, I'm not here to talk about him. It's about me …'

51

The discovery that her father doesn't care should have been enough to send Meredith over the edge. News like that seems worthy of trellises on all the walls and ceilings; perhaps even seeding the carpets with grass, too. But here she is, days later, and things remain eerily calm.

The prospect of Chelsea's departure has helped. As much as she likes the girl, the last few days have felt akin to a sunrise of sorts: the darkness slowly giving way to brighter and brighter light. She'd imagined the actual moment of Chelsea's departure would be momentous, akin to Aslan rising from the dead to save Narnia, but in reality it was a mere williwaw of teenage chaos: a sudden rush of last-minute packing, a flurry of bags and then she was gone.

As Meredith walks around the house, she realizes there's nothing to indicate Chelsea was ever here: Jemima's room looks no more jumbled than usual, and across the hallway Luke is quietly organizing his collection of odds and ends, everything neatly bagged for posterity. In this post-Chelsea silence, it's easy to believe their guest was merely a group psychosis, an elaborate symptom of stress.

*

Jack returns at much the same time that Chelsea's flight takes off, as if he didn't even consider it safe to come near the house until she'd left British soil.

'She asked after you quite a lot while you were gone,' says Meredith, the two of them sitting at the kitchen table with cups of coffee. 'I'm sure she would have liked the opportunity to say goodbye.'

'No doubt in a loud, very irritating voice,' replies Jack. He sips his drink, appears older and wearier than just a week ago.

'What did the doctor say?'

'I'd like you to visit some nursing-homes with me.'

'You don't need to do that yet.'

'Look, it's all beginning to unravel.'

'Those surely can't be the words your doctor used.'

'Melly, you have this chronic need to take refuge in syntax and, frankly, it's not helpful.' He takes a deep breath, speaks more calmly. 'The symptoms are getting worse.'

'Then you'll stay here with me and the kids. For the next ten, twenty years, for as long as it takes.'

'Thank you, and I'd like that. But one day we're going to get to the stage where I need full-time care. And I want to choose the place now, while I'm still me.' He gives her a weak smile. 'I was thinking somewhere with a decent art collection, Swedish nurses, that kind of thing.'

'And what about your flat, your car?'

'I'm not going to risk driving any more, but I'd like to keep the car for a while longer, just for the pleasure of looking at it.'

'It can stay there for as long as you want.'

From beneath the table, Reggie sighs in his sleep; a sound of pure contentment, everything right with the world.

'And when are we going to tell the kids?' says Meredith.

'Soon. But I'd rather do it my own way.'

The next morning

It's some time after Meredith and Luke have gone shopping that Jack notices Jemima slip from the house dressed in a style better suited to late-night Soho than a Sunday morning in Surrey. He opens the front door and calls to her as she nears the end of the driveway. 'Jem, where are you going?'

She glances back at him as she strides away; the perfect angle at which to appreciate her black hot pants and sequined top. 'I'm meeting friends,' she says, her tone indicating that further questions are not welcome.

As she disappears from view, he hurries up to her bedroom, the air still thick with the scent of cologne and hair spray, the bed littered with outfits that were clearly deemed too modest and age-appropriate.

'Something's not right, is it?'

Reggie sneezes once, twice, three times, stares up at him through watery eyes.

'We're going after her ...'

On the other side of town, Meredith and Luke are buying seeds, every sachet seeming to her like an opportunity to start life anew.

'These will look especially lovely,' she says, handing a packet of asters to Luke, today's official Keeper of the Seeds.

'I think we should invite Miss Hardy to dinner,' he says.

'Darling, it's a nice thought, but I don't think she'd want to socialize with her pupils.'

'But she doesn't have any friends.'

'Luke, you need to ignore what the other children say about her.'

'No, she told me herself. Most days, she invites me for chocolates in her office.' He says it in an off-hand manner, as though it's the most natural thing in the world for an eleven-year-old boy to be hanging out with his headmistress. 'When she told me she was lonely, I said she should join a club. I thought that might be a good way for her to meet people. But I still think we should invite her to dinner too.'

Given that Luke has years left at the school, it's obvious that resistance is futile.

'Perhaps once the garden's ready,' says Meredith. 'Miss Hardy can be our first guest.'

Luke appears happy with this idea, is clearly unaware that it will take months, maybe even longer, before the garden looks anything other than a stark, ill-considered mess.

'I was also thinking,' says Luke, 'Uncle Jack may want to marry her.'

'Darling—'

'Don't worry, she's already said no. When I described him to her, she didn't seem very keen. She said she'd rather have a man with "meat on his bones".'

The deep, throaty roar of Jack's car is ill-suited to stealth, but there's no other option. He cruises through the neighbourhood,

Reggie perched on the front passenger seat beside him, seemingly more interested in Jack than the world outside.

'You're supposed to be looking for Jem,' he says, slowing down as they pass yet another street, still no sign of her.

Aware that he shouldn't be driving at all, he's about to give up when he thinks he spots her, far away at the end of a side-street. He brakes sharply, takes a second look.

Even from this distance, it's definitely her: the sequins on her blouse catch the light as she stands on the roadside, a heliograph flashing out some unknown message.

As Jack pulls onto the street, he sees a small hatchback stop in front of her. Seconds later, she's getting in and it's accelerating out of sight.

Reggie stands proud and wags his tail as Jack chases after them.

'I wouldn't be so happy if I were you,' says Jack. 'I'm the one wearing the seatbelt and I'm scared shitless.' He squints at the street ahead, no longer sure of his ability to judge the distance between cars parked on one side and cars approaching on the other. 'Hold on ...'

Through some combination of luck and good timing, they make it to the end of the street, but what they find when they get there is yet another junction, and no sign of the hatchback.

'Left just takes us back towards the house. Unless I'm thinking of right ...' He glances at Reggie, hopes for some kind of animal instinct, but Reggie's only response is to lick his hand. 'That's not terribly helpful, but thank you.' From behind, a car honks at him. 'That settles it, we're going right.'

He accelerates away with a shameless roar of exhaust. The

street is wider here, much better suited to a powerful car being driven by a man on the cusp of dementia. Within thirty or forty seconds of blatant law-breaking, the hatchback comes into view again, some five cars in front.

'Now we just follow,' says Jack, slowing down.

This prompts more licking from Reggie, all the while his tail thumping against the passenger window.

'You're supposed to be keeping me alert and sharp. Why don't you howl or something? Can you howl? Like this ...'

He attempts a demonstration, but it comes out more like a sad yodel, the kind of thing one might hear in the valleys of Austria after a farmer's wife has run away with the postman. 'Okay, maybe forget that. We can do sums! Five times five is twenty-five. Twenty-five times twenty-five is ... Christ ... it's ... Well, ten would be two hundred and fifty, so it's, er ... six hundred and twenty-five.' Reggie cocks his head, looks confused. 'And six hundred and twenty-five times six hundred and twenty-five is ... well, God, it's a lot, lot more.'

They're nearing the edge of town now, the road ahead stretching into open fields. And still the hatchback bobs along five cars in front, everyone in a convoy of sorts, venturing out into the great unknown.

Much like Meredith's vision for the garden, her shopping spree has run out of energy; her ideas need more time and gentle encouragement before they can take on a life of their own. Instead she and Luke sit in a café, eating ice-cream, while Luke arranges her seed packets in an order known only to him.

'Will Grandpa be coming to see us?' he says, his full attention on the glossy pictures of peonies and clematis.

'No, I don't think so. Sometimes even grown-ups prefer not to talk about things in the past. They find it difficult.'

'Like Dad.'

'Why do you say that?'

'Because he doesn't want to be around, does he? Not really, I mean. He finds it easier to be away from us. I think he'd be happy to forget us all.'

'Luke, your father loves you very much. He just doesn't always know how to show it.'

Luke takes his time to respond, smiles to himself as the geranium seeds find their rightful place in his secret filing system. 'I don't blame Dad for the way he feels. He's like these seeds, really, isn't he? They all just need to be planted somewhere they can grow.'

Jack's odyssey ends at a lakeside picnic area, the whole place screened from the outside world by a small woodland. He pulls into the car park just moments after Jemima and her mystery chauffeur. On this cold, grey Sunday in March, they are the only people there.

Jemima's still in the car when Jack approaches, first taking a photograph of the hatchback's registration plate, then moving round to the side of the car to take a picture of the driver himself: a fat, balding man who looks to be in his late forties.

He sees Jack, starts to get out. 'What the—'

'What are you doing with my niece?'

Jemima gets out too, looking angry. 'For Christ's sake, this is just his fat brother.' She shouts into the woods, 'Tim? Tim?'

Jack ignores her, stares at the man. 'You do realize you're breaking the law, don't you? Preying on a fifteen-year-old.'

The man turns to Jemima. 'You said you were seventeen!'

Her jaw drops. 'You dirty bastard.'

'Does she *look* seventeen to you?' says Jack.

Jemima now seems offended by him too. 'I look very mature for my age, thank you very much.'

'I've got your registration number. If you come near her ever again, I'm reporting you to the police, is that clear?'

'I haven't done anything. I didn't touch her.'

Jemima pales. 'You asked for a picture of my tits.'

'Did you send it?' says Jack.

As Jemima nods, the man appears to freeze, too stunned by her revelation to notice that Jack is now swinging at him with a clenched fist.

Jack watches as it slams into his face, a sharp right hook that sends the man tumbling to the ground. 'Shit,' yells Jack. 'That hurt.'

'You're a bloody maniac,' says the man, scrambling to get up. 'I could report you.'

'Of course you could. And while you're at it, you can explain to the police why you brought an under-aged girl all the way out here. Now piss off.'

Evidently feeling the need to participate more, Jemima shouts at him as he hurries back to his car. 'Bad things happen to creeps like you in prison.'

He reverses away in a spray of loose gravel. As he stops to change gear, he winds down his window and yells to her, 'Anne Frank died at the end, you stupid bitch.'

He grates the car's clutch before speeding away.

Jemima stares as he disappears into the distance. Finally, she turns to Jack. 'Happy now?'

'Jem, I just saved you from … from God knows what.'

'And now you know my secret.'

'What? That you're human? I can see how that might damage your reputation.'

She crosses to his car and gets in, slamming the door behind her. By the time Jack joins her, she's fighting off Reggie, who seems determined to remove her makeup with his tongue. 'Are you going to tell Mum?' she says, pushing Reggie away only to have him come back again and again.

'No,' Jack replies. 'She'd worry, you know that. And she wouldn't be able to keep it in perspective.'

'Which is what?'

'That we all want to be loved, Jem. There's no shame in that. I just don't think this was a very smart way of going about it.' She doesn't respond or even look at him. 'Look, I'm not going to be around for ever—'

'And what does that mean exactly? That you're just going to stay in our lives until you feel like pissing off? Because you wouldn't be the first.'

'I have dementia.'

She stares at him.

'I don't know how long I've got left,' he says. 'No one knows, but the symptoms have been getting worse recently.'

'You're going to end up like Grandma?'

As he nods, her eyes begin to fill with tears and she gives up trying to fight off Reggie.

'The time is going to come when I can't look out for you,' he says. 'I need to know you're going to be okay.'

'I'll be fine. I'm always fine.' Reggie dotes on her now, licking away her tears so gently she doesn't even seem to notice.

'I'm sorry your dad left.'

'But he didn't leave, did he? He was never really with us in the first place.' Her chest heaves as the tears come faster. 'And you'll be gone too.'

'Not by choice.'

'You're going to forget who we are, aren't you?'

'No, never,' says Jack, unsure where the words come from, but certain they're true. 'It may eventually seem like I don't remember, but for as long as there's life left in me, I will always love you.'

She looks at him through big wet eyes while Reggie sniffs her hair. 'That's not what you say about Grandma.'

'Then maybe I was wrong.'

52

The first thing Meredith notices when she and Luke get home is that Jack's car is missing. After their last conversation about it, she'd expected it to become a permanent fixture in the driveway; an expensive piece of installation art. Yet it's gone.

It doesn't take long to verify that Jack's gone too. Even though the house is crowded with plants, it feels strangely empty without him, as though something bigger than a person is missing.

She tries telling herself there's no cause for concern – he's taken Reggie out, he's popped to the shops – but still she calls his mobile phone. It's only when she hears it ringing in the living room that she starts to worry.

'Maybe he and Jemima have gone somewhere together,' says Luke.

'I'd imagine Jemima is out with one of her friends,' replies Meredith, dialling her number anyway.

The call goes straight through to voicemail. 'Darling, this is Mum. Can you call me when you get this message? All right? Love you.'

She hangs up, aware of Luke studying her every move. 'Are they going to be okay?' he says.

'Of course, darling. I'm sure they're fine.' And yet the words feel so untrue that there's only one thing that offers the prospect of comfort right now. 'I'm going to work in the garden for a little while.'

It's an act of blind faith, this process of pushing seeds into the cold, damp soil. As she kneels on the freshly hewn earth, she realizes she *needs* the garden to look raw and bare like this for a while longer, if only better to appreciate where she is in her own life and what she may yet be capable of.

She pauses to look at some of her honeysuckle seeds, mere specks in the palm of her hand, each of them so insignificant, so seemingly useless that she feels more like a magician than a gardener. With a mere sprinkle and a turn of the soil, she's hopefully sowing years of long summer evenings, the air thick with scent. She moves on to the foxgloves, smiles to herself as she settles them into their new home, can already imagine the stately columns of tubular flowers that they will become every spring, their very presence a reminder that life goes on.

And so she continues working her way around the garden, creating a future that she alone can see. It's only as daylight fades that she goes back indoors, finding the house too dark and quiet for Jack or Jemima to be at home.

She shouts, into the gloom, 'Luke? Has the phone rung?'

From upstairs, his small voice: 'No.'

Meredith rings Jemima's mobile phone again, but still gets shunted through to voicemail.

Needing to keep busy, she moves from room to room,

turning on lamps, lighting the whole house as though it's a beacon to guide them home.

It's as she's rearranging the tendrils on a chain of hearts in the living room that the phone starts to ring. She hurries to answer it, already certain it will be Jack with a story to tell – perhaps a spontaneous shopping spree that spiralled into outrageous self-indulgence.

'Jack,' she says, almost laughing with relief, 'I was worried about you.'

'Mrs Thomson?' replies a woman, her voice so formal, so official, Meredith instantly feels the room constrict around her. 'I'm Police Officer Burton. I'm calling in regard to a Mr Jack Harris—'

'He's my brother.'

'And a minor—'

'What's happened?'

'I'm afraid there's been an accident.'

Forty years earlier, 1972

Sunrise. The air heavy with the scent of frangipani flowers. She pushes open the heavy wooden doors, the sill worn smooth by centuries of pilgrims. She's barely stepped inside the garden when she sees it in the distance: the Taj Mahal, so perfect in every detail that the very sight of it brings tears to her eyes.

Tears. She knows plenty about those.

She tries to hang on to her vision of the Taj Mahal, but it's disappearing, sunrise over the plains of India replaced by the incessant crying of a young child on a grey morning in England. And now here are her own tears again, not of joy but of despair.

She glances across the room at young Meredith, the child's face red with crying, the floor between them littered with rubbish.

'What do you want?' she shouts. 'Just stop it. Do you hear me? Shut up.' She wants to go there and scream at the child. To wail in her face until there's silence. But there never is silence. Yelling, threatening, hitting: it's been three years and nothing works.

At least her brother is quiet for now, a young child who's grown accustomed to the discomfort of a dirty nappy. He sits there looking as numb and hopeless as she feels. And all the while Meredith screams, her tiny body capable of inhuman noise.

She sees the way other people look at her in the street: their eyes accusing her of being a bad mother. Even when John walked out on her, there was no sympathy.

'You've driven him away,' her mother had said. 'As if living in sin wasn't enough for you, now you've driven him off with your depression and self-pity. While your children sit in their own filth.'

Naturally her mother didn't leave it there. She'd had plenty more to say on the subject of shame: that the stupid young girl of her youth should still be ashamed of herself for what she's become; for feeling so hopeless, so bleak.

She arrives at the local graveyard, already feels a little calmer. These visits have become something of a habit in the last year or two. It felt odd at first, coming here without a grave to visit, but it quickly became a sanctuary of sorts: a place she could retreat to, no one to disturb her with their judgemental glances and whispered criticisms. The children are so young, they still don't know the difference between a graveyard and a park, and on the rare occasions that she meets someone else here, they always seem to make allowances for the way she looks, the way she acts: grief, after all, is a terrible thing.

She pushes the pram deeper and deeper into the cemetery, not wanting to slow down until she reaches her usual spot. Jack and Meredith sit quietly now, both of them looking as unkempt as she feels. Perhaps they're wondering where the other children are, she thinks, wondering why they have such a large playground all to themselves.

She lets them out once she's reached her destination: a bench among the trees and tombstones, a private place all of her own. It seems fitting to sit here among the graves because she and the children are dead to John, she can see that now. It's not just that he's never coming back: they won't even hear from him again, she's certain. And all the while the children stumble around in blissful ignorance, staking their claim on this place in squeals and shouts and occasional tears.

It's Meredith's prolonged silence that finally catches her attention. She looks up, sees Meredith sitting on one of the graves, seemingly content to stay there all day.

She gets up, wanders closer, not interested in her daughter but rather the grave itself. It's only now that she realizes she's never seen flowers here. Has never seen any evidence that this man is missed or mourned.

'George Cooper,' she says, reading from the headstone. Meredith looks up at her, clearly likes the sound of the name. 'That's George Cooper. He died four years ago. The year before you were born.'

And as she hears herself say the words, she knows what needs to come next. Not a lie at all, but a necessary truth. A reworking of the facts to help protect Meredith and Jack from life's sharp corners.

'It's your father,' she says. Meredith looks more puzzled now. 'Yes, that's where your daddy is buried. He's with the angels.'

A time of slow goodbyes

53

It's not a nice place, but compared to other parts of the hospital it's an oasis of sorts. There are far worse places Meredith could have been called to: hospital wards for people caught in far worse accidents.

The car came off the road: that's what Meredith has established. It didn't hit anything, didn't flip over, didn't sink into a lake. Much like Jack's mind, it simply rolled to a stop at an inappropriate time and place.

'It was my fault,' says Jemima, huddled in the corner of the waiting room. 'I'd gone out and ... Jack rescued me.'

'What do you mean, rescued?'

'I'd met this guy online—'

'Oh, Jemima ...'

'Jack wasn't going to tell you because he said you'd worry.'

'Of course I'd worry! Who was this man? Where did you meet him?'

'Does it even matter any more? It was a dumb thing to do. It's done now.'

Meredith speaks more gently: 'Jack's going to get worse no matter what happens.'

'But maybe the stress of driving the car. Of worrying about me ...'

'We like worrying about you. And Luke. That's what family do.' She watches as Jemima processes the words, finds a measure of comfort in them. 'How worried do I need to be about you and this other man?'

'It was nothing, it was … it was just a stupid idea.'

'Jemima, love is never a stupid idea. It's where we look for it that matters.'

After another two hours of waiting, Meredith intercepts a passing nurse. 'I was wondering when I'll be allowed to see my brother, Jack Harris.'

The nurse frowns, couldn't look more affronted if Meredith had spat at her. 'If the doctor hasn't told you anything yet, there's nothing I can do.'

Meredith is already backing away, almost bowing her head in obeisance, when the woman speaks again, a hint of malice in her voice: 'Your brother had to be restrained. He was a risk to himself and the nursing staff.'

Meredith feels an unexpected rush of anger. She's no longer worried whether she's considered yet another pushy relative. 'Why on earth would you need to restrain him?'

'He was angry and disoriented.'

'Well, if your manner was like this, I'm not surprised. I want to speak to the doctor.'

The nurse starts to walk away, doesn't even bother to look at her as she says, 'He's not here right now.'

'Then I want to see my brother.'

Getting no response, she storms towards Jack's room.

'You can't go in there,' calls the nurse.

'Do not tell me what I can and cannot do for my family.' She pushes through the doors, finds herself in a starkly institutional space, the lighting seemingly designed to make people look even sicker than they are.

Jack's bed is in the far corner. He lies there in a pastel green hospital gown, his eyes closed, a thick band across his arms and chest tying him down to the bed.

The nurse catches up with her. 'I told you you're—'

'*This* is how you treat a man with dementia?'

'You need to wait outsi—'

'I'm taking my brother home.'

'You can't do—'

'I'm taking my brother home. Right now.'

54

Although it's only Jack's mind under siege, it seems to Meredith as though the whole house is on a wartime footing. Edna would surely be proud of them, the way this unseen blitz has brought them all together, changing them as a family and as individuals.

Jack hasn't said a lot in the days since he got home. It's not that he's a different man so much as there seems to be less of him now; an enormity of spirit that Meredith can only recognize by its absence.

Luke comes into the kitchen, stands on tiptoe by the sink as he fills the kettle. 'I'm making Uncle Jack a drink. Would you like one?'

'No, thank you, darling.'

'We're going to have a cup of tea while we compare our photographs.'

'Just be careful not to tire him out.'

'Don't worry, it was his idea. We're going to make an album of memories. So when he doesn't have any left in his head, he can still look at them on the page.'

The kettle full, he carries it to the socket, struggling to hold it even with both hands. He puts it down on the counter with a thud, water splashing from the spout.

'Tell you what,' says Meredith, eager that he doesn't try to plug it in too. 'How about you go back to Uncle Jack and I'll bring your tea up in a moment?'

She finds them in Jack's room, both of them sitting on his bed, the duvet between them littered with photographs.

'Two cups of tea,' she says, already feeling like an intruder.

Jack doesn't speak, is still in his pyjamas. It's Luke who drives the situation, his enthusiasm seemingly enough for both of them. 'These are all the pictures we're putting in the book,' he says.

'They're lovely,' replies Meredith, casting a quick glance over them. To be fair, many say more about Luke's past than Jack's: sunlight coming through winter-bare trees; a blade of grass poking up through concrete. But Jack is in a few: laughing behind the wheel of his car; playing with a still-coned Reggie.

Meredith notices one photo in particular. 'When did you all go to the zoo? And you're in your school uniform.'

Jack looks unsure how to respond. Luke cuts in: 'Uncle Jack took us after school. The day before we went to France.' He says it with such certainty that Meredith doesn't even think to doubt him. 'It was only a short visit, but it was fun.'

She peers closer at the picture, not entirely convinced their expressions suggest fun, but who is she to argue?

As she heads back downstairs, Meredith knocks on Jemima's door. 'Do you need anything?' she says, poking her head into the room.

Jemima lies on her bed, homework spread out in front of her. 'No, I'm fine,' she replies.

Meredith is already retreating, the door closing behind her, when Jemima says, 'Are you going to get dementia too?'

'What makes you think that?'

'I'm not stupid. It obviously runs in our family.'

Meredith stands in the doorway, marvelling at how a teenager can take years of fear and condense it all into such an offhand question. 'I don't know,' is all she says.

Jemima simply nods and, without another word, turns back to her homework.

55

It's the wartime analogy that helps her make sense of it: as the bombs fall on her family life, she's found a courage she didn't know she had. Rather than cowering amid the wreckage, she's standing tall, shaking her fist at the sky and daring it to do its worst.

That's certainly how it feels at the doctor's, getting the blood test she's avoided for so many years. And although she won't have an answer for six weeks, the test alone feels like a statement of intent, a declaration that she's a fighter.

It's the right mindset for meeting Alastair too. As she waits for him at Seeds & Leaves, it strikes her that this is the first time she's simply *meeting* him – meeting him rather than pining for him, grieving over him, kidding herself that he's something other than he actually is.

When he arrives, he appears to sense the change in her. His look of wearisome inconvenience vanishes within seconds, and for the first time in her life, Meredith has the sensation that they are equals.

'I was rather surprised you wanted to meet so urgently,' he says.

'We need to talk about the children.'

'Is there a problem?'

'They need to see more of you.'

'Meredith, you know I'm—'

'We're all busy, Alastair. Your children need their father.'

'Is this about money?'

'Of course not. It's about you spending more time with them.'

'I took them to France, for Christ's sake.'

'I mean, on a regular basis.'

'Good Lord,' he mutters. 'As if one madwoman in my life isn't enough.'

'It's not just about being in the same car as you or the same house. They need to be with *you*.'

'What on earth is that supposed to mean?'

'You can be a little distant, you surely know that.'

'And that's now a crime, obviously.'

'I'm not criticizing you—'

'Oh, really? And yet it sounds remarkably like it.'

'I'm simply telling you your children feel neglected. It doesn't matter whether or not you agree with the statement, that's how your children feel.'

'So what exactly are you suggesting I do with them?'

'Perhaps see them every Saturday.'

'Dear God, and do what?'

'Hug them.' She sees him wince. 'Tell them you love them.'

'So you want me to ... what? Become all touchy-feely? To flounce through life with my arms wide open?'

'Yes, actually. That sums it up perfectly.'

She's barely finished speaking when he stands up. 'Meredith, when you called me here, I expected a serious discussion. I don't have time to waste on this nonsensical psychobabble.'

'They won't be young for ever, Alastair. If you miss their childhood, you'll never get it back.'

'Good day to you, Meredith.'

He strides away in his usual dignified manner, though all solemnity is lost when he forgets to duck beneath the branches of a giant ficus.

Meredith replays the conversation in her head as she drives home, her only regret that she didn't say it years ago.

Compared to her own wisteria-like personality – clingy, fast-growing, but a pleasant addition to the garden – Alastair is more of a cactus, all thorns and leathery skin; a man who conserves emotion as though he lives in perennial drought. She can see now that he's beyond her skills as a gardener: having watered him with words, she can do no more than leave him to draw his own conclusions.

She gets home long before the children are expected back from school. As she enters the house, it feels so silent, her first thought is that something bad has happened.

'Jack?' she shouts, up the stairs.

His voice calls back from the kitchen. 'In here.'

She hurries through, finds him at the kitchen table, an unopened package in front of him. Even at first glance, it looks crudely wrapped with too much tape. On the top, a long row of stamps jostles for space above the address, scrawled in a jagged, staccato script.

'It's from Scotland,' says Jack. 'It's from him.'

56

On closer inspection, it's a recycled shoebox, its battered walls and vague stains entombed in so much packing tape it could probably have survived a Martian landing.

It's the first time their father has entered their lives yet there's something fundamentally unnerving about the experience. Not just the way the box is wrapped – like a kidnapper sending the severed fingers of a missing child – but the way their names are written too: 'Jack and Meredith' spilling across the top of the address in an odd, bunched-up manner, as though their father found the words hard to write.

Deciding that even the nastiest surprises can be softened with a cup of tea, Meredith sets about making a pot, breathing in the rich scent of the tea leaves like some kind of anaesthetic. Now that she's begun the process, she feels her defences also require a plate of biscuits, everything arranged just so: a statement of order and comfort to barricade herself against a world of frightening possibilities.

Only once everything is in position does Jack begin the slow process of opening the box.

The first thing they learn about their father is that he obviously believes in the fundamental evil of the postal service; that a parcel is an open invitation to thieves. Even the seams are taped over so tightly, so thoroughly, that Jack struggles to get any leverage with scissors. By the time he's finished cutting through the endless layers, Meredith can only imagine it contains something priceless: a precious family heirloom of some kind; a literal silver lining to her parents' legacy.

Jack begins to lift the lid, hesitating a moment to look at Meredith. Here they are, brother and sister, young children once more, learning about life all over again.

Moments later, the lid comes free with a slight sigh.

There's so much scrunched-up newspaper stuffed inside, it begins to rise up of its own accord, expanding into its new-found freedom.

As Jack removes it by the fistful, Meredith unfurls one of the balls. 'It's from … June last year.'

'If you'd seen his house,' replies Jack, 'that wouldn't come as a surprise.'

He lifts out a letter: a single sheet of paper folded into quarters. Beneath it, a bundle of old photographs tied together with string. The topmost picture is in black-and-white, its edges faded with age. A pretty young woman, early twenties at most, stands on a beach, laughing, as waves splash against her bare legs.

Putting the photographs to one side, Jack and Meredith pore over the letter together, both of them flattening it out against the table.

Spidery handwriting fills the entire page, the lines crammed in so tightly, it appears more like art than communication.

'It makes my head hurt,' says Jack, letting go of the paper. 'You'll need to read it to me.'

'That'll be easier said than done.'

She squints at the first line, fairly certain it says, 'Dear Jack and Meredith'. With that small Rosetta Stone, she begins to decipher the rest of it word by word, so engrossed now she's not even aware that she's reading aloud.

'Dear Jack and Meredith, you shouldn't have come here. Let bygones be bygones. There's nothing to gain by trying to blame one another. I've lived my life as I needed to live it and I dare say you've done the same. I'm not surprised your mother said I was dead. I was dead to her long before I walked out. Maybe it's true I wasn't the man I could have been, but those were hard times for both of us. She was drowning in her own mental sickness. If I hadn't left I would have drowned with her too . A man can't apologize for having the will to live. You were almost two at the time—'

Meredith stops, looks at Jack. 'Two. My God.'

'That means we met him,' says Jack. 'We knew him.'

'I have to say, you weren't like normal children. It's like you didn't know how to love. And I don't think it made much of a difference to your mother whether I stayed or not. She didn't cope well with having you. It wasn't planned, you see. Had it been a different time and place, I doubt you'd be here now. It was your lucky break, I suppose, but it was at our expense. She was a rare bird when I met her. It had been a tough life I think, though she didn't much talk about it. She had such a beautiful smile, but I've never seen motherhood change a woman like that. Almost like Jekyll and Hyde, it was. I want to be fair to her, of course, and maybe it would be different today, people understand things like that better now, but if you ask me it wasn't natural for a woman to act like that, not with her own children. She'd just cry and cry or she'd spend the whole day in bed while the two of you sat in your own filth.'

Meredith pauses. 'Postnatal depression,' she says. 'It sounds like she had postnatal depression.'
'And a useless husband,' replies Jack.
Meredith returns to the letter.

'I suppose it was a nervous breakdown of sorts. I waited for her to get better, but after a year or two it was obvious she'd never be the same again. There was nothing left for me, so you can see I had no choice. I had to leave. If you're angry with my decision, you need to remember I was as much of a victim as you, perhaps even more because I lost something when you came along, whereas you had your whole lives ahead of you.

'I want you to know, there are no hard feelings on my side. Like I say, let bygones be bygones. I'm sending you these pictures so you can see how it was before you arrived. How she was. I was sorry to hear how she's ended up. That's no way for a human being to end their days, especially after a life like hers.

'I'll always remember her as that young girl I first met. Such a sparkle in her eye, and that smile. I'm not saying we would have been together for ever, but they were happy days.

'Regards, John Chapman

'PS If you're after money, I don't have any, so don't try any sob stories. After all these years, I think it's best we don't contact each other again.'

Meredith sits back, glad to get some distance on the words. 'The late sixties would have been a terrible time to have postnatal depression,' she says. 'I don't think anyone really understood it back then. And without the support of her family …'

Jack takes the letter, folds it back into quarters and slides it under the box. 'What a bastard.'

'On this occasion, I think that's exactly the right word.' She reaches for the bundle of photographs, carefully unties them and spreads them out on the table. In picture after picture, their mother smiles for the camera, thick curls of dark hair framing her youthful face.

'She really was beautiful,' says Jack, the words coming out so softly, he could almost have been talking to himself.

There are some colour photos in there too, each of them in garish saturated hues, a testament to when colour film was new and exciting. In several pictures, their mother holds a brightly coloured beach ball, as though wanting to take full advantage of this daring new technology. And always looking so happy, a smile full of hope.

'Where is that?' says Meredith, peering closer at the background: the stretch of shingle beach, the silhouette of a pier. 'It looks familiar.'

'It's not Brighton.'

'Southend, maybe?'

'No. I don't think so.'

They reach the final picture. She sits at a table with a young man of a similar age. He gazes at the camera with a cheeky smile, a cigarette in one hand and the other clamped around her shoulders.

Meredith is the first to break the silence. 'He was handsome, I'll give him that.'

'Mum was right,' says Jack. 'He did look like Cliff Richard.'

57

Jack stands in the kitchen window, watching Meredith work outside. He's already been here for twenty minutes or more, observing the way she smiles to herself at the blank earth, seeing something in it that others won't see for months, something that Jack might never see.

He understands now how this garden restores some balance to her world: that it will burst into life and grow larger even as he slowly retreats; not a death so much as a reversal, shrinking into something smaller and smaller, budlike, until eventually he will be gone completely.

Reggie lies at his feet, staring out at the sunshine but committed to staying with him for as long as necessary.

'Come on,' says Jack. 'We can't both act like miserable sods.'

Reggie springs for the back door with the athleticism of a dog half his age. As soon as Jack opens it, he bounds across to Meredith, rouses her from her green-fingered reverie. 'Hello,' she coos over him. 'Aren't you beautiful?' While he sniffs her hands and clothes and the soil beneath her feet, she turns to Jack, is evidently trying not to look or sound too concerned. 'How are you feeling today?'

'Oh, I'm fine,' he replies, certain that such a vacuous word is appropriate; that if he's lucky he will always feel fine as he recedes from this world, sliding away to a place of perpetual fineness. 'It's going to look great out here.'

'Isn't it?' She beams at the empty space, her muddy brown canvas. 'Hopefully it will be a riot of colour next spring.' She appears to regret mentioning the future, quickly turns back to Reggie. 'Just wait until you smell all the flowers.'

Reggie wags his tail, seeming thrilled just to hear her voice.

'It was Hastings,' says Jack. 'I was looking at the pictures again this morning. That beach in the background, it's Hastings.'

'Well, aren't you clever?' Reggie's tail wag becomes more of a full body wag as he nuzzles against her. 'Yes, and you too ...'

'I was thinking we could go there,' says Jack. 'If you don't mind driving?'

'To Hastings? No, it might be fun. I've not been there for years.'

'I thought we might take Mum.'

Meredith stops nuzzling Reggie. 'Are you mad?'

'That's hardly a good choice of words, Melly.'

'You know what I mean. She's not exactly mobile.'

'But she's not dead either. What does it matter if she's slouched in the nursing-home or slouched in your car?'

'And when we get there?'

'We shove her in a wheelchair and push her up and down the seafront. Some fresh air might do her good. Might do all of us some good.'

Meredith begins to stroke Reggie again, an act that now appears to be more for her sake than his.

'It's just I've been thinking about that letter,' he says. 'I feel sorry for her. She had a bit of a shit life, didn't she? I thought it'd be nice if, you know, before she dies, we could take her back to a place where she was happy.'

'Are you sure you're up to it?'

'Well, if she is, I can't really complain, can I?' He heads back indoors, pauses in the open doorway. 'I was thinking we could go this Sunday.'

He can see the look in her face, that it's too soon, too rushed, but she swallows the words. 'I'll call the nursing-home today. Talk to them about it.'

'And think of the photo opportunities. You, me, Mum and the kids on a proper outing. Our first and last.'

Forty-five years earlier, 1967

She didn't know what to say when John offered to buy her a drink. She wanted to say that anything would be all right.

'I could get used to this,' she remarks, as he brings her a Babycham, the first time in her life that anyone's bought her anything purely for the pleasure of it.

'I could get used to this too,' he replies, giving her a cheeky wink and pressing up alongside her. 'So what do you think of Hastings?'

From their table by the window, she can see people sunbathing on the beach, dancing out on the pier. 'It's lovely,' she says. 'I wouldn't mind living here.'

'Oh, yes? Once you've met the right man, you mean?'

She feels him press closer. 'And once I've travelled a bit,' she replies, laughing and relaxing into him. 'It'd be a nice place to raise a family, don't you think? To have a couple of children. To play with them every day on the beach.'

It's such an appealing thought, she doesn't notice that he makes no attempt to reply, just drinks his pint of beer while his free arm snakes its way around her shoulders.

He seems like such a good catch, she decides it's best not to talk about the future. After all, she doesn't want to scare him off. That's what her mother would say if she was here: that she's talking too much, her head full of dreams and nonsense, that she's always been such a foolish girl.

As John's arm locks around her, she can feel the warmth of his body through her blouse. And even though she's spent so many years wanting to get away from home, she wishes her mother was here right now just to see this moment. To see that she's not good for nothing. That she's here with a handsome man, the two of them falling in love.

She turns to the woman at the next table. 'Excuse me, would you mind taking a picture of us?'

John clearly needs no encouragement to pose for the camera. 'Hold on,' he says, putting his pint down. 'I want to be smoking a fag.'

'Why?'

'Because it's like James Dean, isn't it?'

He quickly lights a cigarette, puts his arm back around her. 'Righty-ho,' he says, pulling her closer. 'Smile for posterity …'

And that's exactly what she does. She doesn't just smile for the camera, she smiles for the future, for the family they'll have together, and for all the happy memories that will grow from this single moment in time.

Full circle

58

To their credit, neither Luke nor Jemima questions the sanity of this trip; neither of them seems perturbed that they have to share the back seat of the car with a senile old woman on the brink of death.

Luke takes five or six pictures of her en route, as though his grandmother is not catatonic but is rather modelling this season's collections of knitwear and incontinence pads. 'That's an especially nice picture,' he says, as the shutter clicks yet again. 'Another memory!'

Meredith catches his eye in the rear-view mirror. 'Luke, darling, we don't want to bother Grandma.'

'I'm not.'

She glances at her mother slumped beside him: she appears so mentally vacant that they could probably set fire to her and she'd never know. 'Well, we're going to be there in a moment. You'll want to save some pictures for the beach and the pier.'

As she says the words, it starts to hail, chunks of ice raining down with such force, it sounds more like the car's being pelted with stones. Luke takes a picture of this too, though fails to say whether it will be classified as an official memory.

So it is that they arrive in Hastings to empty streets, the few other visitors taking refuge in overpriced cafés and tea shops.

'I'm sure it will brighten up later,' says Meredith, even as the clouds thicken and the day grows darker.

As the hail turns to torrential rain, Meredith pulls to a stop on the seafront.

'This is where the battle of 1066 took place,' she says.

'What – right here?' asks Luke.

'Well, no, not in this exact spot. It was . . .' She notices the pier in the distance, a burnt-out wreck. 'Oh.'

'Is that also from the battle?' asks Luke. 'It looks a bit like Edna's house.'

Meredith turns to Jack. 'Did you know about this?'

'It happened years ago. I thought they'd have fixed it by now.'

She kills the windscreen wipers, watches as the pier's tortured silhouette melts into a blur of wet glass. 'That's better.'

'I'm going to get us some ice-cream,' says Jack.

'Jack, it's cold and w—'

But he's already opening his door and getting out, rain splashing on his empty seat. 'Melly, we're at the seaside. Some traditions have to be maintained.' He slams the door and hurries to an ice-cream van, sitting forlorn and neglected a hundred yards up the street.

'Jemima, darling, could you go with Uncle Jack, please?'

'I'm not doing that,' she responds, her first words since leaving home. 'It's pissing it down.'

Meredith turns to face her, speaks more firmly. 'You can take an umbrella. I just think Uncle Jack *may need some help*.'

Whether prompted by charity or guilt, Jemima sighs and leaves the car, squealing as she runs after him, clearly trying to dodge every puddle, every raindrop.

'Will they get an ice-cream for Grandma too?' says Luke.

'I don't think so.'

'She can have some of mine.'

'It's a lovely thought, Luke, but that won't be necessary.'

She wipes at the condensation on the window, but still can't see much: Jack and Jemima reduced to diffuse blobs of colour.

When Jack had suggested this trip, Meredith had known it wouldn't be much of an experience, but now they're here, she can think only of everything the day is not and of all the things her mother will never do: how she'll never float across the Canadian Rockies in a hot-air balloon, or stand in the Australian Outback and watch the sun set over Ayers Rock. Those are places her mother had talked of for years, a lifetime of anticipation finally drawing to an end on a cold, wet day in Hastings.

From the back seat, the shutter click of Luke's camera.

'It was a picture of you this time,' he says. 'You looked so beautiful. So sad and beautiful. It's another memory.'

The ice-cream sees them through the worst of the weather, everyone eating in contented silence, nothing to see but car windows thick with condensation.

It's not much later that the rain stops and they begin peeling themselves from the vehicle, everyone stretching cramped limbs as though they've just been emptied from a tin can and must now restore themselves to their usual size.

Once Meredith sees her mother in the wheelchair, a tartan blanket tucked across her lap, she's glad that Luke is there to take his endless pictures. Compared to the woman she remembers from her childhood, her mother looks oddly happy like this. Instead of her usual frown, her face has the supple, relaxed quality of old leather. Even the way she sits slumped in her chair is a welcome change from the woman who was always too self-conscious to relax; too worried as to what other people might say.

Two hours later, Luke still seems thrilled with the novelty of a grandmother on wheels, a life-size toy. Jemima, too, appears happy simply to drift along, a pair of headphones negating the need to be mentally present.

Jack pauses on the promenade, looks tired. 'Do you mind if we just take a rest?'

Meredith calls to the children: 'You can keep going. We'll catch up with you in a moment.'

She watches as Luke, Jemima and her mother move into the distance; the past, present and future momentarily overlapping.

'I'm glad you suggested this,' she says to Jack.

'You and me both.'

'How are you feeling?'

'Okay … not ready to say goodbye to it all.'

'We can stay as long as you like.'

'That's not what I mean, Melly.' He stares out at the sea: slate grey, crested white. Gulls cry to one another as they pick through the rubbish along the shoreline. 'It's funny how even a place like this seems beautiful when time is running out.'

'I've had the test,' says Meredith. There's such a long silence, she thinks he hasn't heard her. She's about to say it again when he speaks.

'I'm very proud of you. It was the right thing to do.'

'I haven't got the result yet, but no matter what it is, we're all going to be okay. I'm certain of it, I really am.'

He gives her a tired smile. 'I've been waiting years to hear you say that.'

They travel home in silence: Jemima immersed in her music; Luke dozing against his grandmother; Jack staring out of the window.

Meredith thinks of the garden as she drives: of those small seeds stirring into life; a slow awakening beneath the soil.

Comforted by the thought, she glances at Jack beside her, his head resting against the door, his eyes gazing up at the clouds.

At first she thinks she should say something to distract him, to entertain him, but he looks so beautiful. So sad and beautiful. Better, she thinks, just to cherish the moment. To save it as another memory.

Acknowledgements

I'm grateful for the support of many people. In particular, I would like to thank my extraordinary agent, Juliet Mushens, and the whole team at Constable & Robinson, especially Victoria Hughes-Williams, Dominic Wakeford, Lucy Zilberkweit, Grace Vincent, Martin Palmer and Zorana Rzanicanin.

I would also like to thank everyone who expressed their enthusiasm for *Lost & Found*. Writing is often a difficult and solitary task. Your words meant a great deal to me.

If you enjoyed *Arms Wide Open*,
read on for the first chapters from
Tom Winter's debut novel

Lost & Found

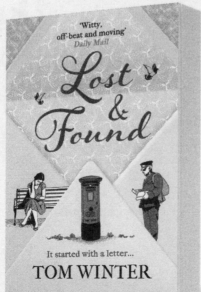

'Witty,
off-beat and moving'
Daily Mail

Lost & Found

It started with a letter...

TOM WINTER

'Original
and surprising ...
It left me glowing.'
Saga

'A touching tale,
full of pathos and
laugh-out-loud
moments.'
Candis

In paperback: 9781472101617   In eBook: 9781472104892

1

CAROL WANTS A disease. Nothing deadly, and nothing crippling. She doesn't aspire to disabled parking, for instance, despite its obvious advantages.

'It's true I haven't done much with my life,' she wants to tell people, 'but it's the . . . the leprosy.'

She imagines how they would nod sympathetically, albeit while backing away, and even she might feel better about looking at herself in the mirror each morning: a middle-aged woman who hasn't accomplished much because she can't, because she's been too busy peeling off dead skin and looking for missing body parts.

'Yes,' she'd say, as she arrives at work late yet again, 'I know I'm crap at this, but the good news is I've found a couple of my fingers.'

But, no, there is no disease, no excuse to hide behind. She has a husband who's a certifiable dickhead, but this isn't her disability *per se*. And her daughter – well, what can she say on that subject? In the months prior to giving birth, she read every book on child-rearing she could find. In retrospect, Sun Tzu's *Art of War* would have been a better choice, or perhaps a field study of rabid primates.

Naturally, this isn't how she'd expected to feel about motherhood, but watching her baby daughter morph into a teenager has been an alarming experience, like cresting the first hill of a rollercoaster just as she realized her seatbelt was broken.

Now seventeen, her daughter stands on the cusp of independence, the whole world at her feet. And Carol is on a bus home, staring at a window too wet with rain to offer a view of anything; an indeterminate cityscape, as fractured and abstract as her own life – the hint of a street sign, the edge of a shop front, but nothing complete, nothing she can look at and say, 'Ah, that's where I am.'

So, nearly twenty years of married life have come to this: 'I'm leaving.'

She savours the words for a moment, already regretting that she'll only get to say them once. Condensing so many years of frustration into two small words has given them a curious, almost nuclear power, as if they might slip from her mouth and accidentally level the whole of London.

She knows she'll tell her husband over dinner tonight, though she still isn't sure how she'll raise the subject. The only certainty is that she'll serve a nicer dessert than usual – her favourite, as it happens – though she'll try her best to make this seem like an act of consolation rather than celebration.

2

IT'S STRIKING HOW much can change in twelve or thirteen
miles. Carol has seen runners on half-marathons, everyone crossing the finishing line with rosy cheeks and
broad smiles. The same cannot be said of London. In the
twelve miles between Westminster and Croydon, London
is reduced from a city of parks and palaces to this, an
unrecognizable commuter belt, a grey concrete mess. To
say London ends at Croydon is only half true: stripped of
hope and worn down, London really crawls into Croydon
and dies.

Of course, this isn't something people are inclined to
admit in Carol's part of Croydon, where the overworked
middle classes still want to believe in the dream – waxing
their cars on Sunday afternoons, decorating their window
ledges with scented candles and porcelain figurines.

Carol tries not to think about her neighbours' habits as
she walks home from the bus stop, tries not to care that the
whole estate is a labyrinth of cul-de-sacs, more a communal

Petri dish than a place to live. Tonight she will be cutting her ties to this place. Soon she will float free.

'Carol!' Mandy Horton comes running from a nearby house, her every move a clatter of bangles and costume jewellery. 'Bob and Tony are playing darts tonight. They want us to meet them at the pub.'

'What?'

'Bob and Tony—'

'No, I mean Bob never mentioned anything about going to the pub tonight.'

'So?' replies Mandy, with a dismissive snort.

For a brief moment, Carol wonders what those snorts would sound like if she held Mandy's head underwater, perhaps even kept it there, submerged, until she went limp and cold to the touch.

She realizes Mandy is talking.

'. . . and it is Tuesday. It's not like there's anything else to do.'

Carol steals a glance at her shopping bag, the dessert almost poking from the top. 'I was hoping to have a chat with Bob, that's all.'

'But you can do that at the pub, silly! How about I come by in thirty minutes?' Her eyes flit across Carol's dress, a hint of pity in her face. 'It'll give you time to change.'

When Carol gets home, the house has a burgled look: not messy so much as strewn, as if the entire building has been lifted from its foundations and kicked around while she was out.

She hesitates at the foot of the stairs, certain that her daughter Sophie is up there somewhere. For Carol, the fact that a teenager can achieve total invisibility in a modest three-bedroom home says it all: Sophie has guerrilla instincts that could put the Viet Cong and the Taliban to shame.

'Sophie?'

Silence.

She ponders going upstairs to say hello – perhaps have another stab at that mother-daughter thing she's aspired to for the last seventeen years – but then thinks better of it. The simple act of dialogue with Sophie has become so rare, it seems better to save the moment for when she has something important to say: 'Yes, I'm leaving', 'No, I'm not coming back'.

She feels a stab of guilt, not at the prospect of having that conversation, but at the possibility of enjoying it. It isn't that Sophie's a bad child, she's just not the sort Carol would have chosen had it been a mail-order process. The only things she really understands about her daughter are the qualities she inherited from Bob – an ability to reduce the house to chaos, for instance, and an expectation that Carol will always be there to deal with the aftermath. Everything else just seems oddly foreign and incomprehensible. Even her intelligence feels redolent of a manufacturing error: how could a bright, studious child have been assembled from this genetic material? It's a question Carol can't answer; a question that leaves her with the vague sense that, in getting the daughter everyone thinks they want, she missed out on the kind that could have loved and needed her.

Thinking the sound of the refrigerator being restocked might provoke a visceral reaction – after all, even clever people have to eat – she labours over the dessert: slowly peels away the packaging, carefully puts it on a plate, slides it into the refrigerator, with the heavy-handed clank of porcelain on metal.

In the loaded silence that follows, she decides she won't go to the pub tonight – might not even answer the door when Mandy arrives in the inevitable cloud of perfume. Instead, she'll wait for Bob to return and will then set about destroying their life together, much as a butterfly must destroy its cocoon in order to live.

3

Yes, she went to the pub after all, succumbing to the same emotional paralysis that has seen her spend years wanting to leave Bob but never quite finding the courage to make it happen; a life that has been dedicated to other people's happiness even at the expense of her own. Yet as she watches the evening unfold around her – a room full of people drinking to forget the futility of their own lives – she knows tonight is still the night she breaks free.

When the time finally comes for them to go home, Carol and Bob drive in an unusual silence, insulated from the tragedy of late-night Croydon by the suburban bubble of their three-door hatchback. Carol's heard of animals sensing earthquakes hours and even days beforehand. Is the same thing now happening with Bob? She glances at him behind the wheel, certain that if she could peel back his skull she'd find just a hollow, empty space, perhaps a single red light flashing in the darkness.

'I didn't expect it to be a pub night,' she says. It feels

good to initiate The Conversation, her first move towards freedom.

'No, it was a last-minute thing. I . . . I thought it'd be good to get out.'

'Actually, I was hoping we could talk.'

Bob looks alarmed. 'What – you and me?'

'Yes, Bob, you and me.'

His eyes widen, and for a moment Carol thinks he might be having some kind of aneurysm – a convenient end to her marriage, it's true, but not what she wants when travelling at sixty miles an hour.

'Bob, are you all right?'

Still those wide eyes.

'Bob? Bob, stop the car.'

Nothing.

'Bob! Pull over! Now!'

They begin to slow.

By the time they pull to a stop, Bob is slouched in his seat. 'You know, don't you?'

Carol stares at him, so confused she momentarily forgets that she's supposed to be leaving him. 'Know what?'

'That's why I wanted us to spend the night at the pub.'

'Bob—'

'You know, to relax.'

'Bob—'

'I thought it'd be a distraction.'

'For fuck's sake, just say it.'

He begins to cry. 'I've got a lump. On my testicle.'

'Oh, shit, I'm sorry . . .' She tries to reach for him, but

her seatbelt snags. She struggles to unbuckle it, turns to face him. 'Look, Bob, it's going to be all right.'

'I was hoping it would just go away, but . . .'

She holds his hands with an affection that surprises even her. 'Look, it's all okay. I understand.'

'I just thought a game of darts . . . I don't know, it sounds mad, but I thought it'd bring me luck.'

'And did you win?'

'No.' He begins crying harder.

'Bob . . .'

'What if I lose my balls?'

Even in the auto-pilot of Carol's compassion, it strikes her that Bob is a forty-something man in an almost sexless marriage – under the circumstances, his testicles became unnecessary baggage years ago.

'And what if it's spread?' he says, more panicked now.

'Bob, it might be nothing. Just a lump.'

He chokes back the tears. 'I don't want to die.'

And, right then, she does feel sorry for him, this grown man who's been reduced to helplessness.

'We're going to the doctor first thing in the morning, okay?'

She imagines the doctor laughing and telling them it's nothing, a mere physical expression of Bob's mental decrepitude. On their way home, Carol will tell him she doesn't love him, has never really loved him. With a sharp dose of reality and a course of antibiotics, both she and the lump will disappear from his life for ever.

And yet here he is, looking up at her, imploring,

desperate, terrified. 'God,' he says, 'I love you so much.'

'I know,' is all she can manage, but still he gazes at her, a frightened man with an ominous lump; a man for whom a few simple words would make all the difference.

'And I . . .' she adds, with barely a stammer '. . . I love you too.'